# A journey to find a Love

Estella Hopetoun

# Contents

# CHAPTER 1

♥

S ammy pressed the doorbell once more, becoming more tense by the second. She knew she shouldn't have gone, but she had little to no choice. She was aware of how it appeared, and she detested being in this circumstance. No one had ever been in a scenario like this, not that she had ever been, either. Things like this don't just happen to people; they are the result of a curse, which was unquestionably punishing her as usual.How in the heck was she supposed to say it? What the hell was she supposed to say? Even so, would he recognise her? Even if he did, Sammy was aware that he wouldn't accept the news well. His family's background didn't help them because it was clear that she wanted something from him—from them.Sammy turned to leave, saying that she had no business being there and that she could easily manage the situation by herself. She was unsure of why she had allowed Vicky to persuade her to come down here. Who was she kidding, Vicky and she both knew that she couldn't manage anything on her alone. She was such a wimp that she had to deliver the news to a complete stranger at his home on a Sunday afternoon, even though she knew he wouldn't want to hear it.She went around and rang the bell once more, telling herself she should leave if no one answered this time. In all honesty, she was hoping they wouldn't answer the door so she could at least tell Vicky she tried.When the door opened, a small woman popped her head out and grinned, "May I help you?"The invisible lumps that had developed in Sammy's throat were swallowed.I have come to see Jason. Jerry McCarthy?Sam cleared her throat as the woman's gaze caused it to go dry. "Do you have an appointment?" she said.An arrangement? Why hadn't she considered that before? You couldn't just barge in and demand to see individuals like this. Jason was most likely quite busy.She observed as the elder woman scowled a little before saying, "I don't, but I really need to see him."When she sensed that the woman was about to eject her, she begged desperately for her to stop by saying, "Please."She inhaled deeply, widened the door, and ushered her inside.Sammy had thought the home was enormous from the outside, but the interior was far more daunting; it was so large that Sammy was certain it could contain half of New York plus two of her studio apartments.As they came to the sitting area, the woman said, "I'm sorry you had to wait a while before I could get to the door, the employees had the day off, and I was busy upstairs.Jason isn't at home right now, but I'm sure he will be soon. Sammy asked for water, Vicky said she had to cut back on the caffeine so she was going to attempt to, and the woman added, "Make yourself comfortable while I get you a cup of coffee."Sammy closed her eyes and muttered a prayer because she knew she needed all the support she could get right now. The woman responded with a smile, "Of course," and then she walked away.

Nick laid on the bed and took a break from everything; it seemed like all he did recently was take breaks. But that's what happens when you get caught up in things you shouldn't, leading to a crash that almost killed you. At least he was no longer in the hospital, and the arm cast would soon be removed, allowing him to leave this place in peace.He didn't go on the picnic with the rest of the family, however, not because of the accident, but rather because the idea of being in a small place with them at this time made his head spin. Charlie would fuss and worry despite the fact that she was supposed to be the one being fussed and worried over, and Luca would give him that troubled expression whenever he so much as lifted a finger. Additionally, Jason would be looking for an opportunity to hit him or an excuse to break his other arm, which would be uncomfortable for everyone. Then Chase? Well, aside from how to approach his next lay, nothing ever upset or worried that one.They couldn't possibly be back already if they were knocking on his door in short, unpleasant rasps, right? He hadn't had much sleep, so he'd have heard them coming.He stood up and thought about putting on a shirt when he heard the door again. He was the only one in the house, wasn't he?"Who are you?" "It's me." From the other side of the door, Mrs. James' voice could be heard.Although she was now in charge of managing the estate, the woman felt more like a part of the family than an employee. Nick was unable to recall a period when she had not been present.The petite grey-haired woman entered the room as Nick opened the door, and he knew that if there was anything out of place, she would give him that look and tell him to put it back in its proper place. Joanna James continued to terrify him despite the fact that he was a fully grown man and that he was living at home for the first time in his adult life.She announced, "There's a lady downstairs, she's here to see Jason," after making sure everything was to her satisfaction. "Why would someone come to see Jason on a Sunday?" "Is it about work?" she asked. Nick pleaded, "Please let it be about work," saying that he had no imagined he could miss work so much. However, this is what happens when you stay in a hospital bed for an extended period of time."I didn't ask, but she seemed very distressed."a distressed woman visiting Jason. Nick questioned whether Mrs. James should have shared this knowledge with him. Not with the current state of affairs between him and Jason.He said, "So what do you need me to do?" "Talk to her perhaps"Nick shook his head, realising that it wasn't the best time to be looking into Jason-related matters. A second before, when he believed it to be about work, he had been intrigued, but a distressed woman to see Jason just screamed trouble, and if he had even one functioning brain cell, he would keep out of it.This would just take a minute, and I guarantee I'll make sure no one disturbs you for the remainder of the day. "Mrs. James, I have a disturbing headache," wasn't exactly a lie.Deeply sighing, Nick. Mrs. James was not someone you could readily reject. He was aware of that from experience. Nick said, "I'll be down in a second.

Nick wondered what this woman wanted with Jason as he descended the stairs. He had only come to the conclusion that she might be a reporter trying to acquire an inside scoop on all that had transpired the previous year or the events that followed. People had made a lot of assumptions about what had happened, but nobody was certain of the facts, and his family preferred that they remain unknown.Rich people had advantages, but there were also drawbacks. People would do anything to obtain even the slightest piece of information and dirt about them.Nick took a short breath when he saw her slumped on the armchair. She was really petite. She could as well have been a teenager because of the way she was seated, which made it difficult for him to see her face.She had on an extremely vivid yellow blouse with black polka dots and blue jeans. Her hair was worn so short that Nick imagined running his hands through it. He also felt that the length of her hair was chosen to highlight her extremely long neck, which a lengthier hairstyle would have concealed. Once more, Nick imagined what it would feel like to wrap his hands around her hair.He shook his head, pushing the thoughts down despite not knowing where they were coming from.He said "Good afternoon" and watched her startle and stand up."Hi... Pleasant afternoon... Samantha here. She stumbled, "Samantha Baker," he responded, "Niklaus," and extended his hand to shake.She grasped his hand, wiped her it on her jeans as she quickly apologies for it being sticky and damp. "You are here to see Jason?" he said as he motioned for her to seat. She still nodded even though it was more of a statement than a question.He questioned, "Is it a business or a private matter?"

as he observed her swallow, which was a clear indication that she was anxious.She paused before responding."There's just something I need to talk to him about. I would say inform him. But if he's not here, I might be able to return later or never.She wanted to talk about something that truly attracted Nick. She would have stated that it was not business, and Nick felt confident that he would have known her if she had done business with his family.I'm Niklaus McCarthy, Jason's older brother, I don't think I presented myself well, he informed her. She was visibly anxious, but Nick knew he wanted to know right away if it was something crucial or involving their family.He watched her swallow again before saying, "Okay," "If you can tell me whatever it is, I'll make sure Jason gets the message," but she remained silent. She then started biting her bottom lip.Sammy gave it some thinking, but before she could decide otherwise, she said, "I'm pregnant. Is from your brother.She observed the shift in his facial expression from neutral to astonished to alarmed before she saw it all return to neutral."You are expecting? She nodded as he said, "And it's Jason's."She didn't appear to be pregnant; rather, she simply displayed fear and discomfort. This wouldn't be someone's first attempt to defraud their way into their family. Not that he was suggesting the girl was lying, but what were the chances that Jason would have had a hookup with her right when he was attempting to get his life back on track? What were the chances that she just so happened to be in this location at this precise time when Jason was away to deliver such news?In all honesty, he was stumped as to what to say to the girl, and it didn't help that she appeared visibly terrified."So, you and Jason...?" He didn't anticipate having this conversation at three in the afternoon."Yes. Seven weeks ago, we first met in a New York pub. last seven weeks. She was correct; Jason was visiting several bars in New York at that time. However, that didn't prove anything because everyone knew about Jason's promiscuity, and this girl might have learned about it from a variety of places and made the decision to try to make money off of it.This was a conversation that should have taken place in front of everyone concerned, so he asked, "Seven weeks ago?"As if on schedule, Nick began to hear the chopper noises as they arrived; at this point, everyone present would be asking, "What's happening?" Samantha questioned, feeling the cynicism in his tone, "Well, your baby daddy's back... and so is everyone else."Why in the world did he say that everyone else is doing the same? Sammy was left wondering what in the name of God she had just walked into.She inquired, "who is everyone else?" and he gave her a sly look that made her cringe."everyone in the family"So, she just announced that she, a girl he only spent a little over five hours with, was pregnant in Jason McCarthy's family home?She was in the position of the girls she and her closest friend had been making fun of, and she almost laughed at herself. She was going to be the mother of a child for a person she hardly knew.

THE FIRST GUY entered the room holding a very pregnant woman in his arms and grinning at what she was whispering to him. If it weren't for his blond hair and the fact that Jason went in behind him, Sammy almost mistaken the man who was following them for Jason. There was no doubt that the older man walking behind Jason was their father because he was holding hands with a younger female.Sammy struggled to control the beads of sweat that began to gather on her face as the entire McCarthy family stood before her. To all of these people, how would she introduce herself?When they spotted her, all the conversation stopped; it was as if they all noticed her at once.She stood up at the same time as Nick did, and with them both on the same side, the newcomers began to stare at each other in a competition to be the first to spea k.This is Samantha Baker, Nick said after clearing his throat, glancing at his brother Jason as though waiting for him to respond.Sammy realised that he didn't recall her when he didn't. He didn't know who she was as they stood face to face gazing at each other, despite the fact that she hadn't stopped thinking about him ever since. However, she had thought of him, the man who had left her to awaken alone in a hotel room, the man who had only given her a first name, and the man who had forced her to throw caution to the wind and take a leap into the unknown. It wasn't because they had the most memorable time; in fact, she honestly remembered very little to nothing about their entire encounter that night. Well, if she remembered correctly, her friend Vicky had also played a significant role in the previous one, so it had been partially his fault.Nobody spoke, as if anticipating him to go into greater detail about who she was, which he definitely did.The stillness that followed "She calms she is expecting Jason's child" really made her uneasy; this would have been the ideal time for the ground to give way and swallow her, but it didn't."What do you mean, you're expecting Jason's child?"

A closer look at her revealed that she was quite attractive and had unusually blond hair that gave the impression that she wasn't really there. The girl who had been hugging their father inquired Sammy. The bright red lipstick made her look as though she wouldn't mind throwing a fight, but the sweetness of her voice revealed that she wasn't really one to raise her voice. She also had double piercings in both of her ears and one on her nose, which gave her character.Everyone looked at Jason awaiting a reaction when he said, "Apparently they met in New York seven weeks ago. Sammy wanted to go because of the stunned expressions on everyone's faces, but as Vicky had indicated, there was no getting away from this. This was something she had to face right now."Can we please have the room?" After the longest period of silence, Jason seemed to have just found his voice.Sammy observed them all leaving, each of them giving her a quick glance, and she already knew what they were all contemplating."This bitch who digs for gold"

He made a modest pace. Before daring to spare her a glance, he made his way from corner to corner. She was genuinely afraid by the fact that he appeared to be a lion circleing its victim. Did he really forget who she was? The silence was killing Sammy, and she would have given any-thing to know what was going on in his thoughts. He didn't appear furious at all, which was good, right?I asked, "What are you doing here?"  Sammy noticed the expression in his eyes and realised that things weren't going to be as simple as she had first anticipated.Sammy didn't comprehend the need for the second question because, of course, he had already heard what his brother had stated before.She started, "we met at a pub in Brooklyn seven weeks ago," and he laughed. Sammy waited for him to speak, but when he didn't, she recognised he was making fun of her. She carried on nevertheless because, after all, she was aware that this would be a challenging talk to have.Vicky's favourite pub in the city was called "Donald's dive," mostly because the management was almost in love with her and always gave her a discount. Sammy had only visited twice because she didn't enjoy going to bars, but Vicky's dragging her to one to celebrate the promotion wasn't a surprise. Even while being an assistant manager might not seem like a huge issue, Vicky enjoyed celebrating both big and small victories.And we shared a bed? She was offended by the subsequent giggle rather than the insulting tone in which he said it. He clearly believed she was lying, and Sammy had little to fall back on but the child they had that night to back her up. Sammy shuddered at the idea; even though it was already a fact of her life, the idea of having a kid with a total stranger still made her uncomfortable.Yes, she muttered, swallowing her pride at how embarrassing and difficult it had been to admit."And now that you are pregnant?" Jason asked once more, his smile never fading.She felt compelled to respond, "I'm not lying. Didn't say you were, but that still doesn't address my question. Why are you in this place?"I just thought you might be interested in knowing,"She was truly astonished when he said, "Nope," "You are not here because of that."Okay, things changed. Sammy had not anticipated"How much?" he questioned. "Excuse me?"How much did you anticipate making off of this con of yours?She whispered loudly, "What?" Naturally, that was his greatest concern—not that he had fathered a child with a complete stranger, but rather that the stranger was here to con him out of his money.Sammy spoke to him in a timid murmur, "I don't... I don't want your money," but mainly because she didn't believe what he had the courage to say to her."Obviously not. He rolled his eyes at her, "Cut the nonsense lady, you obviously want something since you are here. You just came all the way from New York because 'you don't want my money. Therefore, the sooner you tell me what it is, the simpler it will be for both of us.For lack of a better phrase, she reiterated, "I don't want your money. Of course not. The same sarcastic tone he had earlier was employed to say, "We had sex and you became pregnant."Yes," "Lady, I don't even remember you and maybe I didn't pay you enough for that night, and I think you've got the wrong idea if you think that breaking into my father's house on a Sunday was going to help you extort us."She muttered, "I'm not a hooker," once more, before closing her eyes in the hopes that when she opened them again, she would be back in her New York flat and that everything had been a dream."And you slept with me because?" he questioned without blinking."I was wasted. We were buzzed.You don't see them all running up to announce their phantom babies now do you? I was drunk all year and I was with a lot of women. That's because I'm always cautious, whether I'm intoxicated or not.Since she didn't expect to see him again, Samantha sincerely wished she could have told him what happened, but she couldn't even remember. She couldn't be sure since she wasn't the kind of girl who kept a condom in her purse in the hopes of getting laid; all she knew was that Jason McCarthy was the only man she had been with in a long time.I'm not lying," she reiterated."Maybe not, but I believe you ought to seek out the true paternity of your child because I don't buy the whole act you're peddling. After saying "Now get out of my property, before I have you thrown out," he left her there acting foolishly and went upstairs.Sammy only wanted to collapse there in a pool of her own tears, but she was determined to solve this problem on her own instead. She made a mistake by coming here, but she didn't make a mistake by sleeping with Jason McCarthy, and because she couldn't undo it, she decided to go immediately and face the consequences on her own.

He believed Sammy was a liar and a gold-digger as she walked out of the McCarthy manor; nonetheless, she was unable to control her nausea. She hadn't really considered anything other than simply coming here and informing him; while she had anticipated that he would have had some degree of turmoil and shock, she hadn't anticipated the absolute rejection. She hadn't anticipated being labelled a liar in front of others and then being asked to leave the premises. She undoubtedly deserved worse humiliation for allowing herself to become involved in this, so it's not as if she didn't deserve that.She whirled around as she heard her name called out from behind her to see Jason's brother, the one she had initially seen and the one with the cast on his arm, racing in her direction. Sammy wanted to run away from him because of the scowl on his face, but she knew she wouldn't be able to take it if he said something as hurtful as his brother did.He introduced himself as "Niklaus, we met earlier" as though she would have forgotten after only a few minutes.Since everything had been humming when they first introduced themselves, she had forgotten, in actuality."You need to come back inside, my father would like to speak to you," he said, continuing. The way he said it didn't sound like a request; rather, it sounded like someone who was used to delivering instructions and expecting them to be followed .She told him, "I don't think that's a good idea. I wish you had thought about that before you got here." He answered, "I wish you had thought about that before you came here. He sounded upset, and Sammy winced at that, but she followed him anyhow.

For what felt like an eternity, he left her alone in this enormous, terrifying room. She would never confess it, but she was hungry and needed to pee, but she would keep all of that to herself until she left this place. If only she had left.Loudly, the door swung open, and Richard McCarthy entered.Sammy could now understand why he had been called one of the most scary men in America in the article she had read about him back home. Although he wasn't a particularly large man, the instant he entered the room, his aura dominated the space. Despite his slender build and height, he gave the impression that he could fight on his own. He appeared to engage in regular exercise and eat well. He had just grey hairs on his head, which in some strange way enhanced his appeal. In essence, he was really attractive, and Sammy was well aware that he probably broke a lot of hearts when he was younger.He sat down on the opposite side of the table and questioned, "Ms Samantha Baker, am I correct?"Samantha waited while nodding.She consented, not knowing what he meant by "don't waste mine," "I won't waste your time Ms. Baker, so please don't waste mine." "You say you are pregnant, yes?"He responded, "I am""and it's my son's?" "It is""fine, then let's get started. He just stated, "I want you to marry my son Jason. Like he was discussing the weather or any other completely normal topic."what?" Sammy inquired since she thought she had just overheard Richard McCarthy, a man she was meeting for the first time, mention that he wanted her to marry his son.Sammy shook her head as she struggled to find the right words. "I'm sure you heard me, Ms. Baker." What exactly were the words? What would be the appropriate response to this?She said to him, "I don't think I understand what you mean."They were probably using this devious tactic to force her to declare the child wasn't Jason's.Jason lost his wife a little over a year ago, and here she was thinking that she had done extensive study on the man who had knocked her up. He stared at her thoughtfully for a time before saying, "Jason lost his wife a bit over a year ago." "the circumstances surrounding her death left a rather sour taste in everyone's mouth" Didn't death often leave sour tastes in everyone's mouths? In actuality, comprehensive investigation entailed asking Vicky a few questions and letting her tell her the things she knew about the entire McCarthy family. Sammy pondered, but she was genuinely unsure of how it related to him and his ludicrous request for her.I believe you are what he needs right now, sir. "I'm sorry, but I can't marry your son," he said with a pout and a narrowed gaze. This was certainly a man who wasn't accustomed to having his opinions cha llenged.He questioned, "Can't or won't?" "I don't think your son..."He interrupted her by saying, "Jason has little choice in the matter.""Mr. McCarthy..."He commanded her to "hear me out" with a little hand raise."Ms. Baker, I am a very traditional man. If the child you claim to be expecting is my son's, then I would really like him to be a member of the family. I do not want to have a bastard grandson somewhere in the world. Which implies that after we establish your child's paternity, you will wed my son. On paper, yes, but in order to maintain appearances, I would want you to move into the manor. Of course you will be taken care of, and on top of that, you will receive $1,000,000 for each year you spend married to my son.Dollars one million! Sammy gulped. Sammy was certain she would never see money like that in her lifetime.She questioned him, "You'll pay me to marry your son?"Don't think of it that way; it's more like a recompense, Richard McCarthy grinned. A million dollars will be deposited to the account of your choice after each year you are wed to Jason.To be completely honest, Sammy had never felt so embarrassed in her entire life—not even when a patron openly degraded her at a banquet she had worked at. But it hadn't felt this way; in fact, this was the most degrading sensation she had ever had."I'm sorry, sir, but I don't think..."Richard said, "Oh my dear, you do not understand what I'm saying.""My offer is very generous for someone like you, and I hope you accept it. However, if you don't, I will require that you move into the manor immediately and that, after the child is born, you give up both the child and your parental rights to us."Sammy's mouth fell wide, and she nearly pressed her fingers together to confirm that she wasn't dreaming. Was he crazy, or was she the only one? give up her parental responsibilities? What even did that mean?"Mr. McCarthy, I don't think I understand what you mean" "Of course you would be allowed to visit, but if you don't agree to marry my son then you are condemning your child to growing up without a mother"Was there a joke involved here? Sammy was curious. Or possibly a sinister prank?She detested that his words had made her afraid and detested the fact that he knew it from the look on his face when he said, "With all due respect sir, I will not give you my child."Let's not act as though you have a lot to offer this child, Samantha, please. Your single, beleaguered mother, who barely provided for you and passed away when you were sixteen, reared you. You work as a sales clerk in a run-down boutique and reside in a studio apartment in Brooklyn. "What the...She had just met these individuals thirty minutes ago, and now they seemed to know everything about her life?She found herself stuttering, "How... how did... where did..."She wasn't even sure of the question she wanted to ask. "Or did I get any of it wrong, Ms. Baker?" he questioned as he stood up and moved around the table to stand next to her. "Take a week to think this over; I know marriage is a big issue, but I do hope you make the correct option. I shall stay in touch," he said before making his way to the door and holding it open for her.He was done talking to her, thus it was an offer to depart.

# CHAPTER 2

Although Samantha Baker had always been aware of her status in life and had never felt ashamed of it, she couldn't help but be transported back to Richard McCarthy's home office as the airport cab pulled up in front of her apartment complex. She felt like throwing up after hearing him read out her life in a demeaning manner as like it were some tragic tale.He had looked at her. He had conducted a comprehensive inquiry into her life in less than the thirty minutes he had made her wait, to the point where he was aware of the day her mother had passed away.She knew that Jason would reject her and her child, but she hadn't expected to be presented with a marriage proposal along with the prospect of losing her child.All she wanted to do was go up to her flat and sob uncontrollably, but she also wanted to scream at Vicky because it was really her fault because she had persuaded her to travel 2,550 kilometres to find a man she knew very little about in order to tell him he was the father of the child she was carrying.

Vicky calmly listened to Sammy's suffering at the McCarthy manor before yelling, "ONE FUCKING MILLION!" Sammy questioned whether she had heard the whole of the story, in which Jason McCarthy called her a con artist and his father threatened to kidnap her child. a child who had not even been born.She yelled, "One fucking million dollars!" once more, sounding ecstatic. "Yes Vicky, he said that if I marry Jason he was going to pay me a million dollars," she said, in case Vicky hadn't heard it the first time. However, knowing Vicky, the girl only heard what she wanted to hear and blocked out the rest."What do you mean by IF?" Sammy responded to Vicky's question, "You don't think I'm just gonna take the money and marry a man I barely know.""You had a child with a man you hardly know, and I don't see the problem with you marrying him as well," Wow! That was not anything Vicky just said."Wow, Vicky."I realise that and I'm sorry, but you are sober now, Sam. "I'm sorry" "I was drunk, I made a mistake" You ought to choose wisely.What is which? Why would I accept their money and wed someone I hardly know?"Yes! These individuals will take your kid and give him stuff you could never even imagine. Do you want it, exactly?Obviously not. Sammy had only recently discovered she was pregnant, but she already knew she would die if her child were taken away. Simply put, she couldn't bear the thought of her kid growing up without her. "Sammy listen to me, taking that money doesn't mean you're selling yourself or your values, she said. Vicky remarked, "It implies you are a fantastic mother who is willing to make this one sacrifice for her child.Did it, however? Or does it merely make her more ebullient?

Sammy was relieved to have left for lunch because her back was killing her and the store was crowded. Vicky was now constantly in her apartment pleading with her to make up her mind, so she felt as though the rear of the store was the only place she could get some peace and quiet. At the store, it seemed like everyone needed assistance of some kind, but she was in no condition to lend a hand today; rather, all she wanted to do was sleep. This was strange because she had been having a hard time falling asleep for days. She had sat up all night yesterday watching the clock until her alarm went off, at which point she felt incredibly exhausted and wished she actually had a million bucks so she could skip work. which made her realise that her allotted time was almost over. Sammy couldn't help but admit that she felt a little frightened, especially with Vicky's voice present. Since Jason McCarthy had treated her so poorly, she could not imagine herself getting married to him. She recalled that Jason had little choice in the matter, which implied that he would likewise be forced into it. In that case, he was likely to despise her for however long the marriage lasted. Did she truly want to be in a marriage that way?She couldn't just turn everything off and get married to someone who would hate her, so her friend's counsel wasn't really helpful.Hello, Sam. Addison She turned to face the other salesperson when she was called.She informed her that there were two males in the store to see her.To see her, two men? She wasn't sure if she knew any two males who would come looking for her at her place of employment, so that was rather strange.She gave Addison a quick "I'll be right in" as she put down the cheeseburger she was barely starting to eat. She didn't want to keep them waiting if they were clients.She said with a fake smile, "Hello, good afternoon," but as soon as she recognised one of the men, she realised who the other one was.She questioned the person whom she recognised as Niklaus, Jason's brother: "What... what are you doing here?" He wasn't wearing the arm cast, but she could still recognise him as the person she had first met that day at the McCarthy house.He said with a serious and professional tone, "We come to talk to you.Sammy gazed around the shop; her break wasn't over for another twelve or so minutes.She motioned for them to follow her, her heart beating as she led them to the rear where her cheese burger, which had previously been thrown away, was still sitting. Prior to the end of the week Richard McCarthy had granted her, she was meant to have two more days.She questioned again, taking careful not to let her voice quiver, "what are you doing here?" now that they were alone.I'm Chase. Hello. We didn't get a chance to introduce ourselves when you dropped by the house, the other guy remarked with a smile that helped release some of the tension. He was not just younger but also finer than the man standing next to him. His blonde hair was slightly wavy and not nearly as bleached as their sister's. Niklaus McCarthy was very attractive, but in a broody way, so don't get me wrong.She said, "Samantha," and waved back.It was Niklaus who spoke while holding out an envelope to her, saying, "This is a copy of the prenup; look it over before you are picked up on Saturday." Nothing nice from that one.She was totally perplexed and asked, "Wait, what?"collected on Saturday? What was she looking at a prenup for and why was she being picked up on a Saturday?He looked at her as if she were ignorant, "You do know what a prenup is?"She was aware of what a prenup was, of course, but it didn't help her understand why they were giving it to her. "Ignore my brother; he hasn't been around people much lately so he's lacking the basic bedside manner," they said. With a smile that somehow put her at ease, Chase hopped in.We just want to make sure you know what to expect from us, in case you accept the offer my father made you. And what they anticipated of her. Sammy understood that to be what Chase genuinely meant even if he didn't say it.Sammy responded, "Of course you haven't," when he said, "I haven't made up my mind yet." And that's okay," his brother rolled his eyes at Niklaus as he scoffed and stated in jest. However, it would still be nice if you returned to Texas on Saturday. While you're debating, just a few tests," Chase remarked.Sammy was certain that Chase was handling her, but it was still preferable to his brother's approach.She said, "I work Saturdays and I don't know if my boss will let me skip the day." This time, Niklaus inquired, "What time do you get off work?" "Five thirty, six," she replied.Sammy didn't catch the apology Chase threw her before following his brother and instead lowered herself to the chair she had been sitting on earlier, put her face between her legs, and just took deep breaths. He didn't wait for her to respond before turning around and walking back into the store. This was not how things should have gone, and everything about it was wrong. She hadn't anticipated things to unfold in this manner. They were meant to discuss how to raise their child in a way that involved everyone while still making everyone happy after Jason apologised for leaving her in the hotel that morning and perhaps gave her a sympathetic explanation. She didn't anticipate that his entire family would now be involved in the decision-making process, treating her like some sort of gold-digging con artist who had anticipated their father would offer her a million dollars to marry their brother.She wanted nothing more than hurl the envelope she was holding into the trash. While giving Niklaus McCarthy the middle finger, she felt like calling him back. Vicky would have, and he deserved it as well.

SAMIE PERFORMED UNTIL When she was by herself, she took the envelope out of her bag from which she had stuffed it earlier at work. She needed to finish it because she had put it off for too long.She had considered asking Vicky, but she opted to read the papers by herself first since she had a hunch that Vicky would support whatever was stated in the articles as long as they didn't want to kill her or kidnap her child. Vicky could be informed tomorrow, or even better, she could let Vicky read it herself.The first of the four pro-visions in the contract discussed the compensation she was entitled to. It specified that she would be paid as long as she stayed married to Jason McCarthy, but if she ever decided to separate from him, the payments and any other benefits she had previously received from the McCarthys would end.The following sentence was regarding the child and claimed that even if the marriage failed, Sammy would never exclude them from his paternal family's existence. She was informed that she could not leave the nation with the child without first telling either their father or their grandfather. There were many more things, but none of them were actually pertinent to Sammy at that particular time.The prenup said that Sammy was not permitted to discuss any secret she may or may not learn while staying with the McCarthy family with the press.After that, it discussed her rights; it stated that, even if the marriage ended, she would only be entitled to the amounts she received. Most importantly, she had no financial interest in the family business, Luxury.Since she wasn't in it to steal their money or kidnap the child from her father, she could live with any of these conditions. In fact, the only reason she had travelled to Texas in the first place was so that Jason could be involved in his child's life.The situation may not have been as bad as she was portraying it to be, but it all still felt surreal. She was carrying a child for an unknowing father who also happened to be one of the top fifty richest men in America. And she didn't know it until Vicky told her in one of the numerous attempts Vicky made to persuade her to accept the bargain. She was now being courted to marry him. Was she going to get married? Sammy nearly laughed at the idea. Being someone's wife was the last thing she was prepared for, but she also wasn't prepared to be someone's mother, so she would have to somehow buck up and do both.

Sammy glanced at the clock in the shop; it read precisely five. She had been up all night thinking of the countless reasons why this would never work, but she had always talked herself out of them. Now she couldn't stop the beating in her chest. Even though she felt deep down that she was making the wrong choice, she had contacted Vicky twice simply to hear someone else reassure her that she wasn't. She wasn't sure what it was precisely, but she just couldn't get rid of the feeling.But she wasn't going to wed Jason today; rather, she was only going to perform some tests, one of which she knew would be a paternity test.She picked up her phone once more and called Vicky, saying, "It's the right decision." Vicky told her right away that her response, "What if they are a bunch of serial killers?" was absurd because she had previously visited their home and met them."Seri ously? Did they resemble a group of murderers when you first met them?"Well, no, but it was a very brief meeting, so you could never be sure,"They cannot all be serial killers simultaneously.What if they belong to a cult and want to offer me up as a sacrifice?Do you hear yourself, Sam?"I do, but...""There are only a few simple tests to run, and then you'll be back, no buts. Okay?""Okay. But suppose something does happen."Then I'll bring every cop in New York down there," he said."Wealthy people often get away with things""They can't harm you and get away with it."Even though Sammy knew her friend was simply making her laugh, it was still pleasant to hear.The words "I love you"She ended the call with "I love you" and hung up feeling less anxious than before.

After the trip to the airport, Sammy came to understand what it meant to BE CHAUFFER DRIVEN. She was still unsure of her ability to get a flight to Texas at this hour when Levi informed her that the plane was 'this way'. Flying in a private jet and receiving royal treatment seemed unreal at the time. Every member of the crew had personally introduced them-selves, addressed her as ma'am as if she were their boss, and was carrying her suitcase as if it were stuffed with priceless stones.She held her breath, waiting for something to happen to snap her back to reality. It wasn't until she was waiting for Levi to open the car door for her inside the McCarthy manor—a treatment she still wasn't used to—that she finally let go.With a broad smile on his lips and acting as though they were buddies, Chase unlocked the car door for her. Sammy discovered that she was compelled to grin in return; this was all she required to calm her worries. Why had she been so concerned? They were all people like her; there was no way Chase, who had such a charming personality, could be a serial killer or a ritual killer.When Levi, the chauffeur, pulled out her bag, he said, "Is this all you brought with?" "Don't worry, we can just send for the rest later," he remarked dismissively and casually, as if everything had already been resolved."All right, let's enter. Everybody is waiting to meet you. All of you saw Sammy freeze? like everyone who had been present when she had made a fool of herself earlier? She didn't mind at all if they postponed the introductions until tomorrow or later; she had been hoping they would.She questioned, "Everyone?""Well, simply my sister, the estate manager, and my brother Luca and his wife. You ran into her the day you arrived?He was referring to the diminutive woman with the cruel face and loving eyes.He made a joke to soothe her anxiety, "Don't worry, they don't bite."It would be a miracle if she didn't see him until she made up her mind about whether or not she was going to be his wife. He said nothing about Jason's whereabouts or the other sibling, and she didn't bother asking.

They didn't bite her, but as they entered, everyone stopped talking and stared at her as if she had grown two heads overnight. The very pregnant woman was the one to regain consciousness first, and she then stepped forward before jabbing her husband hard by his side with her elbow, saying, "Make her more uncomfortable, why don't you?" She warned them as Chase laughed and her husband made a loud noise of anguish.She extended her hand and said, "Hi... I'm Charlie."Sammy shook her hand and felt quite self-conscious because she thought she was really pretty—no, beautiful—and wished she hadn't driven straight to the airport after working a seven-hour shift at the store.So when the McCarthy boys weren't drunk, these were the kinds of ladies they pursued.Hello, Sammy.She pointed at her husband, who was now standing upright and approaching them, and said, "That blubbering mess over there is my husband Luca."He said to his wife, "You did just punch me in the ribs," before turning to face Sammy and saying, "I'm the husband, Luca. I'm Alex, and as you can see, the only sane person in this family, remarked their sister, who is also quite gorgeous. "And yes, my wife is as vicious as she looks," Sammy replied now with a real smile.Chase said, whispering, "That's not true, she's not sane either," drawing a chuckle from Sammy and a punch to the arm from Alex.Let me just say I'm delighted that you've decided to stay with us, Sammy," Chase said, introducing the older woman with a smile. She reassured her, "Pay her no mind, she sucks up to every pregnant woman in the family. It will be so nice having kids back in the house." Charlie rubbed her belly, and everyone smiled.Sammy instantly realised that these folks wouldn't treat her or her child as though they didn't belong in this place. not yet, at least.I'll take you to your room so you can freshen up and rest when you get there, so come on. Mrs. James informed her before turning to face Chase.She questioned, "Where are her things?" Levi had already taken them."All right, shall we then?"

Sammy was deposited here by Mrs. James almost an hour ago with instructions to ask if she needed anything. She was lying on this incredibly big bed with the silkiest sheet she had ever touched. Her body was now in desperate need of sleep after she took the liberty of taking a shower and changing into new clothes.Vicky was expecting a call from her when she landed, but she postponed making one because it was already late and because she knew her friend would want to know everything whenever she called.After a soft knock on the door, Charlie popped her head inside.She inquired, "Are you decent?" Sammy grinned and nodded, "Good you are. Can I come in? she said, but Sammy didn't bother to answer because she was already inside and had closed the door behind her.She approached Sammy and sat down next to her on the bed, asking, "So, how are you? " Sammy said, "I think as good as it can get," but, in all honesty, she was still unsure of her feelings. Simply put, the situation was too overwhelming."good, is that right? I just wanted to see how you were doing and give you some updates. She inquired, "Have you eaten anything yet?" Her nerves prevented her from saying, "I'm not hungry yet.""That's alright. Feel free to go downstairs and take a snack at any time; the kitchen is right there. Sammy gave a nod.She called, a smile on her face,

"So Sammy..."Sam couldn't help but feel a bit self-conscious since she was so attractive. She wished she had at least brushed her hair when she got out of the shower, but she had assumed she was going to bed right away."Luca is on the phone updating Richie, the old man wants to make sure you got in okay and Chase is gone, he said something about having a date but we all know it's a sex date, I swear that one only thinks about getting laid, Lord knows when we are going to see him next," Richie remarked. Since my sisters won't be able to attend, I advised Alex to cancel her ridiculous shower, but she was having none of it. Of course, Alex is still being a pain in the ass. And I'm here to update you on everyone," she said with a smile. Sammy returned the smile; she liked Charlie. Although it was really soon, she had a Vicky-like quality to her.No updates on Jason? Did the man even anticipate her arrival? She had been here for more than an hour, so Sammy figured he would have at least shown up by now given that the child she was expecting was his.She questioned, "And Jason?"Sammy had a sneaking suspicion that when Charlie said, "Well... Jason isn't here right now, but I'm sure he'd be back soon," she really meant, "I have no freaking idea if he'd be back." Nevertheless, Sammy agreed.Don't anticipate seeing either of Richie and Nick for a long because they are both in Denver on a business trip. Charlie giggled and touched her tummy before saying, "Oh, you are having a boy?" as she added, "Luca would have gone with them but he's turned into this clingy husband since this bad boy started showing, it's a miracle he even let me come in here alone." No, no, we're going to wait until the baby is born to find out the sex, Sammy pleaded. My hubby has a flair for the dramatic. Sammy could tell right away from the way she spoke of her husband that she loved him. She was a little bit upset since she realised she would never be able to share that with the father of her child.She only inquired, "You've been with them long?"Luca and I have been married for a few years, but I've loved that man since I was fourteen, Charlie thought as she scratched her jaw."Fourteen!" Sammy reaffirmed his amazement. She had been shocked by Charlie's early devotion to Luca because she had never experienced love before the age of 24.She smiled and continued, "Maybe before that, and I know what you are thinking, and nope the blockhead didn't always love me back, but I won him over, and now that man would die for me.She stood up in bed.As she rubbed her belly and turned to leave the room, she said, "Okay, I'll leave you alone to rest now but I'm probably going to be the first face you see when you wake up in the morning because believe it or not you are the most interesting thing to happen in my life in well over six months."Sammy pondered whether she would look like this in a few months as she watched her stroll. She still had trouble picturing it; she had never considered herself capable of being a mother, but she also didn't believe she would make a bad one.

# CHAPTER 3

Sunday went by as a bit of a blur. True to her words Charlie was the first person she saw in the morning and they spent the entire day getting her familiar with the property, she introduced her to the staff and everyone that was available for introduction.The woman sure did talk a lot but Sammy couldn't complain, she enjoyed her company which was weird because she didn't enjoy spending time with a lot of people. And it seemed like Charlie genuinely liked her too because she was very friendly.

The three ladies, Charlie, Alex and Sammy had lunch that afternoon and after which they all dispersed. Alex had asked if she wanted to join her to go shopping but she decided it was best she didn't and Charlie? That one just wanted to crawl into her husband arms. She had said earlier that her husband was being clingy but Sammy had a feeling the clingy went both ways. So after she went up to her room she called Vicky just to let her know she was still alive but that had turned into a two hour phone conversation because Vicky wanted to know every tiny detail and had asked a ton of questions after that she decided to take a well-deserved nap.

SAMANTHA BAKER WASN'T much of an eater, not just because she could most times barely afford herself the standard three squared meal but also because she was a really shitty cook and Vicky would say because she was lazy too. But now she was eating for two and the growling in her tommy she would have normally ignored she now couldn't.

She looked at the time on her phone and it read twelve eleven, the well-deserved nap had turned into a well-deserved slumber and she had ended up missing dinner.

Charlie did say she could use the kitchen anytime right? But did anytime also include twelve in the morning when everyone was probably asleep?She didn't want to be caught wondering about their home in the middle of the night but when her stomach growled again it forced her to sit up. She had had lunch, right? So why was her belly crying like it hadn't been fed in days?Maybe just a glass of water or two, to drown the hunger, she thought and then decided to go down to the kitchen.

As expected the lights of the kitchen where out but from the windows facing outside there was enough light coming in that she decided not to bother with turning on the ligh ts.She tried not to make much noise as she made her way to the refrigerator, she had no idea why she was tiptoeing but she did it anyway. Helping herself to the carton of milk she poured the first glass and downed it in one gulp and then poured a second glass and decided to take it upstairs with her. She screwed the cap back on the milk and returned it to the fridge and then made her way out while carrying the glass she had poured.She was almost out of the kitchen when she spotted the dark figure hunched over on one of the kitchen stools and it felt like it was staring directly at her, she let the glass of milk she held drop as she let out a scream.

The lights were on in seconds,"Jesus Christ! Do you want to wake the whole fricking house?!" he asked looking panicked.

It was Niklaus. Shirtless, barefoot and ruffled hair but Niklaus McCarthy and not a serial killer.She still didn't understand this recent obsession with serial killers, it must be the documentary Vicky made her watch last month.

Her hands immediately flew to her chest. Oh, thank God!

"I'm sorry, you startled me" she said really apologetic"I was here first" he informed her dryly."I'm so sorry, I didn't mean to cause any trouble"

That meant he had been watching her the whole time she had been tiptoeing around like a common thief. Her cheeks grew hot with embarrassment. She knelt to the floor immediately in an attempt to clean up the mess she made she began picking up the broken pieces of the glass cup she held earlier.

"What are you doing?" he asked as if it wasn't already obvious"I'm trying to pack this up" she replied without looking at him. She was still too embarrassed to do so."No. No. Stand-up" he told her as she was reaching for the last broken piece"I said stand" he repeated when she ignored him, with the way he had said it there was no room for objections so Sammy stood up with a handful of broken pieces of glass.In three short seconds he was standing in front of her and the mess she had just made with an annoyed look on his face that said this was obviously a disturbance he could have done without.

He went around to fetch some paper towels and Sammy stood watching as he went down on his knees to clean up the mess she had stupidly made.

"What are you even doing in here?" he asked from the ground and from the tone of his voice Sammy could tell he was pretty annoyed at her

"I was hungry and I thought that everyone would probably be asleep, I swear I didn't mean to disturb anyone and Charlie said I could use the kitchen when I liked" she explained

He stood up and gave her a look over that made her skin crawl, Niklaus McCarthy wasn't doing much to hide his disdain for her and that made her wish she was anywhere else but here.She would have dragged her robe closer together if it wasn't that both of her hands where now soggy with milk and one hand held broken glass pieces.

"Give me that and go rinse your hands over there" he demanded relieving her of the glass pieces, he was speaking to her like she was a child and worse she was obeying like she was one.

She was still rinsing her hands when he asked."How do you feel about eggs?""What?" Sammy asked in confusion, how did their conversation go from rinsing her hand to her feelings about eggs?"Do you eat eggs" he asked again this time rather impatiently. Was he always this short tempered or was it just with her?"Yes, I do" she told him"Good. Now go sit over there" he instructed and Sammy scurried into one of the kitchen stools.

They both stayed silent while he worked, the only noise came from the thing he was doing, in few short minutes the aroma filled the kitchen and had Sammy salivating, the embarrassment she felt from him cooking for her faded with huger.

"Here. Eat" the two words sounded more like a command as Niklaus dropped the plate of eggs in front of her not that she minded with how hungry she was.

Using the fork she collected some and shoved it into her and honestly not expecting the taste of magic in her mou th.She smiled,"this is really good" she said with her mouth full before she could stop herself.He was still standing next to her but it didn't look like he was expecting the praise. He walked to the fridge and poured two glasses of orange juice and stretched one out to her without saying anything. She collected it from him and murmured her thanks.He sat back down where he had been sitting earlier and that was when Sammy noticed the slice of cake just sitting half eaten.He didn't go back to his cake, instead he just sat and watched her eat and her usual self would have been too self-conscious to continue eating while he watched but the eggs were too good to just pass out on and she was hungry.

"Why didn't you come down for dinner?" he asked after a while of silence, Sammy looked at him and thankfully he didn't have the scowl he wore earlier and that put her at peace a little.

"I was asleep, I woke up about an hour ago"he nodded and then took a sip from his juice and just when Sammy thought he was going to say something else he picked up his fork and went back to his cake.

"Charlie said you and your father were on a business trip" she said just to fill the awkward silence, he looked at her and then said"yes. But my trip had to be cut short."He didn't have to say it but Sammy already knew it was because of her that his trip had been cut short. She wanted to apologise but then decided against it instead she filled her mouth with more of the delicious egg to prevent her from saying anything.

"So, you are going to marry my brother?" he phrased it like a question but Sammy had a feeling it wasn't one.This was the man who had scoffed her when she had said she was still deciding. It was obvious that these people weren't used to hearing the word no and sadly she was leaning towards being one of the people who wouldn't tell them no.

"or have you still not made up your mind?" he was mocking her. It was embarrassing but there was little she could do about it.

"No. But I'll have an answer soon"she watched him roll his eye and then picked up his fork and then fiddled with the cake on his plate and then shook his head."it's cute the you think my father is really giving you a choice in the matter" he said"Excuse me?""Samantha Baker, let's not pretend there's a lot that you could do for this child. My family would offer you both the stability that you really need""I don't need anything thing from you people""Except that you do. You think raising a child is a walk in the park? No ma'm it requires more than you are capable of and my father is not just willing to let you have a test run with his grandchild" "it's my child too" her voice cracked a little, mostly because she was on the verge of breaking down into actual tears."Yes. And that is why you should be willing to do whatever you can to make sure they turn out okay even if that means marrying a man you barely know""I will do all I can for my child""Which is what exactly? My family is willing to let you raise your child however you want with all the support you can ever imagine and the only thing my father is asking of you is that you sign some marriage license making you my brother's wife"

His family was willing to let her raise her child? Seriously?

The eggs that had tasted magnificent earlier now just felt like chaff. Sammy wanted to be anywhere else, how could a man she had met just three times in her life make her feel like her entire existence was worthless?

"Thank you for the eggs, but I'm gonna go to bed now. Good night" she said and stood up, hoping her legs wouldn't shake she left the kitchen because she knew that if she stayed for one more second looking at that man's face, she was probably going to break down in a pool of tears.

AS NICK WATCHED the woman that was carrying his brother's child walk away he hated that Richard McCarthy had given him this task.He was finally ready to go back to work again and the only thing his father could think of was assigning him to be the one to make sure things went according to his plan."Bring this home" Richard had said like this was some business deal he needed to close. Well to an extent it was a business deal to Richard and Nick decided to treat it as such because if there was anything he did know, it was business and he had never failed at business deals and he suspected that was why Richard but him on top of this.

Drunk or not he could see why his brother would bed her, she wasn't pretty but she was beautiful but you wouldn't tell by just taking a glance at her because she did a good job hiding it.She wore her dark brown hair lower than his, her eyes were slightly big and was a very dark shade of brown that had this weird allure to them and her skin looked as silk as butter. Her ears looked too big for her head but he had a feeling that had more to do with how short she wore her hair than the actual ears themselves. She was thin and not in that sexy way that made you want to bed a woman but her figure suited her well enough.

She had sounded genuinely surprised that his eggs were good and he wasn't sure if to be insulted by that or just amused but it had given him some level of satisfaction to watch her eat. She had eaten like she was hungry, in big bites and with her eyes closed like she was savouring the taste and storing it in her mind for later. And with every bite she took Nick found he could only think of biting her lips, it was such an odd feeling that made him uneasy. He had no business thinking of her in that capacity, she was going to wed Jason and soon if Richard had anything to say about it.

"So you are going to marry my brother?" he asked partly to keep himself in check and also because Richard wanted to know,he hadn't meant for it to come out as rude as it had when he asked if she was still deciding and he normal-ly wouldn't have cared if not for the embarrassment that flashed on her face, it was gone as quickly as it came and she just casually said she'd have an answer for them soon. The meeting he had had with Richard before he left Austin concerning this came to his mind, the girl didn't know the lengths Richard would go to get the things he wanted. He had decided on suing her for the custody of the child and with the background check they had made on her it was obvious that the girl couldn't afford to battle it out with Richard in court and even if by some miracle she did, no judge on the planet would grant her custody over the almighty Richard McCarthy. He had pushed her harder than he had initially wanted.

No child should have to grow up without their mother, he was speaking from experience and he knew that Jason was going to be exactly how their father had been or worse so it was best if Samantha Baker came to her senses soon. And if he had to push her a bit hard for her to make the right decision then that was what he was going to do.

Sammy woke up with the feeling that today wasn't going go as smoothly as yesterday had gone, she also felt it was going to have something to do with Niklaus McCarthy. If she went the entire day without seeing him then she was sure she was going to be fine. Why couldn't he just be as nice as everyone else? They had all made her feel so welcomed until she had spoken to him last night. She had almost forgotten she was here on the conditional basis that she was going to marry Jason but his voice was the cruel reminder that the clock was ticking and they were waiting for her to give them an answer.There was a knock on her door that made her just want to crawl back under the covers but instead she got out of bed and went to see who it was, it was Levi who came to inform her that Mr McCarthy was going to see her in his study in an hour.So that meant Richard McCarthy was back too. Did that also mean that Jason was back too? But Charlie didn't mention anything about Jason being with him but it felt weird being in his home and being expected to marry him without actually seeing him and having a conversation with him just to know where they stood with each other and on the insane idea. Well he had clearly expressed were he stood the other day they had spoken and Sammy suspected he still felt the same way or he'd be here right now with her making decisions. The whole point of all this was for them to raise the child together right? She couldn't see that happening with him being MIA.

CHARLIE AND HER husband were in a heated conversation when Sammy came downstairs, Charlie looked and saw her and then said,"Good, a sane person" she motioned her to come over with her hands, Sammy walked over to them and smiled at both of them"Hi""No time for pleasantries" Charlie said hushing her "Go ahead, tell him" she said placing her hands akimbo and waiting for Sammy to tell her husband something she had no clue of."Could you please tell this knuckle head that nothing's going to happen to me if I go out with Lexie for just a bit""Baby, babe, I didn't say that something was going to happen but I just want you to stay here while I go join Richard for that meeting in Austin this afternoon"Richard? Was he not supposedly waiting for her in his study? Sammy wondered."I am going crazy just sitting around in this house. Look I love you, but if I have to watch another episodes of the real housewives of Texas, I'm going to literally carve this baby out of me" Charlie told her husband"then watch something else" he said calmly for someone his wife had just threatened to carve out their unborn child.Just immediately Chase walked in holding a box of the most heavenly smelling doughnut in his hands"Good morning, lovelies" he greeted no one in particular.Both Charlie and Luca threw him a glance and then went back to their staring contest."you don't want to be getting involved in their arguments" Chase told Sammy"We are not arguing" they both turned in unison and saidFrom where Sammy and Chase stood it did look that way."if you say so" he said to them and then whispered to Sammy "they are totally arguing" and Sammy couldn't help but chuckle."Let's go" he said taking her hand and taking her from the arguing couple,"have you had breakfast?" he asked her when they got to the dining areaSammy shook her head breakfast was the last thing that had been on her mind with Mr McCarthy summoning her like that."good" Chases said as he opened the delicious goodness he was carrying and they both dug in.

Sammy lost track of time while she ate with Chase, he was a wonderful company, at least better than his brother. Sometimes it was hard to tell if he was flirting or just being extremely nice which was somewhat unnerving for Sammy. He did all the talking and watched as she devoured the whole box by herself after he had taken that first one and by the time she realised what she had done there was just one doughnut left in the box and she flushed, embarrassed by her behaviour. Chase smiled at her,"it's all for you carino" he told her as if he had just read her mind"Thank you"  but she was full now so she smiled at him.Just then this girl that was putting on a maid's outfit came in, Sammy was sure she met her yesterday but she couldn't remember her name.She immediately saw Chase and blushed deeply"Good morning, Mr McCarthy" she said and Chase smiled back"I told you Jennifer, Chase. Mr McCarthy is my father"So it wasn't just Sammy with the flirting thing, she was relieved as she watched him do it with Jennifer."I'm sorry" she said with a silly giggle"Chase" she said as if testing how it sounded coming from her"okay Jennifer, do you need something?" Chase asked her and for a moment Sammy thought that they maybe had forgotten she was in the room with them."Yes. Mr McCarthy... the other Mr McCarthy sent me to fetch Ms Baker" she said"Oh Sammy, this is Jenny. She's new here so I'm still teaching her some stuff" it sounded dirty, the way he said it but that was none of Sammy's business, her business was the girl who had come to fetch her."Looks like you are needed somewhere else. Can you go with Jenny?" he asked and Sammy nodded

WHEN SAMMY KNOCKED on the door Jennifer left her there was no response, it was the same room she had been in a week ago with Richard McCarthy when he had made the indecent proposal. She knocked again and still nothing so she just turned the knob. The door gave in and she stumbled in"I'm sorry I knocked and..." she began to apologise but then drifted off when she saw Niklaus McCarthy sitting on the other side of the desk scribbling vigorously.So, when Jennifer and Levi had said Mr McCarthy, they had meant him and not Richard.He slowly stopped what he was writing, looked up at her and frowned when he saw her then he went back to what he had been writing"I knocked but...""Sit down" he said cutting her off without even looking at her.Sammy walked quietly to the chair and sat while he continued with what he had been writing.He took the next minute and then he looked up at her,"Good morning" he greeted in a way that made her feel like she had walked into a job interview."Good morning" Sammy responded after clearing her throat, she suddenly felt really nervous"We will be going down to the hospital now for the tests we talked about earlier""Oh, okay." It wasn't like she didn't know what she had come here to do, she had gotten so comfortable between yesterday and today that she thought she was a house guest.The test in question would have to be the basic pregnancy test and a paternity test right? All of which she was going to pass, so why was she suddenly feeling disappointed?"Are you ready to go?" he asked.Could you ever be ready to be probed and poked by doctors?"Yes. But I need to quickly grab my phone upstairs" and pee quickly too because it felt it was all she did lately. He took a heavy breath, the ones people took when they were bored of something or someone, or just plain annoyed."Fine, but we need to leave in ten minutes" he told her and then when she stood up to leave he called her and when she turned he said,"Please don't waste my time, I do have other engagements""I won't""Good. Be in front of the house in ten minutes" he said dismissively.

SAMMY SAT IN the waiting room of the hospital alone waiting for Niklaus, he had told her to do so when he went into the doctor's office twenty minutes ago. Why did it have to be him who would bring her here? Why couldn't Chase have brought her or Charlie? They were both really very nice and Alex too, compared to the brooding man who never smiled or wiped the scowl from his face.It wasn't like Sammy wanted them to be friends or anything but she would have appreciated it more if he stopped speaking to her like she was a child and had done something wrong.The entire ride down to the hospital they had just sat in an uncomfortable silence and Sammy was grateful for it, she kept fearing that he would ask her if she had decided on the whole marriage thing and then go at her again like he had done yesterday, she was still a bit sore from his words last night."Let's go" he said when he finally came out of the office, she followed him without question to the lab where they were apparently going to take some blood samples.Until the nurse had pulled out the syringe, Sammy had had no clue how terrified she was of needles. Thinking back now she had never gotten a blood test before, never needed it. She bought over the counter medication and had had no major reasons to see a doctor, as a matter of facts hospital in general wasn't really her scene. So there was no possible way she could have known how terrified she would be at the thought of the needle going into her arm.The nurse got up and went to the cabinet to fetch something and that was when Niklaus looked at her,"Are you okay?" he asked after she had taken the chair the nurse had generously offered while he kept standing."Yes. Why?" no, no, nope, I'm not okay at all. Not okay. She wanted to scream."Because you don't look so good"Sammy touched a hand to her forehead and found that she was sweating, her breathing had laboured and she felt like she was going to puke."Well, I might be a bit uncomfortable with the idea that that needle is going into my arm" she told him in panic."Are you kidding me? You are trypanophobic?" he whispered "If that means I don't want the needle going through me then, yes, whatever" she didn't want to give him any more reasons to be more upset with her than he already was but she was in a state of panic.He cursed, she could obviously imagine why this would upset him very much."I'm sorry" she told him"why are you apologising?" he asked"I don't want to give you any more reasons to hate me"  he looked genuinely surprised with what she said and just then the nurse came back with a tourniquet and wrapped it around her arm."Can you give us a moment?" he asked the nurse and then turned to her"Do you want to go and maybe come back tomorrow?" "Do you think this is going to go away by tomorrow?" she asked"I don't think so""Then let's get it over with, can you call the nurse back?" she didn't want him to think that she was trying to avoid this.

"Hey, maybe you should look away" he suggested as the nurse swabbed the insides of her elbow."Hey, hey, just look at me" he said as the nurse began and Sammy turned around and locked eyes with him and then felt him slip his hand into hers and that was all the distraction she needed to forget the needle going into her arm, she felt a pinch and then heard the nurse say it was over. It wasn't the death experience she thought it was going to be, the hand that held hers was the most soothing experience she had had in a long time and even after the nurse was done taking her blood, she found that she still wanted to hold it.

THE ENTIRE RIDE back home Nick found that he felt naked, it was an odd feeling looking into Samantha's eyes. Had her eyes been that large since the day they met or had he just imagined it. It had felt like he had given her access to his soul and she had taken it, it felt like by that one stare she knew all there was to know about him which was mostly ridiculous but it felt like that was the most invasive experience of his life and one that almost terrified him.He had panicked the moment she had panicked, and he held her hand. It was weird because the moment his hand touched hers, he felt the chills run down his spine, if anyone else had told him this he would have rolled his eyes at them and probably thought they were exaggerating but it had happened to him. He wanted to blame it on the AC or whatever but he knew it had more to do with the girl who was carrying his brother's child, which made things much scarier.She thought that he hated her and that was funny because it was the opposite, not from lack of trying because he was really trying. Samantha Baker was just a very difficult person to hate and it didn't help that she was all everyone talked about. Charlie wouldn't shut up about her and neither would Chase and Alex too. Even Richard called three times just to discuss the damned girl.This wasn't going to be another case of Sophie, he wasn't going to let things get out of hand like the last time.He just needed to speak to Richard as soon as possible. Jason could handle his mess by himself and leave him out of it."Can I ask you a question?" Samantha asked him, he turned and looked at her.Did she suddenly get more beautiful over the past ten minutes? This was just ridiculous."I suspect you are going to anyway" he told her"Where is Jason?" she asked and then bit her lips, a habit he observed she did whenever she was nervous."He's out of town" he wanted to leave it vague, she didn't need to know the entire details of Jason's trip."Did he leave because of me?" again, she didn't need to know that so he didn't answer her"Is he coming back?" she asked obviously taking his silence as an affirmation. He didn't miss the disappointment that appeared all over her face."It would be a tad difficult for the both of you to get married if he doesn't come back"she nodded and then began to pull on her fingers.It was on impulse as well as to distract himself from staring at her when he asked,"Are you hungry?" but she did just have her blood drawn so he was purely thinking about the baby's health."Yes"

THEY STOPPED AT a corner café and the smell made Sammy think of the box of doughnut she had devoured in the morning, she normally wouldn't have been hungry by now or for the rest of the day but with the pregnancy and all her appetite was just a hot mess. She was going to definitely get fat soon if she didn't get a handle on her eating pattern.They got seated by the window, Niklaus had picked the seats but they were her favourite. She liked being able to look outside while being on the inside. He ordered for the both of them and they sat waiting for the very cheerful waitress to come back with their order.Sammy couldn't help but let it sink in that Jason had gone away because of her. She had known there was something more to it when Charlie had said he left. She was here on a fool's errand, the man they were all expecting her to marry didn't even want to be in an entire house with her. Lord only knew what type of marriage they were going to have."I was wondering, how long is this going to last?" she asked Niklaus"I'm sure it won't be long now, the waitress said she'd…""I meant the marriage. How long is it going to last?"He looked at her like she had just said something absurd."What do you mean?""The prenup said I was going to be paid for every year that I am married to your brother right?""Uhmm""So how long is that going to last?""Ms Baker the payments don't stop until you decide you are done with the arrangement"Why did he have to call her Ms Baker? Easy, because he wanted to make this seem impersonal.So that meant she could leave whenever she wanted?"But I do have to marry him?" since she could leave anytime why then did she have to marry him in the first place?"Samantha my father is a very traditional man, he doesn't think that you'd want to leave once you are married to my brother"So that was the catch, they thought she'd be lured with the payments that she'd never want to leave.Just then the waitress came back with their order, a cinnamon roll with vanilla café latte for her and a muffin and an expresso for him.They waited while the waitress set it up and then leave before she asked"What if I do decide to leave? What if I marry your brother and in a year or two I decide that I don't want to be married to him anymore?" would Richard McCarthy force her to stay then?"In the unlikely events that were to happen, then there will be a discussion about it" he said as he bit into his muffin, was it weird that she liked watching him eat? That she liked that he spoke with his mouth full and she also liked the little crumb that he didn't know rested under his lower lip."You people are not going to ask me to leave my child, are you?""we would still like to maintain a relationship would the child. But like I said it will be discussed if that happens"

* * * *

NICK LAY IN bed but sleep wouldn't come. Since the accident sleep was now a luxury, one he couldn't afford most nights and that was mostly because of the sore shoulder but tonight felt different. His shoulder was throbbing yes but at the same time he couldn't stop thinking about their houseguest. She wasn't just their houseguest anymore, she was now a person and not just the woman that might be wanting to scam his family. She all of a sudden was this person with fears and hopes.He turned around and adjusted his pillow and closed his eyes, going to sleep was the best option for him right now at least then he wouldn't be thinking about the look on her face when she had accused him of hating her. But closing his eyes just made it worse, he shouldn't be thinking of Samantha Baker in any capacity. If the things that happened with Sophia had taught him anything then he would stay far from this one.She was carrying Jason's child for Christ's sake.He gave himself twenty solid minutes before he decided that sleeping wasn't going to work for him tonight, he got out of bed and headed downstairs to the kitchen. This had now become a routine with him since the insomnia started.He was almost downstairs when he heard the muffled noises coming from the dining area, he took a step closer and then sighted her scrawny figure hunched over the table and sobbing.He stood at a distance and watched her taking quivering breaths as she sobbed."Ms Baker?" he called taking a step closer.Her head shot up and she saw him then followed the look of embarrassment that flooded her face."Oh my God!" she said shooting out of her chair she almost fell"I'm so sorry, I thought I was alone" she sniffled"No need to apologise I'm the one who's intruding" Nick told her as he watched her wipe her face with the back of her hands."I was on the phone with my friend Vicky and…" she trailed off and sniffled again."I'm so embarrassed" she said and shook her head.Nick stood watching her and in that moment Samantha Baker looked so vulnerable, her hair was a mess, her eyes were swollen and her lips still quivered.What had he just gotten himself into? He stood there confused as fuck as to what to do. This wasn't really his expertise, his brothers would always mock him because he sucked at handling emotions and that was usually okay because he had never walked in on the most vulnerable looking woman crying."Should I call someone? Charlie? Or maybe Alex?" that would be the best thing to do now because anyone else would probably handle this situation better than him."No, no. God no." she said wiping the remainder of her tears."I'm just going to go back upstairs" she said"Maybe you should sit and calm down first" he cringed. Why did he just say that? He should have just let her go back to her room and sort herself out, but he didn't know why the thought of her crying alone in her room left a weird taste in his mouth."I feel ridiculous. I didn't even know why I'm crying" she said and ran a hand through her hair which left them rougher than they had been."It's the pregnancy, it messes with your hormones and stuff. Charlie wouldn't stop crying the first month she was pregnant"She nodded and then bit her lower lip"Sit, I'll make you some tea to calm your nerves""I really don't want to bother you""Sit. I'll make tea"She squinted her eyes as if trying to figure him out which was weird because it always felt like she could see into his soul with those eyes of hers, then she nodded before sitting back down.

WHEN THE KETTLE whistled, Nick already held one of Mrs James' tea bag in a mug so he poured the hot water in it and then turned around to carry back to the dining area but there she was standing by the door. The only evidence that she had been crying was her red puffy eyes."Are you going to come in?" he asked her setting the mug down.She came in, but barely. She stood biting her lip for about five seconds before she said,"I came to apologise"Nick frowned, was she really apologising for crying?"Come drink this, you'll feel better" he said ignoring her apology.He didn't know for sure that drinking the tea would make her feel better but it felt like that was something Mrs James would say.She hesitated a moment before coming close and picking up the mug."Peppermint" she said after taking the first sip."thank you"He didn't say anything, he just kept watching her drink the tea slowly. She looked really sad."Is being here making you sad?" he asked before he could stop himself"Of course not. No. Everyone here is really amazing""You were crying in the dark""You said it was the hormones" she reminded him"You weren't crying because you were happy now, were you?" he was only asking so he could give Richard a full report, Nick told himself. He didn't care what she wanted to do and why.She looked at him and then sat down,"I wasn't crying because of anything your family did or didn't do. My friend just told me that my boss has refused to excuse me from work today and she said I shouldn't bother returning. So, I'm jobless" she made that last part like a joke but taking a glance at her Nick could tell she wasn't joking.She slowly took another sip from the cup of tea in front of her and then said"I'm going to marry your brother""Okay" he just said it as if he had been expecting it, because honestly he had had no doubts that the girl would end up a McCarthy. The question had always been how long before she agreed to become one and how long she would stay one. What he never imagined was that it would take her being unemployed to get her to agree, Richard would have gotten her fired long ago if they'd know that her job was a determining factor.What would happen if it turned out that the child, she was expecting wasn't actually Jason's? What if she had just come to find Jason because of the McCarthy name attached? But she didn't look dubious like that. Nick had dealt with many people that had tried to deceive him in his life but never one that looked like Samantha Baker, she had the most honest eyes he had ever seen."what?" she asked him"What?" he asked too"What's with the face?" she asked"What face?" he hadn't realised he had made a face, he knew he had the most excellent poker face and most people could never pick up on the things he felt."You know the face" she said trying to mimic him."so, you are marrying Jason. Because you are jobless?"he didn't expect it when she said,"Yes" and he couldn't hide the surprise on his face. He had honestly expected her to deny it."oh""Your father is going to pay me a million dollars for every year that I'm married to your brother, I'd like to pretend that I'm going to do it just for the child but that kind of money would change my life forever."That shocked him, any other woman would say she was going to do it for their child but the fact that Samantha Baker had admitted she was doing it for herself was really surprising. But she wasn't the only woman he knew who had put the money first."And what about your child?" he asked her"What about them?""Most mothers would say that they were marrying the father of their child because of their child not because of the money attached"If he hadn't been paying attention, he would have missed the shame that flashed on her face, and for a moment he wanted to take back what he had said."I didn't know who your brother was when we slept together," she began"My friend Vicky got a promotion and she dragged me out to celebrate. When we met him, he was already half way drunk but he still joined us for more drinks. One thing led to another and then I woke up the next morning alone in a hotel room. And I know that that makes me a woman with loose morals or whatever scurvy name you wish to call me. But when I found out I was pregnant, my first thought wasn't to race back to him. I mean I didn't even know who HE was." She was staring her tea absent mindedly,"And what was your first thought then?" he asked her purely out of curiosity"I was going to have an abortion" she frowned, as if just realising what that would have meant."You were?" that was information his family didn't have."why didn't you?""There was a magazine in the waiting area of the clinic, Vicky picked it up and there was my one-night stand on the back cover. I didn't even recognise him, she did. She thought it was fate." She chuckled with that last bit.In that moment Nick found out that he no longer doubted her, it was stupid yes, because there was no evidence to back up her story but it was those damned eyes, the look on her face and the sincerity in her voice. They were all he needed to decide in that moment that Samantha Baker was telling the truth."I thought he deserved to know but I honestly didn't expect a marriage proposal, I figured he'd help with raising his child. Maybe visit New York when he had the chance but I promise I didn't come to steal your family's fortune or anything like that""No one said you did" Lie."Is that not what the prenuptial agreement was for?""The documents protects you as well as it does us""If you say so" she said with a shrug."I do. Now finish your tea"She didn't drink the tea instead she raised her brow at him"What?" he asked"Why do you do that?""Do what?""That. Now finish your tea?"He still didn't see what the problem was,"It's the way you talk. I know you are used to dishing orders to your employees and stuff but you don't need to speak to me as if I were a child""I don't do that""Yes, you do. Last night it was, sit and eat the eggs and tonight it's sit and finish your tea. The way you say, it shows you are not used to being disobeyed"He chuckled, which honestly surprised him and her too by the look on her face."Well your tea's going to get cold""Then let it. I don't like tea""Then why drink it in the first place?" he asked"Because you've gone through the trouble of making it and quite frankly because you scare me a little""I scare you?""Why do you sound so surprised? You must know how intimidating you are. I mean I read an article last week that said you were your father's child with the most resemblance to him because you were as ruthless as him in business, I don't believe business is the only place you can be ruthless" she cringed,"I shouldn't have said that""You didn't write the article" he told her"I shouldn't have said it. I'm sorry"The girl had a habit of apologising when she'd done nothing wrong, he watched her bite her lower lip and then stop. He had no idea why the habit he discovered she did when she was nervous bothered him a lot.“It's nothing compared to the time you called me hateful” he was kidding, but she didn't pick up on it, which really made it more fun for him as he watched her squirm.“I didn't...” she began to deny it“I think you did. At the hospital, when you accused me of hating you”“I didn't mean it that way” She said and then did the lip biting thing again and that was when Nick discovered why it bothered him so much.It made him want to do the biting of those lips himself, in an entirely different context. He shouldn't be near her right now, at least not until he figured out what it was about the girl that made him loose part of his senses.“I don't hate you Samantha Baker” with that he got up and left without saying any other thing to her and as he walked out from the kitchen, he realised that Samantha Baker was going to be more trouble than he had anticipated.

# CHAPTER 5

It was the banging on Sammy's door that woke her, she had gone to sleep really late because she found out that her talk with Niklaus McCarthy was all she thought about. It didn't help that his chuckle had played in her ears hours after she had heard it. But it wasn't entirely her fault he had a really nice laugh.She sat up the moment Alex barged into her room looking rather angry,"I'm going to kill my brother. I will plunge a knife into his eyes until he's crying blood"What a nice way to say good morning, Sammy thought. She was almost sure plunging a knife into someone's eyes wouldn't leave them crying at all, but hey, what did she know?She sat up and supressed the urge to rub her eyes or yawn, she couldn't remember the last time someone woke her up in the morning. Boy was she glad that she hadn't decided to go to sleep naked."is everything okay?" she asked getting out of bed"What do you mean is everything okay? No, nothing's okay"Oh boy. What had she done this time?It would have to be something serious to make Alex hurl her out of bed this early.Sammy couldn't help the panic that rose inside of her,"What's the problem?" she asked"The problem is that my brothers are idiots, the problem is that I'm going to murder Nicky and Chase and probably wind up in jail" Alex said pacing about the room, she made these really weird hand gestures when she said murder that creeped Sam out.Sa mmy let out the breath she had no idea she was holding. So, her rage was directed at her brothers."What happened?" she asked"They both bailed on me. Can you imagine? Nick decided that today he just had to be in a meeting. And Chase? I'm sure that man whore is probably inside a woman's panties right now"Sammy cringed, that was a mental image she didn't need in her head at all. What she still didn't understand was why Alex was waking her up by, she took a glance at the clock to make sure, six thirty-two in the morning to tell her this."That's bad right?" she said for lack of anything better to say"Of course it's bad, Diego said that today is the last time the store will be open. And my idiot brothers decide today is the day they go about doing God knows what"Honestly speaking, Sammy wasn't following her at all. Her sleep deprived brain didn't understand why Alex was speaking to her as if she knew what she was talking about. Who the hell was Diego and what store was she talking about?Alex turned and looked at her when she said nothing and Sammy tried to pretend this wasn't the most awkward conversation she had ever engaged in."I'm sorry" Alex said as if realising that Sammy had no idea what she was talking about.She ran a hand through her hair and sighed in frustration."I found this vintage crib for the nursery for Charlie's baby and Nicky and Chase were supposed to pick it up because the store's closing today. Actually, they closed last month because the owner died, not Diego, his father and Diego's going to donate it all but I talked him into selling me the crib because I started the negotiations with his father before he died. And he says today is the only day he got to clear it all out because he already sold the store and the new owners were coming tomorrow and now my brothers both bailed on me and I have this wine tasting in Florida that I can't miss, plus I think I maybe hung over, so please forgive me""it's fine. It's good to vent a little" or a lot but maybe leave out the graphic murder images next time"What about Luca? Couldn't he maybe pick the crib up?"she shook her head,"It's supposed to be a gift for the shower on Saturday. I can't ask him. And speaking of gifts, could you maybe get something for the Charlie's baby shower? Nothing too extravagant or anything""Of course" "So how do you feel about a road trip?""Road trip?" Sammy asked, confused how their discussion had jumped from the crib to the shower and now a road trip."I was hoping that you would maybe join me to Houston to pick up the crib?""Oh" so that was what all the ranting was about."It's barely an hour drive and I promise to bring you back in one piece. Well maybe not in one piece but, alive." she said with a smile.Sammy considered it for a moment, alive was good enough for her. It wasn't like she had anything else scheduled for today since she was now jobless, she had a lot of time on her hands."I guess we are going on a road trip"Alex squealed and then gave her a hug,"You are the best. I gotta make a call but you should go get ready, we'll leave in half an hour" she said and then she was gone, as loudly as she had come.

When Sammy came to the front of the house, Alex was in a heated conversation on the phone in front of the car. She couldn't exactly make out what she was saying because she was speaking French but Sammy could tell she was angry. All the McCarthy siblings had the same angry face that quite frankly scared her.Alex suddenly put the phone to her mouth and yelled into it before hanging up and then taking an angry breath."Gabriel won't put the tasting on hold for me. I offered to buy out his next supply but he said that a bunch of dignitaries were coming so his hands are tied. His hands are tied my foot. I hope whatever woman Chase is fucking is worth it because I'm gonna make sure it's his last"Sammy suspended the 'hi' she had been about to say, she didn't think Alex was in the mood for pleasantries at the moment."What if we went to get the crib tomorrow?" Sammy asked"I told you Diego is shipping everything to Europe today""My sister never makes anything easy on herself,"Alex and Sammy turned simultaneously to find Niklaus walking towards them. Alex walked over to him and gave him a punch on the shoulder,"Ouch""I called you like a hundred times" Alex complained not bothered by the fact that she had just caused him actual pain."I know, my phone wouldn't stop buzzing. Thank you very much" he said waving his phone at her."And you couldn't be bothered to answer?""Alex I was in a meeting""Well I have a meeting in an hour so,""You have a wine tasting" he mocked her."I hate you" Alex told him and he stuck his tongue out to herIt was weird for Sammy, seeing this side of Niklaus. He wasn't frowning or being mean or intimidating, he just looked like a brother who was with his sister in that moment. And watching him smile for the first time since they met Sammy couldn't help the butterfly that danced around in her belly. He wasn't just the broody man anymore."Where's Chase?" "Nicky, I don't know because if I did, he'd be dead""Did you call?" he asked "Yep. And I also had Levi stop by his apartment. You should go now and Sammy's going with you"Sammy watched the smile on his face get replaced by the usual frown at the mention of her name. So, it was indeed her? She had thought they had left things on a better note after last night, not that she would go as far as to think they were friends but she had thought things would definitely be friendlier.Seemed like Alex didn't notice any change from him because she turned back to her with a smile on her face,"Guess I can make it to the wine tasting after all" 'Please take me' Sammy wanted to say.she turned and headed back to the house and then turned back,"if he starts misbehaving, just give him a punch on his arm. It resets his brain every time""Not funny" Niklaus yelled at her as she matched back into the house.

"I'M SORRY ALEX is making you take me" Sammy said breaking the heavy silence in the car.They hadn't said anything to each other since they left the house and that was several minutes ago, and before then the only time he had spoken to her was when he asked her to get into the car."It's fine" he replied without taking his eyes off the road.Since it was fine why then was he making her feel like she had done something? Sammy wondered.She watched as his frown deepened and then he turned to look at her,"I mean she really likes you"That really came to Sammy as a surprise, she had been in that house for just two days, and she hadn't even spent a lot of time with Alex so it surprised her that Alex liked her."Really?" she asked"Yes. And so does Chase and Charlie, and I'm sure Luca does too. Everyone at the manor likes you" he told her. And instead of it making her happy it kinda made her sad, everyone but him."well I like them too. Everyone is really nice""Did you have breakfast?" he asked out of the blue"No, Alex got me out of bed and I didn't have time to grab breakfast""There's a diner ahead and they make the best cheesecakes but don't tell Mrs James I said that"

True to his words the cheesecake was amazing delicious and he didn't hide the fact that he was enjoying it because he ordered another slice half way into his first one and encouraged her to do the same."How did my sister rope you into this?" he asked"Well she painted a colourful picture of how she was going to murder you and Chase, so when she asked I couldn't refuse" he laughed, his mouth full of cake and somehow he still managed to look cute. Sammy couldn't help the thrill that passed through her, she liked making him laugh. It was odd but it made her feel good."Alex is all bark and no bite, she the sweetest girl ever" spoken like a true older brother.Just then the waitress came back with their second slice and placed it on the table and then turned to Niklaus,"you should watch the carbs, we don't want you ruining that amazingly built body of yours""We don't want that now do we?" he said in that overly intimidating tone that Sammy was starting to get used to. The girl scurried away which almost got Sammy laughing."You know she was just flirting with you right?""She was educating me on my eating habits"Oh boy! Chase did say that he hadn't been around people a lot lately, that was the only explanation why he would miss when a really pretty waitress was trying to flirt with him."Trust me, she was flirting" Sammy told him stuffing her mouth with more of the glorious cheesecake."In that case, I'm not interested"No doubt.

The little store in Houston was being packed up when they got there. A short stubby woman approached them and introduced herself as Angie, her husband owned the store before he died."My son Diego has most of the things packed up, the boy is one stubborn mule. It's going to take a while before the crib is ready to go" she told them and asked them to sit and wait."I have a freshly made pot of coffee, I'll go pour us some while we wait" she leftWhen she came back she was carrying a tray, she set the first cup of coffee down in front of Nick,"Coffee for the gentle man and another for me," then she set out a glass of orange juice for Sammy,"and some orange juice for the expectant mother""You can tell?" Sammy asked surprised, she couldn't even tell she was pregnant sometimes and this woman could tell by just being in a room with her for less than ten minutes."Of course I can tell, you have all the looks of an expectant mother. The shiny hair, look, you are even beginning to get the mask of pregnancy" Angie said taking her arm and pointing out the dark patches on her arm."I've never seen this before" Sammy said surprised"They were there last night" Niklaus said"Your husband is very observant. Mine didn't notice until I looked like a zebra" Angie said with a chuckle."No, he's not my..." Sammy was interrupted by the loud banging coming from the back"I'll be right back" Angie said leaving them to head to the noise.Sammy didn't know if it was just her but the atmosphere became super awkward. Why on earth did Angie just assume Nick was her husband,"I don't know why she said that but once she gets back, I'll set her straight" she told Nick but he said nothing. Great! He was already mad at her, again.Angie came back and then smiled at them,"Diego's found your crib but he's going to need some help loading it up. Do you mind?" she asked Niklaus, he nodded and then went through the door Angie came in from.Angie sat down to her cup of coffee and took a long sip with her eyes closed and then smiled,"You got a good eye, the crib was crafted in the 1950s by the Herter brothers after the civil war. Not the original Herter brothers obviously, but you get the point. This could be one of their last pieces left" Angie explained.Sammy couldn't believe that Charlie's baby was going to be peeing on something created by famous people."With a few modifications your baby will have an amazing crib""Oh the crib is not for my baby, it's for Nick's sister-in-law" Sammy told her"Well then, your husband's sister-in-law is going to have an excellent crib for her baby" Sammy cringed, that word again? She had been willing to ignore the first one but now she just felt like she was misleading the poor woman."Nick's not my husband" she decided to set the record straight before Nick came back."Oh my mistake. I just assumed," she paused for a moment and then"but if I might ask, what are you two waiting for? That fine gentleman, if you ask me is crazy about you" Angie said"No, he's not. Nick is just my...""Please don't say friend. I've seen a lot of couples in my day and anyone that looks at his woman the way that young man looks at you has definitely lost his mind over her"Sammy couldn't believe what she was hearing, she also couldn't believe that she felt her cheeks heat up. She was blushing. It was either the old lady had lost her mind for noticing things that were clearly not there or Sammy had lost hers because of the way she was reacting to said things."You are mistaken, I can assure you that Nick doesn't have those sorts of feelings. It's not like that"Angie chuckled."Child, it is you who is mistaken. Admitted I can sense that he is a little hesitant and maybe even conflicted but ultimately time will reveal what it ought to"just then Nick and some other guy came out and Nick walked to her,"are you okay?" he asked and Sammy nodded,"yes, why?""Your face, it's all red" the statement just made her blush harder, if only he knew why her face was red."Oh it's just the weather and the pregnancy" Angie said with a smile on her face and a knowing look."Are you ready to go?" Nick asked and Sammy almost leapt in joy, she needed to get the hell away from here before Angie opened her mouth again.

# CHAPTER 6

Nick took a glance at the digital clock hanging over his head, it was thirty-one minutes past twelve. He turned around and buried his face in his pillow. His shoulder was killing him and it was worse since he stopped taking his prescription drugs, they made him fell drowsy and mostly tired and he didn't like that feeling especially now he was going to begin working again. But the alternative was insomnia which somehow was almost worse but if he really wanted to get back to work, he needed to find a balance without the drugs.He got out of bed and took out a bottle of water from the mini fridge, he took a gulp and looked back at the clock, twelve thirty-three. Just two minutes had passed.He decided it would be futile going back to bed so he decided to help himself with a cup of coffee and then he thought about going to the kitchen and then his thoughts went back to Samantha Baker. He had spent time with her the past two nights he had gone downstairs in the middle of the night and for some reason the idea of her being there again tonight thrilled him more than it should.There was something really wrong with him, he had spent most of the day with her and had had nothing to tell her but the minute they had come home and had parted ways he had actually missed her.

Nick told himself it didn't mean anything when he walked into the kitchen and the place that used to provide solitude and peace now felt empty."Fuck!" he muttered under his breath, this was not normal, not at all.He put the coffee maker on, that was after all what he had come to do right?He had barely sat down when he heard,"Hi"

SAMMY TOLD HERSELF as she tiptoed downstairs that the only reason she was going was because she needed a glass of water. With the amount of fluids leaving her body it was only right that she replenished. She was just going to go grab a glass of water and then head back to bed despite who may or may not be there.Of course he was there, she watched him set the coffee maker and then sit down,"Hi" she said and watched him get up from his chair before replying her"Hi""I wanted to grab a glass of water" she told him without waiting to be asked,He looked at the refrigerator and then sat down.Sammy's leg felt heavy as she walked to the fridge, she could feel his eyes on her which made her mostly uncomfortable and a bit nervous."Your test results will be ready by tomorrow" he said while she drank her water"Oh. So fast," that was a good thing, at least now she could go back to home to New York."You could come with me to pick it up if you wanted"Did she want? Did she want to be stuck in a car ride with him again? It didn't really matter, he could give her a ride to town since he was already going.She turned to face him"Yes. I mean, I have to go into town tomorrow and since you are going you could drop me off""You are going into town?" he asked"Yes. Alex asked me to pick out a gift for Charlie's baby shower""Do you have anything in mind?" he asked as the coffee maker beeped, he stood up a went over to the machine"Not really," she had never been to a baby shower before. What did people usually get?"and you, what did you get?" she asked him and watched him take his sweet time pouring his coffee and taking a sip from it."Luca had this stuffed elephant my mother got him, he had it for the longest of time. Even as a teenager I remember that elephant still being in his room. It was like his comfort... everything. So I tracked down the company that makes it here in America and had them inscribe Charlie's favourite quote, so it'll be a part of both parents for the baby"Wow."That's so thoughtful" she said returning her glass cup,she had been unsure of what to get now this just made it worse."good night" she said and turned to leave.She was almost out of the kitchen when her stomach growled, she paused and turned around to see that Niklaus was staring at her, probably horrified the sound that came from her insides"That's embarrassing" she said and felt her cheeks heat up"Did you have dinner?" he asked, "yes, I ate with Charlie and Luca after we came back" that was several hours agoHe shook his head at her"you don't eat enough, you are too small" that only added to her embarrassment,Sammy knew she wasn't like most girls, curvy or full but she had never had any problems with her figure. At least not until Niklaus McCarthy had used the word small to describe her with a frown on his face."I'm not that small" she told him hating that she sounded a bit defensive"Trust me you are. As a matter of fact, you look like a malnourished boy and sometimes I wonder what my brother saw in you"It was the words as well as the condescending way he said it. A slap on her face would have stung less, suddenly Sammy felt so small. So the reason they doubted she was carrying Jason's child was because they didn't think Jason would bed someone that looked like her."I should go to bed, I feel tired" and nauseous and she didn't want to cry in front of him because she really did feel like she was going to cry."Sit down, I'll make you something to eat""Don't worry I'm...""Sit down" he repeated and this time he wasn't asking and like a good little girl she obeyed.More like foolish little girl.

THE SILENCE IN the room was deafening as Nick worked and so that gave him time to think about the stupid thing he had said. It had been thoughtless, saying that to her but he honestly didn't mean itA malnourished boy? Really? Admitted Samantha Baker had a smallish figure but that didn't mean she wasn't attractive because he could testify that she was. She had such tiny waist and slender legs that made her look taller than she was, her boobs weren't that prominent but there was no mistaking that they were there. Though she had no cleavage but that was only because of the type of clothes she wore, it was as if she was trying so hard to hide the fact that she was a lady. Her eyes seemed a little too big for her face but it suited her because they gave her the most innocent look Nick had ever seen someone wear.He shouldn't be thinking about her body but she should have already put on a little weight by now, her breast should have grown along with other parts of her body but she wasn't eating well.Charlie ate so much in her first trimester that

Luca began to worry but not Samantha, he watched her the three days she had been here, the girl barely ate and when she did she ate very little as if afraid someone was judging her."I shouldn't have said that" he turned back to where she sat with a pout on her face and she just shrugged. he knew he had hurt her feeling a little bit with what he had said,"you don't look like a malnourished boy, your figure suits you well" that was mostly true.She said nothing so he went back to the pancakes he was making.Maybe her feelings were more than a little hurt."He was drunk" she said"What?" he turned back to her"Your brother, you said you wondered what he saw in me? He was drunk that's what""I'm sorry, I shouldn't have said that""It doesn't matter, I just want to go to bed" she said with a sigh"Stay and eat, please" she nodded."I feel like you are always feeding me" she said while he served her pancakes,"at least now I know why"He liked to watch her eat, she ate like she enjoyed food. He didn't remember the last time he ever cooked for someone,"this is really good" she murmured"don't you want to have some?" he wasn't hungry, he felt oddly content watching her enjoy his pancakes."I'm not hungry" he said and poured her a glass of orange juice, she took it and murmured her thanks."Well you are missing out" she said, she obviously not crossed with him anymore. Seemed like the way to this woman's heart was through her stomach.He settled down opposite her and took a sip from his now almost cold cup of coffee, he swallowed despite it now tasting bland before abandoning it. He reminded himself that he wasn't looking for a way to her heart, just taking care of his brother's baby mama almost bride until he returned to handle it himself."How can you cook this well?" she asked"I've seen the number of kitchen staff you people have"Well there was that time he thought he wanted to be a chef, well those were times he didn't like thinking about."I've lived on my own more than I've lived at home" he explained"You have?""Yes. I left when I turned sixteen, I managed Luxury's oversees assets""At sixteen?" she asked genuinely surprised"I didn't start immediately, I learned the business from bottom up but at eighteen I knew everything there was to know""you were by yourself?" she asked"it gave me the freedom I craved, I travelled a lot and I liked it""You were a child" why did she sound so sad, it wasn't like anyone had forced him"I was sixteen, not really a child. I was ready to take the position and I did?""Your parents were okay with that?""it was my father's idea""And your mother? How could she be fine with her son being away from home like that?"Nick frowned, his mother, that woman couldn't be bothered with anything that had to do with her children. "She didn't care enough" he didn't mean for it to come out as harshly as it did but that was the way he felt. His mother was not a subject he liked to discuss.Sa mantha took a long gulp from her glass and the poured more syrup on her pancakes,"but you are back now" she saidFor a second Nick had thought she was going to ask more about his mother but the girl could at least read a room"For now, while I'm still in recovery""But it must be nice to be back home with your family?""It was" until Sophia Jamieson turned his life upside down."Finish your meal" he said before she could ask him any more questions. Who knew how inquisitive she could be."If I eat anymore, you'll have to carry me upstairs" she joked rubbing a hand over her belly.Nick had a mental image of carrying her upstairs but in an entirely different context.Sophia Jamieson! He reminded himself"Fine. Hand me the plate, I'll rinse it out. We don't want Mrs James to know I was playing chef in her kitchen" he said getting up.She also got up shaking her head,"You've fed me, the least I can do is to wash my plate" she told him and then emptied the remaining content of her glass cup into her moth.Nick backed down and let her carry her things to the sink, he watched her stand and look around,"where's the..." "Soap" he finished and was already on his way to show her.The soap was kept in the compartment under the sink, "it's right here"he told her and stooped down to get it, when he picked it up and raised his face he didn't realise that Samantha had bent down with him so their lips locked.They both froze.Nick didn't know if he was imagining the bolt of electricity that passed through him as if bringing him to life for the first time.He was going to pull away and apologise when he felt Samantha move her lips, but not to pull away. His brain was obviously asleep because the next thing he knew his lips were equally moving with hers.The kiss started off slow, Samantha's lips tasted like pure heaven, soft and sweet. Her lips parted the same time his did, their tongue joined, dancing to a music only them could hear. He could taste the orange juice she had taken earlier which just somehow made her taste sweeter.Somehow, they managed to stand erect with him pinning her against the sink without their tongues stopping the intimate dance. It was weird having her this close and still wanting her closer, there was no need for any further persuasion because she was moving closer, wrapping her arms around his neck as he deepened their kiss.Nick wrapped his both arms around her tiny waist, lifting her off the floor and she in turn wrapped her legs around his.His head was about to explode, she was driving him insane. The mere nearness of her was driving him insane. Her scent, he had never been this close to her before, no wonder he was still sane. She smelled like vanilla and the only thought in Nick's head was finding out what she felt like, what her skin felt like underneath the pyjamas. This was no malnourished boy at all, she was all female. Head turning, knee weakening female.He carried her to the top of the counter without breaking their kiss, his hand found its way into her pyjama top, she shivered when his hands found her breast. She let out a moan when his mouth left her and went down to her neck and he thought his head was going to explode. He caressed her breast but all he wanted to do was cover it with his mouth, he wanted to know what they would taste like.He wanted to do more than that he realised when she moaned again and threw her head back giving him all the access he needed

SAMMY COULDN'T COMPREHEND how the fuck she had gotten in this situation but all she knew was that she didn't want to get out of it.All her senses had never been in overdrive all at the same time before but as Niklaus McCarthy had his hands on her, she couldn't help but feel like she was going to explode. She had never been kissed like this before, never been ravished before and that was what Nick was doing. He was a glorious kisser, and his hands? Those were an entirely different ball game.The assault on her neck made her feel dizzy, she wanted to touch him but she was in sensory overload. She had never felt this sexually aware in her entire life.She was unbuttoning his shirt before she realised her hands had moved and in three fast seconds the clothing was on the floor.Hard, solid, male. So she touched him. Niklaus McCarthy shivered stopping the assault on her neck and raised his face to look at her.Pure lust. Arousal. Was this what her face mirrored? Sammy wondered. And then suddenly he was withdrawing his hands from her body and then taking a step back so hers fell away from his. The look of arousal quickly fading and getting replaced by realisation and regret.She wanted to say something, anything, but she was still too out of breath and her head was still spinning. Plus, what could she have said?He gave her a look over that made her skin crawl,"I have to go" he said and without waiting for a response he picked his earlier discarded shirt off the floor and was gone, leaving her almost half naked, alone and still confused as fuck.

# CHAPTER 7

The phrase 'sleepless night' had never been truer, Sammy had lain awake till morning. Her brain wouldn't shut off and there was only one thing in it, Niklaus McCarthy. She honestly didn't realise or remember how the whole thing happened but she sure was aware of how it had ended.The look he had given her before almost physically running out on her was horrible, Niklaus had looked at her like she was disgusting. She had pictured that look on his face over and over again all night.How was she going to face anyone today? And she was supposed to go into town with Niklaus today but the mere thought made her feel like throwing up.She dragged herself into the shower, she was barely out when she heard the commotion from downstairs, her heart almost flew out of her chest. She was sure she knew what the com- motion was about and she knew that before long the entire McCarthy clan would be at her door.She hurriedly dressed up and matched downstairs to explain herself. It wasn't what she was expecting when she got to the parlour, for peo- ple who were planning on murdering their houseguest they looked rather chipper."Good morning" she said to no one in particular.Chase was the first person to notice her so her came right over wearing his usual charming smile. It had been a while since she had seen him around, Sammy thought."Hey, you sleep well?" he asked and she nodded which in reality was a lie."What's going on?" she asked him in a whisper"Dad's back" he said pointing and then Sammy noticed the McCarthy senior sitting on the couch and Alex hanging on one of his thighs.Oh, so that was what the ruckus was about. Not that they had found out what she did last night and wanted to murder her."And so is Jay" her heart sank because as if on cue Jason McCarthy strutted in with Charlie on his arm and laughing at something only both of them knew.The smile on his face froze when he saw her and Sammy didn't know whether or not to run. The last time they had seen each other he hadn't been exactly happy to see her.Jason was already walking to her before she decided what she was doing,"Hi" he said and actually smiled at her.Sammy felt a sudden tightness in her throat, she cleared her throat,"Hi" she greeted back"I'm sorry I wasn't here when you got in, but I'm thinking maybe we could have dinner tonight and talk?" he asked and she could only nod.This wasn't how she expected today to go, not after how her night had ended.Jason was back. The father of the child she was carrying. The man she was supposed to be marrying.Only problem was, he wasn't the man she couldn't stop fantasising about.

Nick always prided himself on control, he liked that he always had control on everything, it was one of the reasons he was so great at everything he did. He had never lost control like this, most especially not of his feelings or his emotions.

Last night had been a whole different ball game, Samantha Baker was a whole different ball game. He hadn't slept well ever since the accident but after the thing had happened and he had come upstairs and hit his head on a pillow he fell asleep and got a solid five hours.His throbbing shoulder that would have normally bothered him didn't. The phrase slept like a baby had never been truer.The pleasant surprise from his father and Jason hadn't been that pleasant for him because he was suddenly assaulted with the guilt from last night.Guilt, that was a feeling that Nick couldn't quiet put a lid on. He knew it was going to eat him alive.The only thing he could think of was the whole Sophia debauchery. At least then he had nothing to feel guilty about. Yes, he had had something with her but that was long over before his brother had married her. And even after she had lost her mind and had come for something Nick couldn't let himself give her, he knew he couldn't because he knew his boundaries.So why then were those boundaries blurry now, why then did he let himself lose control with Samantha last night?Kissing her last night had been the biggest mistake ever and he hadn't realised how much until he had looked his brother in the face this morning. If only he had stopped at kissing her, he had done worse than kiss her. He had touched her, tasted her, ravished her and wanted her. And now having her was all he thought about. He had been so close to that last night and if he hadn't taken a moment to realise what he was doing he could have easily had sex with his brother's fiancé on his father's kitchen counter. It made him sick to the stomach thinking about it, he made himself sick. Why was he having all these thoughts about her?Sex wasn't something he usually obsessed over, yes he did have sex at his disposal whenever he did want it but it was usually on his own terms and just to get the release he needed, but he knew that God forbid he found himself in bed with Samantha Baker it would be a different story. And different wasn't what he wanted or thought he could handle, different gave room for other stuff like say feelings, attachment and worse... abandonment. So there was no room in his life for any of that most especially not with the woman who was going to be marrying his br other.At least his father was back now so he could wash his hands off every and anything that had to do with the girl. Jason could man up and take his responsibilities seriously or not, it wasn't his business anymore. Nick decided it was time he got back to work and that wasn't just because he thought it was best to put an ocean between Samantha and himself. But also because he felt he had been away from his responsibilities for too long and since Samantha obviously wasn't that anymore he was free to go about his business.

The whole day passed and Sammy neither heard from nor saw Nick, she knew it shouldn't bother her but it did. The mood of the house was high but that didn't stop her from dreading her dinner with Jason, how would she sit across from him discussing marriage when she had already defiled the marriage even before they were wed and worse with his brother?The more the time drew closer the more she felt like running, she wished she had spoken with Nick then maybe she wouldn't be this nervous. She thought of calling Vicky a thousand times to give her words of encouragement but she knew her friend was going to skin her alive over the phone. What she had done was unforgiveable, and worse she had enjoyed it.She spent the entirety of the day relieving the kiss in her head over and over again, she had never been kissed like that before, not in a head turning life changing way. It was an experience she won't be soon forgetting.

Dinner with Jason was good, he had been a complete douche to her that first day and from all indication he had gone away when he realised she was coming so she hadn't expected things to go well. She had been a bit sceptical in the beginning but the more they spoke the more she felt terrible about kissing his brother.He was willing to try with her, he said so himself. And he was nice and friendlier than his brother. He even smiled more than Nick which was a bonus for Sammy, she didn't want to have to spend the rest of her life with a man that rarely smiled no matter how good of a kisser he was and boy was he a really good kisser. Jason was just a blend of both Nick and Chase but mostly Chase because he didn't scare the crap out of her.She tried really hard not to think of Nick throughout the dinner with Jason but it just felt like the more she tried the more Nick was the only thing she thought about, she tried to tell herself that it was because of the guilt she felt because Jason spoke about a future that honestly scared the shit out of her. She honestly didn't remember what had attracted them to each other that first night at the club, except for the fact that they had both had a bit to drink Sammy couldn't think of anything else. She was sure he must have been charming and maybe because

Vicky had nudged her a bit to loosen up, that was mostly why she had indulged in more than one glass of cocktail.

The next couple of days were the longest of Sammy's life, it wasn't just because Jason wanted to hang out and get to know each other a bit more but also because she hadn't seen Nick in three days. She didn't want to ask anyone about him because she felt that if she did they'd figure out what had happened between them. No one spoke of him or his where-abouts which only added to Sammy's consternation.Sammy was in Alex's room waiting for her while the later went to take a call, the door opened and in walked Nick looking like something that had fallen out of the sky,"What are you doing here?" he asked in that his usually annoyed look"Hi" Sammy couldn't help but say, this was not what she thought their next meeting would be like. Scratch that this was how she had imagined it would be, he would wear that scowl and she probably would be nervous. And boy was she nervous.He ignored her greeting,"Where is Alex?" he asked"She... she is... she went downstairs" she stammered, embarrassing hersel f.Nick turned to leave and she blurted out,"Where have you been?""Nowhere that concerns you" he said before hurriedly leaving.The kiss had been an accident, neither of them had planned it but from all indications both had enjoyed it – at least she had enjoyed it. So why was she being the one getting punished for it? His rudeness wasn't something new so why did this time sting more?Did she really expect that things would change because they shared a stupid kiss?And so it was for the days that followed, Nick was back but it made no difference. He walked out of a room once she walked into it, he totally ignored her and though Sammy didn't make any attempts to speak to him again she couldn't help but be little hurt by his actions. She decided that she was going to focus more on what she had come here to do, which was Jason at least he was being kind. He was really interested in wanting to know her, he was nicer than his brother and he didn't make her feel like shit.

WHEN JASON HAD said drinks with his friends, Sammy had imagined two or three friends sitting to a bottle or two of wine but that hadn't been the case. There had been a total of six men and there was no wine, they all indulged in stronger stuff, made inappropriate jokes and laughed at things Sammy had found offensive or not very funny. Like the time one had asked when she was going to be blotted instead of how far along she was, they all laughed, including Jason, but that might have been because most of them were half way drunk already.All she wanted to do was go to bed but she didn't want to seem rude, if these were Jason's friends they would most likely be the people they hung out with for the rest of their lives, which mostly made her nauseous.T hey didn't try to include her in their conversations, talking about the things that had happened in the past and leaving her out.She helped herself to some orange juice since she couldn't indulge with the spirit they were having. She felt so out of place and she wished that Charlie was home, she would have definitely come down stairs to save her from all of this. The girl couldn't stay at a place to save her life. But since the rest of the McCarthy clan went out for dinner Sammy didn't see anyone saving her.She wanted to tell Jason to slow down when he downed his fourth glass of vodka, she wanted to tell all of them to slow down but she decided to mind her business as she continued to nurse her glass of lemonade. They were all fully grown men after all and should know their limits.One of Jason's friend Bryant decided all of a sudden that he wanted to toast to their friend, who after everything he had been through was brave enough to get married again,"I don't think you can ever love her like you loved Sophia but... good luck" he finished and raised his glass before tossing the remainder of what was in his glass into his mouth.Sammy knew it wasn't a love match with Jason and they probably would never have that but she couldn't help but feel a bit self-conscious. Did Jason tell his friends about their drunken encounter and everything that followed? Sammy couldn't help but wonder."Now you may kiss the bride" Bryant said before stumbling to his seat.He was probably drunk but Sammy couldn't tell if he was joking, but the joke was when Jason got to his feet dragging her up with him, a second later his mouth was on hers in a slobbering wet kiss. She squeaked and he had the opportunity to plunge his tongue into her mouth. Sammy was sure she had never been violated like this in her entire life, his mouth tasted hot from the drink he had been indulging in and Sammy felt like she was about to puke. She tried to shove him away but he grabbed unto her waist, holding her steady.Sammy could hear the catcalls from his friends, which only repulsed her more. Everything about the kiss felt wrong and that was because it was neither consensual or acceptable.Sammy used both hands and all the strength she could muster to finally shove him away and looking at his smog face Sammy saw that he seemed unapologetic like he had just done nothing wrong. All she wanted to do was to give him a sounding slap but she restrained herself, she wasn't one to ever slap anyone, ever."Welcome home guys" Jason said looking past her and at the door, Sammy turned around to see the entire McCarthy clan standing looking at them. They had obviously witnessed that awful kiss.Nick was the first person to react and his reaction was to turn around and head upstairs, and with the strides of his steps Sammy could tell he was ticked off.

Hours after Nick had witnessed the kiss between Samantha and his brother, he still felt nauseous, it had been the most terrible thing he had witnessed in a long time. It was the way she had looked at him afterwards, apologetically but not really. He shouldn't feel this way, that girl meant nothing to him. Rather she was supposed to mean nothing to him. But how could that be when the sight of her in the arms of Jason made him feel actual rage? He had felt a variety of things in the span of the one minute he had watched them kiss for, things that he had no business feeling.Hadn't this been what he wanted all along? For Jason to come back and take responsibility? But that was before he knew what Samantha Baker tasted like, that was before he knew the feeling of having her in his arms. She was responsive like no other woman he had ever been with, her skin felt like pure silk and he had never wanted a woman like he had wanted her.He went away because he had thought that taking a couple of days would assuage the things his mind was thinking he was starting to feel about this woman carrying his brother's child.

But that didn't happen, he had seen her standing there in Alex's room and everything he had worked on not wanting came flooding back.He slapped his laptop shut and took a gulp from the glass sitting in front of him, he enjoyed the burn of whiskey in his throat, he wasn't one to ever turn to alcohol for comfort or whatever but the sight of Samantha and his brother had done a number on him. It was the middle of the night and he should head up to bed, but who was he kidding, it would surely be a sleepless night and his aching shoulder wouldn't be what would keep him awake but the dreams about his brother's baby mama.He had stayed in his study tonight because he still dreaded going into the kitchen, the thoughts of what could have been still haunted him.He threw the remainder of his drink into his mouth and headed to the mini bar to replenish the drink, he heard the kitchen cabinet shut with a tiny bang and then he paused. He knew she would be the one there by this time of the night, she was obviously having insomnia because of the pregnancy.Before he could talk himself out of it Nick began to make his way to her, maybe if hadn't indulged in the glasses of alcohol then maybe he would have shown a bit of restrain. But with inhibitions lowered Nick knew just how futile it was going to be trying to talk himself out of seeing her.

HER BACK WAS turned when he came into the kitchen, he didn't mean to seem like a creep but it was hard not to stand and stare at the woman that had haunted his dreams for nights now.She filled her glass with water and he just stood and watched in silence, she turned and startled spilling the water a bit"You scared me" she said casually.All the while

Nick had walked the distance from his study to the kitchen he had had no idea what he was going to say to her but as he stood watching her the images of his brother's lips on hers flooded his head and he knew in that moment what he wanted.He wanted to brand her his, he wanted to put her in the same mental state he had been in all week, wanting something that was so close yet so far away. He wanted her, period."Nick?" she called dragging her robe together and re-knotting it.Was that fear he saw in her eyes? Good. She had once told him that he scared her, well she should be scared of him. Now most especially, because if she had a glimpse of what was going on in his head then maybe she wouldn't even be standing here with him."Samantha" he called in response and before he realised he had moved, he was standing right in front of her."I noticed you were enjoying yourself earlier when we came in" he told her hoping he didn't sound as jealous as he felt."Jason had been drinking…" she began to explain and then trailed off and eyed him suspiciously,"apparently so have you" she took a step away from him"I didn't hear you complaining when it was Jay" he said and took a step forward closing the distance between them."Nick" she called him in a warning"Samantha" he hadn't meant for it to come out as flirtatiously as I did, but he didn't mind at all.

Nothing about this woman should appeal to him yet everything about her suddenly excited him. From her short-ruffled hair, to her sleep deprived eyes. She looked totally exhausted but at the same time so appealing. She shouldn't cause him this much grief, Nick thought. She was just a simple girl that shouldn't have the power to mess with his head like this."I think maybe you should go upstairs and..." she began to say before he silenced her with his mouth.The kiss didn't start off soft and slow like the other day, instead it was hot and overpowering. Nick didn't want soft and slow, he wanted her, he wanted it all. There was no hesitation and in seconds she was kissing him back with equal fervour, wrapping her arms round his neck. Their lips parted at the same time allowing the other full access. Her response thrilled him because maybe then it meant that she wanted him as much as he wanted her.She moaned when he bit her lower lip, something he had been wanting for a very long time. She had no idea how crazy it drove him every time she bit her lip nervously because then he was aware of how full those lips were and how much he craved to graze his teeth over them. He moved down to her neck parting her robe to give him better access, her head fell backwards and she grabbed unto the counter behind her for support. His mouth hot and heavy found her breast from outside of her clothes and bit it lightly, that wasn't enough, he wanted to know what they tasted like when he wrapped his mouth around them. So he did, he parted her robe some more and took her breast in his mouth,"Nick!" she moaned as the shock coursed through her. Her fingers now at his back scratched him and Nick knew that if it wasn't for the shirt separating his body from her nails, she would have left marks.He dragged his mouth back to hers all the while knowing how wrong this was but not caring a lick what the consequences would be tomorrow. No one else would kiss her the way he did and he wanted to make sure she remembered that the next time she put her mouth on anyone else. He wanted to imprint himself on her so that the next time Jason as much as held her hand, his mouth would be all she would be able to think about and nothing else.He lifted her off the ground and she wrapped herself round him as he carried her to the floor. She dragged her robe off in one quick movement without breaking their kiss.When he dropped her on the floor he knelt between her thighs and for the first time since this madness started looked at her.She looked like the sexiest woman alive, her eyes had somehow managed to become bigger, her pupils dilated. Which just showed how aroused she was. Her face flushed and her lips swollen from the assault and he couldn't help but feel a little proud that all this was because of him .She looked completely how he had imagined she would be writhing beneath him as he made her his completely."Nick" she whispered and sat up and kissed him, he pulled away, he wasn't done devouring her with his eyes but they were way passed that now. The simple kiss he had intended to steal had now turned into a whole thing and they both knew what was going to happen in mere seconds. And watching her in nothing but her underwear Nick realised that he had never wanted anything as badly as he wanted Samantha Baker in that moment,"Tell me you want this" he ordered, his voice coming off more rugged and rougher than he had intended."I want this" she said immediately looking him dead in the eyes, Nick couldn't help the smile that crept onto his face, he was pulling off his shirt even before he thought about it and as soon as the piece of clothing landed on the floor the lights came on,"What in the name of Christ is going on here?" a very familiar voice askedThey both startled and looked up only to find a very petrified looking Mrs James standing above them with both hands on her chest.

AS SAMMY GATHERED UP herself, she could picture Mrs James shocked face. She wished the ground would open up and swallow her, she didn't understand how things had gotten so out of control so fast to the extent that she was just in her underwear in the middle of a kitchen that didn't even belong to her.She could hear Mrs James scolding Nick from the hallway and she honestly didn't want to be in his shoes, the look the older woman had given them had made her want to crawl into a cave and die. It had been so humiliating, being literally caught with her pants down like that.What had she been thinking, engaging in such a heinous activity but it had felt so good she didn't want to stop. How was she ever going to face Mrs James ever again?It took all of fifteen minutes before Nick came back in, the look on his eyes showed that things had changed. He wore that scowl on his face and Sammy could tell he was angry.The eyes that had been filled with warmth and passion now looked cold and dead.Was he angry at her? She couldn't help but wonder.They both stood in silence staring at the other, Sammy wished that he would vault over and continue the assault on her lips but the mouth that had been giving her so much pleasure was now set in a frown."That shouldn't have happened" he began, breaking the eye contact."it was a stupid mistake and I take full responsibility. I had been drinking and I wasn't thinking clearing" he was just on the other side of the room but he felt so distant.Sammy hated the way her heart sank, the disappointment nearly brought tears to her eyes. How could he just stand right over there looking at her that way and saying those things to her? A stupid mistake? The disappointment soon faded to anger. It was the casual way he said it, reducing the best kiss of her life to a stupid drunken mistake on his part."of course" she said, grateful that her voice was steady. She'd be damned if she let him see how hurt she was over a dumb mistake, putting it in his own words. She made to leave, she was almost past him and he grabbed her arm,"I'm sorry" he said. Sammy took a step back, she didn't want him touching her right now, not after the wall he had just built between them."I got it, the only way any of the McCarthy boys would ever want me is if they had been drinking right?" she asked and then her body betrayed her by letting a single tear drop, not sad tears but angry ones. She doubted he'd even know the difference."Samantha that's not...""I completely understand what you meant" she told him and without letting him say anything else she scampered away, there were just so much emotions a girl could take before she lost it.

# CHAPTER 8

♥

When Sammy had pictured a baby shower, she hadn't pictured this much people, the McCarthys really went all out when they threw a party and according to Charlie the engagement party Alex had thrown her had even been more elaborate than this. They were over thirty girls and they were apparently all close friends with Charlie. Sammy had just one close friend – one friend period, so it surprised her how someone could claim that all these people were her close friends.She had never felt out of place in the McCarthy manor until she the girls for the party started to arrive, she wanted to crawl back upstairs to her room until they all left. She didn't belong with them at all. They were all shinny and elegant and she was just plain.The dress she had carefully picked out for the occasion now made her feel like a simpleton, which would have been fine by her if it wasn't for the looks the girls had been throwing at her. One had even mistaken her for the maid and asked her to be a darling and fetch her a pomegranate spritzer and didn't even wait for a response before going to take her seat, Sammy had no idea what that was but she didn't have a chance to tell the very hot and very beautiful blond before she left.Charlie seemed like she was having the time of her life as Alex went about terrorising the workers who were doing their best waiting on the arrogant brats they all were. She couldn't imagine how Charlie could be friends with people like this but she seemed right at home with them."You having fun?" Charlie walked up to where she stood in isolation and whispered. Sammy smiled, how could she tell her that she wasn't?"Everything is so amazing" she said instead, which was in fact the truth. The house had been transformed from the classy home it was to this very glamourous looking place."Well I'm glad one of us is" Charlie told her, which surprised Sammy. She had looked like she had been enjoying herself earlier."You're not?" Sammy asked and she shook her head before taking a sip from the virgin daiquiri she held."These girls are driving me crazy. Alex included. She has put in so much work into this that I didn't have the heart to tell her that none of these girls are actually my friends"Sammy felt so relieved to hear that because she honestly couldn't relate the Charlie that she had come to know with someone that would actually want to be friends with these girls."I mean, the last time I saw Edna was the week before graduation" she said pointing at a girl who was laughing at something neither Charlie or Sammy knew."And Chrissy," she continued"I'm sure that girl has been in love with my husband since we met her in France two years ago. But Luca hates women with tiny legs so she doesn't stand a chance" Sammy's eyes fell to the gorgeous blonde's legs and boy were they tiny. She didn't help the chuckle that escaped her and Charlie laughed too and just like that she stopped feeling out of place. Charlie was still Charlie so everything was right again."And speaking of Luca, I still have a murder to plan. His murder. The son of a bitch chose today of all days to leave me alone with his nut job sister. I told Lex I wanted something intimate, just family, but that girl is as stubborn as they come so I'm just here pretending to be having the time of my life to make my sister-in-law slash BFF happy"Just then Alex came strolling in and Charlie plastered a smile on her face,"This is great, I'm so happy" she told Alex and Sammy concurred."Really?" Alex asked,"because I'm freaking out. I just need everything to go smoothly" she said looking really stressed."Everything is amazing, you should sit and have fun, have a drink" Charlie said and lifted a drink from the nearby server and handed it to her.Alex took a swig and then frowned,"why the fuck is this champagne not cold?" she asked no one in particular before storming out."that's her murder face" Charlie informed Sammy,"Good to know, at least now I can be able to know when she's about to kill me" Sammy replied and just then two of the girls came and dragged Charlie off.

Sammy decided to have a moment alone before someone else came to ask her how she knew Charlie, she had answered the same question at least seven times already and she was sure she would still answer it again. They all apparently wanted to know what a low life like her was doing partying with them, she was wondering the same thing too. She couldn't possibly tell them that they met a few weeks ago when she found out that she had been knocked up by Charlie's brother in law and her father in law had offered her money to marry his son and now she was almost a member of the family but only if her baby daddy ever came back because he took off after he had stolen an unsolicited kiss from her and had taken off the next morning and now no one was sure where he was but they all hoped he would be back for their wedding, the wedding no one was talking about if she might add. So instead she had just smiled and said that Charlie was her friend, which was only a half lie. She hadn't even found the time to give Charlie her gift yet because there were just so many gifts to be opened and honestly because she was beginning to have doubts about the stupid locket she had picked out. Everyone's gift was so flashy and expensive that she had tucked hers back into the pocket of her dress, there was no way in hell Charlie would want something as low cost as it.She heard Alex's voice from the kitchen and she sounded pissed, she could also hear Charlie's usual calm voice coming from there too so she decided to see what was happening,"it's just ice" Charlie said rubbing her temples"so what? The guests are just going to drink hot champagne till the idiot gets here?" Alex asked looking rather furious, maybe it had been a bad idea coming in here."Sam," Charlie spotted her,"please can you help me calm her down?" she asked."What's wrong?" Sammy asked them"The ice maker is broken and the guy said it would take another twenty minutes before he gets here" Charlie explainedTwenty minutes wasn't that much time, Sammy wanted to say but taking one glance at Alex she decided to bite her tongue, the girl still wore her murder face so Sammy decided she wasn't going to say anything that would tick her off."I just remembered, the freezer in the storage room downstairs, I think there's ice in there" Charlie said"Yes?" Alex asked, her whole face lighting up"I haven't been down there in a while but I think so" Charlie was being careful not to make any assurances but all the girl heard was that her party was saved."Oh Charlie you are a life saver" she said and gave Charlie a peck on both her cheeks."You two go back to the party, I'll get someone to check for the ice""I'll do it!" Sammy volunteered immediately, the thought of going back into the party just made her want to take to her heels."You sure?" Charlie asked and she nodded, anything to get a few moments away from those awful girls."Good. I'll go start up the games, Charlie come with me" Alex said and then dragged Charlie off.

SAMMY HOPED SHE knew where she was going to, she had only been down to this basement once when she had accompanied Alex to fetch some wine. So, as she descended the stairs, she hoped she was on the right path. She let out a huge sigh of relief when she sighted the door marked 'storage'. She opened the door and it gave way with a creaking noise, not loud, but just enough to cause annoyance. She stepped in,"Don't bang..." too late she had already let the door shut behind her"...the door" Nick still completed from where he stood by the corner."You banged it" he said coming to stand in front of her.If Sammy hadn't been so surprised to see him, she would have said something, anything. Instead of staring like a fool. She hadn't seen him since that night in the kitchen and she hadn't even realised he was home."I'm sorry, I didn't realise anyone was in here" she apologised when she finally got a hold of herself."I asked you not to shut the door" he said wearing his usual frown."I'm sorry, I wasn't paying attention" she said and turned around to grab the door handle, she turned it and nothing."It's not going to open" he told her when she turned the door several times"Why not?" she asked but she wasn't stopping with turning the door handle"Because it's jammed""What do you mean jammed?" Sammy asked getting alarmed, the last thing she needed right now was to get stuck in some basement."Can you stop that?" he said when she wouldn't stop trying to open the door.She stopped and then turned to look at him,"why is the door not opening?" she asked"Because you banged it" he accused,"it can only be opened from the outside now" he told her"Then we should call someone" she suggested and felt her pockets for her phone but came up empty, it wasn't in her pocket."I don't have my phone" she told Nick looking expectantly at him"Me neither. I didn't anticipate being locked in here on my way down" he said and then ran his hand through his hair."I'm sorry, I didn't know that the door...""it's fine. What are you doing down here?" he asked"Alex sent me to go get ice"Alex, shit! The girl would definitely murder her now."what are we going to do now?" she asked him thinking of Alex's furious face"We wait" he said settling on the floor by the side of the door"Maybe if we banged on the door someone would..." she stopped talking when she saw the way he was looking at her.She joined him on the floor but on the other side of the doorframe, she was already starting to feel hot and she hated that the room started to feel smaller than it actually was."Someone is going to find us right?" she asked after a while of silence"Alex knows where you are so hopefully she's going to come looking for you""Hopefully" she repeated.

It was weird, just sitting there in silence with him. The air was tense between them, of course it was, the last time they had been in a room alone together they had had their tongues down each other's throat and that had not ended well. That had been days ago.She took a sneak peek at him, he had his head resting on the wall behind him and his eyes shut. His breathing was even and she wondered if he had maybe fallen asleep.How could he look this peaceful when she was having all these emotions? It wasn't just about being trapped in a room with him, it was about the images that now flooded her mind. The memories.Two days, that was how long it had been. Two long days where all she thought about was the taste of his lips and the feel of his skin and now, he was this close it was as if nothing had happened. He even felt more distance than when they had first met and somehow the thought made Sammy feel like throwing up. That could've been because of the pregnancy or because she had been trapped in a room for more than twenty minutes now.She stood up and he opened his eyes,"Are you okay?" he asked.No. No, I'm not okay. I'm pissed."I'm fine" she said and took a couple steps away from him.He sat up and didn't stop looking at her, which wasn't really helping the way she was feeling in that moment."Are you sure you're okay?" he asked again,I'm trapped in a room with the world's meanest man. So no, I'm not okay"I'm trapped in a storage room and I'm pregnant which means I have to pee every five minutes. So all I can think about right now is what I'm going to do when that happens""Try not to think about it" he said dismissively and closed his eyes again, as if she was in control of her bladder."Okay then, I'll just think about other stuff like when I can go back home" that got his attention, she had been meaning to ask someone that for days now."What do you mean?" he asked"When you came to New York you said that this trip was just for a few days, to get some test done and now I've been here for nearly two weeks" she told him."You agreed to marrying Jason" as if she needed any reminding,"And Jason's not here!" she ran her hands through her hair in frustration, she felt like she was going crazy and she wanted out from this basement immediately."Jason's gonna come back" he told her and she hated that he was still wearing that calm exterior as always."Your brother doesn't want to marry me""He has very little choice in the matter""Just like me then""Ms Baker...""Can you stop with the whole Ms Baker thing"Your tongue has been down my throat for goodness sake! I was this close to letting you have sex with me on your kitchen floor!"I am not your employee" she told him even though she always felt like she was."What would you rather have me call you""My first name maybe?""Okay then Samantha, maybe you should sit down, you don't look so good"She hated that him asking still made her want to obey, she hated that she was maybe having a nervous breakdown and all she wanted was for him to hold her, she hated him period."I just want to go home" she said while taking her position on the floor again"Why?" he asked and when Sammy looked at him, he looked genuinely intrigued,"Why do I want to go back to my home?" she asked him.Easy, because you are not there."I meant, if it's about your things they are just things, they could be replaced"Her things weren't just things, they were all sacred to her. Everything she owned was sacred to her. Maybe he wouldn't get it because he had lived in luxury all his life but she had to work really hard to get the little she had, and so him saying that her things were 'just things' really struck a nerve."It's about my best friend, it's about my apartment and it's about my favourite mug that has this crack on the side but I love the taste of coffee when I'm drinking from it. I have never lived in a different city from Vicky, ever. Even when she got into college, she got an apartment off campus just so we could live together.And my apartment? It's the first apartment I've ever owned. I didn't have enough for the first and last month's rent so Vicky and I had to work in her mother's diner for a week and she hates that place.I just didn't imagine that the last time I was standing there would be the last time I'd be standing there" she told him and then cringed inwardly, she didn't want to be sharing herself like that with him"We could keep the apartment, pay for it for as long as you want" anything just to make sure her marriage to his brother went off according to plan right?"I would never ask for that. If this is my new home now, I just want to go back to my old one and say a proper good bye. Plus, I'm running out of clothes" and I need time away from this fastmoving car that was the McCarthy manor she had been stuck in."I'll speak to Richard about it but I'm sure it can be arranged"She threw her face away and closed her eyes, could someone please find them already? She really, really wanted to leave. As if being stuck in a room alone with him wasn't embarrassing enough her stomach decided it was time to remind her that she had skipped breakfast and it was well over lunch time by rumbling loudly.She cursed mentally, why was this always happening to her? And always when she was with him."You're hungry" it wasn't a question so she said nothing,"Was there no food at Charlie's party? With the money Lex is spending you'd think there'd be a feast" he asked herShe hadn't gotten around to eating anything, she had been too distracted being intimidated by everyone."I was going to eat once I got the ice for Alex""And breakfast? What did you have for breakfast?" he asked againWell about that,"Nothing" ever since Mrs James had caught her in the most unnerving situation she had avoided the woman like a plague, and since the woman was mostly always in the kitchen she also avoided the area completely. So the only time she ever ate was when Charlie or Alex invited her and Alex didn't eat breakfast and Charlie always ate with her husband, so for days now she completely ignored how hungry she was every morning. Hunger wasn't something that was new to her so she could totally take it."What do you mean nothing?" he asked"I wasn't hungry" she lied."You can't be skipping meals like that, not in your condition"Of course that was what he cared about, the baby she was carrying."I know" she said just so the conversation could end.He got up and she watched him walk to one of the shelves at the end of the room and dig up two bags of chips, he came back and tossed her one of the bags."This is the only edible thing in here or maybe you'd prefer raw meat from the refrigerator" he said as he settled back down on the floor."This is just fine" she told him.At least one problem down, but the problem of still maybe having to pee was looming around the corner and Sam knew that before long she would really have to relieve herself."Are you going to eat or are you going to keep staring at the bag?" Niklaus asked her when he noticed that she wasn't eating.She gently opened the bag and then tossed a chip into her mouth, it really reminded her of Vicky. The girl could have potato chips for the three designated meals of the day. This was the first time in days she was thinking of her friend, which was really weird but she had been so occupied this past couple of days and the only time she had managed to think about anything it had always managed to be one thing."Is that okay?" he asked forcing her to look at him, had he been watching her the enter time?This was the Niklaus she always managed to think about whenever she thought of him. She didn't think about the one who ignored her or spoke to her as if she was retarded, it always managed to be this one who took care of her. The one that had held her hand at the hospital, the one that had made her tea because she had been crying and the one that cooked for her. The one who despite how annoyed he was at her always managed to make sure she was comfortable and well taken care of. And that was the one she had genuinely missed."It is" she replied and then added"are you going eat yours or are you going to keep staring?"He looked at her for the longest of time and then something like a smile appeared on his mouth but it was gone before it formed properly and he opened his own bag of chips.They both ate their chips in silence for a while before Sammy began,"I lied earlier,""when I said I skipped breakfast because I wasn't hungry that wasn't exactly true" she told him for no reason."You were hungry but you chose not to eat?" he asked,"I didn't exactly choose. Since the night Mrs James caught us, I haven't been very eager to return to the kitchen" she told him."So you haven't been eating?" he asked"Breakfast, no. But I usually have lunch with Alex or Charlie""And dinner?" he asked and she said nothing but he got the memo "So you've been starving?" it wasn't exactly a question.Starving was such a strong word, starving was that time when her mom had been sick and she had to work two jobs to cover her medications and didn't have enough left over to feed properly. Starving was the month she had lost her job and couldn't get another for a whole three weeks so she had almost starved to death that month. Being served a buffet every afternoon wasn't starving."I'm not starving" she told him"I've been so preoccupied this past couple of days helping Alex with Charlie's shower that I don't even notice the skipped meals""Well you should. You are pregnant.""I know" you've said that before"You can't be careless about this""I know""How do you expect to be in good health to carry this child to full term if you are barely eating?"She spared him a glance expecting to be met with his disapproval face instead it was genuine worry that covered his face. Was he worried about her or about the child? Sammy thought but she wasn't going to delude herself with the thought that Niklaus was worried about her, it was obviously his brother's child that he was concerned for."I didn't want to cause any trouble. Mrs James seemed pretty angry after she saw us and I just wanted to avoid her.""You're going to have to face her at some point because you live here now"That sounded weird, the fact that she lived here now. In her head she was avoiding Mrs James until she went home and never had to see the woman again. but agreeing to marry Jason meant that this was home."I'm sorry I kissed you" he said when she said nothing."what?" she asked turning to face him"I shouldn't have put you in that position" he said.How could she tell him that she wasn't angry because he had put her in the position over the counter and on the floor? How could she tell him that the only thing she was crossed about was him saying it was a stupid mistake? Which in all honesty it was, but hearing him say it really hurt her more than she was willing to admit."I think that I let myself get carried away and I'm glad Mrs James came in before we went any further"You let yourself get carried away? I almost had sex with you on your kitchen floor!"I was angry and I didn't think things through. What I did was selfish and that is why I left"What exactly had he been angry about? Sammy didn't dare to ask. What was it about kissing her that drove them away? Jason too took off that night after he had violated her lips without permission and as weird as it was, she hadn't thought of him since then. Maybe it was because her mind was on someone else. It was weird because when she got here Niklaus had been her least favourite, the thought of seeing him when she woke up in the morning made her want to crawl under her bed and die. He was still honestly the same person and treated her the same way but things had somehow managed to change on her part."I promise it won't happen again" he said"I honestly didn't think you remembered" she told him"What?"

he asked"Kissing me""Why would you say that?" how could he sound so surprised?Where to start from?"For starters, you called me Ms Baker few minutes ago""I thought that would make it less uncomfortable""For whom?" him perhaps because it made her just want to hurl things at him."Fine, Samantha it is then"she hated that she couldn't help the smile that crept into her face at the sound of her name coming from his mouth. She tried to remind herself that it didn't mean anything, except for maybe the fact that he remembered what kissing her felt like. Except that he remembered how much he had wanted her that night, how much they had both wanted each other. He had said he had been angry and that was why he kissed her,"You were angry?" she askedHe looked at her and then looked away and went back to eating his chips and just when Sammy thought he wasn't going reply he said,"Yes. I was very angry""At me?""At me, at Jason and maybe a little at you""Your brother kissed me, I didn't want...""You really don't have explain yourself to me" he told her"I want to" she said it before she could stop herself."Why?" he asked. Yes why? Why did she want to explain to him that she didn't want Jason's mouth on hers?"Because we are friends" that was laughable the notion of them being friends, friends didn't do what they did. And if they were friends, she certainly wouldn't want a repeat of that."Friends? Is that what we are?" he asked"Maybe not yet, but I'd really like it if that happens" was that even possible at this point?"Okay" He said after a pause,"Friends, it is"

# CHAPTER 9

I t was nice, being friends with Niklaus McCarthy was very nice. Admittedly it had only been thirteen hours but it felt like it was going to be a really long and good friendship, why wouldn't it be? They already had the bases of any long-lasting friendship, a secret. They were keeping a massive, mutually destructive secret from the rest of the family, well not entirely the rest of the family because one person knew about it but that wasn't the point. The point was they now had a secret that felt like an explosion hanging over her head.It had been different when he was gone, their sordid deed had felt boxed up and tucked away when he wasn't there. It had been a memory that felt surreal. But he was here now, which was a game changer.It wasn't the fact that he had made her dinner last night after a help named Nigel had found them hours later, not Alex or Charlie, just Nigel. Apparently neither noticed she had been missing because the handy man had come and fixed the ice machine and they forgot about her. That almost didn't surprise her.They didn't talk much but it was the intimate setting of watching him as he cooked for her again that made her realise that maybe she didn't just want to be friends with him. But what she wanted was out of the question so she was just going to have to take his friendship, it was indeed better than being disliked by him.And this morning, she had woken to the knocking on her door and a breakfast buffet. Apparently, Mr McCarthy had made a request for her before he left. She didn't have to imagine which Mr McCarthy it was, she also didn't try to hide the smile that had covered her face or the quiet butterfly that had danced their way into her belly. He cared, and maybe it was more about the baby and not quite about her, but whatever, but he cared and that made her happy. Not a lot of people cared about her, not even the father of said child gave a damn but Niklaus did, so she would let herself be happy about it whatever his reasons were.

Two hours after she had had breakfast, she was barely out of the shower and she still had her towel wrapped around her when there was another knock on her door. She guessed it would be Charlie, the girl was energy draining but consistent. She probably needed company for some weird thing she decided to do today, which mostly meant she wanted someone who she was going to talk at while they just sat and listened. But Sammy was okay with that, the alternative would be to just sit inside her room and do nothing so however much exhausting it was going to be, Sammy was still grateful to be somewhat included.The smile she had carefully plastered on her face froze once she opened the door and it wasn't Charlie on the other side of it."Nick?" she called and he gave her a slight wave before letting his eyes travel down her still dripping body."You're wet" he stated"Yes, I was just in the shower" she told him.They both stood at the door staring at the other for what felt like hours but in reality was just a few seconds before Sammy finally said,"Did you need something?" she refused the urge to add 'friend' at the end of the question.He had never been to her room before now and she was pretty sure this was the first time she was seeing his face without the usual scowl and she didn't think it was possible but he had somehow looked more handsome than ever before."Of course. We are going out, you and I. We have some errands to run" he was back to sounding distant, not like a friend would. Which almost worried Sammy."So dress up and meet me downstairs" he was gone before she could reply him and this definitely worried her.

AS NICK SAT waiting, it felt like he was waiting for his doom. This being friends thing, was definitely NOT GOING to work, at least not on his end. He had fricking gone to her bedroom! Why did he do that? She had been in a fricking towel, dripping wet and smiling like some sort of sex symbol and then he had froze. Staring at her like the idiot he was. When she had asked if he needed something, all sorts of ideas came to his mind and the friendly gesture he had come to make then felt like a seduction tactic. He shouldn't even have come home, but considering that Richard McCarthy felt like treating him like his employee the man thought he could use him however way he pleased and since Dr Brenda still hadn't cleared him to leave the country, he was stuck being a baby sitter. Her baby sitter. And even though his first instinct was to run like hell because he felt more like a pervert uncle than a baby sitter he somehow still wanted to be around her but he wasn't going to do that. He wasn't going to let himself get caught up in another scandal, especially not when it involved another woman that had something to do with Jason. That would just be begging for trouble and he wasn't really ready for trouble.This was quickly turning into another case of Sophia Jamieson and this time he was Sophia and Samantha Baker was an innocent bystander that was about to get caught up in his perversions if he didn't get a hold on himself.

The cheer on Charlie's face somehow made Sammy want to smile, the girl was just so good at being happy. She was standing at the foot of the stairs as if waiting,"Have you heard the great news?" Charlie asked and she shook her head trying not to seem as impatient as she felt, she was sure that Nick would already be pretty tired of waiting for her and she hadn't meant to take so long getting ready but nothing in her bag felt right for the occasion. She had no idea what the occasion was but she wanted to look right and even though she would never admit it she wanted to look right for him."No, I didn't" she said trying to sound as cheerful as Charlie, but no one could ever be as cheerful as her."Well, Luca has gone down to Dallas"That was the great news?"I know what you are thinking, I love that man but I swear to God, if I stay cooped up in this house for one more day I'm going to lose my mind. And that man would never let me leave, unless it's for a doctor's appointment"She was trying to sound like it was hectic being with her husband all the time but Sammy knew that wasn't true, the woman was equally as bad as the man."So," she continued,"me, you and Lex are gonna go have some fun" she told her the smile returning to her face,"No, I cant. Nick and I have plans" Sammy couldn't help the thrill that rushed through her body. She had plans with Nick. She almost giggled like a school girl, It probably didn't mean anything, but it made her really super happy."Oh no. He's gone. Said to tell you that something came up""He left?" she asked as the disappointment washed over her."Yeah. But he asked Lex to take you into the city and I've managed to squeeze myself into the plans" Charlie said in a really excited tone,"Lu is probably going to have a fit when he finds out but nothing some hot sex wouldn't fix" Sammy cringed, information she really didn't need. She now had a mental image of the very pregnant Charlie and her husband doing things she didn't even know was possible at this stage of her pregnancy."Okay then, I'm going to go drag Lexie down. She always takes too long to get ready" Charlie said and then started going upstairs, she was practically racing up the stairs for a woman in her condition. Sammy immediately understood why her husband worried all the time, she wanted to yell 'be careful' after her but she was sure it would fall on deaf ears.Nick had left, Sammy thought hating the feeling of disappointment that had now overshadowed her earlier excitement. She shouldn't have spent so much time getting ready, he had probably gotten tired of waiting for her and that stung.

* * * * * *

NICK SAT IMPATIENTLY as he waited for Chase to discharge his guest as he had called them. The two women were almost as reluctant to leave as Chase was to see them go and if Nick wasn't in crisis mode, he would have been a tad sorry for interrupting them but he needed to talk to the only man whore he knew. The boy was the proper definition of what a hedonist was and somehow the entire family including Richard had managed to be fine with it. Maybe fine was an over statement, more like learned to live with it."You better have a very important reason for being here this early and you are not moving back in" Chase said walking back to Nick after had just watched him give the two girls individual goodbye kisses that were very passionate and very extensive, one had even given him a little squeeze on his butt."You mean a very important reason for interrupting your ménage a toir? And I wasn't living here, I stayed a few nights" Nick said and his brother laughed."It's not my fault that everyone wants a piece of this" Chase said referring to his body, Nick rolled his eyes,"You are disgusting, go put on some clothes" not that he wasn't enjoying staring at his brother's fantastic figure in the boxer briefs he wore but he would prefer it if they were both clothed for what he wanted to discuss."So, talk" Chase said after he got dressed and came back,"and please don't take too much of my time I have a busy schedule today""Oh, more women coming over?" Nick asked sarcastically"Well if you must know, I'm flying to Spain for a very special introduction to a Spanish heiress"Nick rolled his eyes,"You know, if you had a job like the rest of us then maybe you wouldn't just be getting out bed by this time of the day, discarding two girls and still thinking about getting another into your bed""Well first of all, you don't have a job either. Unless babysitting now pays as much as being an exec in a large corporation. And secondly, you know that I don't want to work for Luxury. I wouldn't feel comfortable working for dad or you""You're literally a dick brain, you don't feel comfortable working for Luxury but you have no problem spending Luxury money. And you wouldn't be working for me or dad, you'd be working with us""Yeah, right" Chase said sarcastically"And I'm not a babysitter, I'm just taking care of the girl until Richard convinces your brother to come home. But that's not the point, I don't want to talk about the girl or Luxury I have more important things to talk about" Nick told him"Wow, that's a first. Niklaus McCarthy having something more important than Luxury to discuss" his brother was mocking him but he was desperate enough to take it"Are you going to shut up and listen or should I just go?" he asked"Fine, let's hear it" Chase said getting more comfortable on the sofa. He crossed his legs and rested his head on the back of the chair and in that moment, taking a look at his brother's face Nick wasn't so sure if coming here was a good idea anymore.He took a deep breath before he began,"I met a girl...""A girl, oh la la""Seriously Chase?""Sorry, it's just weird. You coming to me about a girl" he said.Definitely a bad idea coming here, and an embarrassing one too. In his thirty one years of existence he had never had to have a talk like this but he felt like his brain was literally going to explode if he didn't talk to someone and thinking about it now that person should not be Chase, Charlie maybe but the woman was definitely going to figure him out if he told her anything about it. She was too smart for her own good. And yes, she was his best friend but he still wouldn't want her to know any of this.He took a deep breath and rubbed his hands over his face in frustration, Chase just sitting and staring at him wasn't making this any easier."...and all I can think about is having sex with her" if only it was the constant want to have sex with her. It was the always wanting to be near her, to talk to her. It was the obsessive thoughts about her, the anger he felt every time he thought about her marrying his brother, it was all the weird feelings that nauseated him and angered him at the same time. It was the abnormal want to always cook for her and watch her eat, to take care of her. He wanted to do things with her and to her and that was the problem.Chase waited for him to continue but when he didn't he asked,"So what's the problem, she doesn't want to have sex with you?""She's married" better to stick close to the truth but not tell the entire truth."Okay. I still don't see what the problem is?" Nick sighed, of course he didn't see what the problem was in wanting a married woman"She's married to a friend of mine" it hadn't been his intentions to lie to his brother but he couldn't possibly just get out and tell him the real reason he was in a turmoil now, could he?"You don't have any friends" Chase told him"Of course I do" Nick said but that wasn't exactly true."You don't""I do, and I'm not arguing with you about this. Just tell me what I can do" Nick said shushing him."You could maybe talk to your 'friend'," Nick decided to ignore his air quotes Chase made  when he said friend."...offer him some money or something""Do you even hear yourself?" he asked his brother"Well I don't know, I have never had to do much work to get a woman into bed not even if she's married" leave it to Chase to find a bragging moment in this"I don't want to get her into bed, I just want to make it stop. The wanting her, I just want to turn it off, turn her off. How do I do that?" was that even possible?"How should I know?""Well with the number of women you have sex with there must be one that have gotten stuck in your head and you had to shake""Uh uh. I don't get stuck on a woman. If I want to get a woman out of my system, I fuck her. Maybe you should try that with your married friend"This wasn't helping at all, of course Chase's solution was going to be more sex."Jesus! Chase I'm not sleeping with her" he said sternly, so his brother would know that that was off the table.If Chase had a clue of who he was actually talking about then he would stop making these impertinent suggestions."Fine. Maybe fuck someone else instead. I mean, how do you even know it's about her? Maybe you just need to get laid"Of course it would be another stu... okay, maybe that was not actually the worst idea. Maybe if he had sex with someone else then Samantha Baker wouldn't be an issue anymore. It was scary that Chase was beginning to make sense but truth be told it has really been a while since he had gotten laid, not since the accident and he knew someone who could help. Maybe a few people but just one he actually wanted to help him with the problem."I gotta go"

SAMMY'S SKIN HAD never felt so good in her entire life, admitted skin care wasn't something she usually indulged in or at all to be honest. Up until she had come to the McCarthy house, she had used the same kind of soap and shampoo for no other reason but because they were quite affordable. So, as she, Alex and Charlie left the spa she felt like a million bucks. It was a feeling she feared she could get comfortable with.The next stop was a high-end boutique, Sammy was sure she was going to have a heart attack just being in the place, she had never been in a place that was so chic before. The attendant that had introduced herself as Anna looked like she just crawled out of a modelling catalogue not someone Sammy could ask for directives on clothing acce ssary.The prices on the tags where outrageous and Sammy was sure that unless Richard McCarthy paid her the million bucks he was going to give her for marrying his son there was no way she would be able to afford to buy anything from the store not even a handkerchief.That wasn't the case for Alex and Charlie, they looked rather at home, gushing over shoes and other accessories as she just stood in the corner watching them."How do you like this?" Charlie asked coming to stand next to her with a pair of silver stilettos that was trimmed with black at the edges."It's quiet nice" but Sammy was sure there was no way the very pregnant woman standing in front of her could possible walk in those but taking a glance down at the ones she was wearing now made her have a rethink.It seemed like it was at that moment that Charlie noticed she wasn't in on all the fun they were having,"Sammy why aren't you picking out stuff you like? We won't be here all day you know" she asked and Sammy turned a shade of pink."I don't... I couldn't..." how should she say this right now? Best to just come out with it.She reduced her voice so only Charlie would here,"Charlie, I can't afford anything here" "oh my God" Charlie laughed"What do you mean you can't afford anything here? You're not paying" "No, no, I can't let you pay for me, everything here is so expensive and I don't want to…""Oh honey I'm not paying either. Nick is. This whole thing is his idea"Well that was a shock,"It is?" Sammy asked"Of course it is, he wanted us to show you a really great time and it's a good thing I have his black express card and we are going to try to max that baby out" she sounded really excited when she said that last part.Sammy couldn't help but smile too, Nick had wanted her to have a good time. He didn't just abandon her.

WHEN NICK HAD called Allison West and asked if she was still in  town and available to see him, he had left out asking if she wanted to have sex but he was sure she already got the memo.Allison was a prima ballerina Nick had met in France, he had watched her in the Nutcracker and he had been totally mesmerised. And when he met her again in Venice he just had to introduce himself half hoping to get her into his bed, that was three years ago.It had been nothing serious obviously but the six weeks they had spent together in one of Luxury's hotel suite in Milan had been mutually satisfying. They ran into each other six months after that in Paris and she was seeing a Swedish prince but it didn't really surprise Nick when she called him a week later to ask if he was still the city. Apparently, the prince wasn't as fun as she had hoped in the beginning. They spent a week together in Paris and Nick invited her back to Milan with him and that was how it was from then on, when they ended up in the same place, they kept each other company. It was a thing of convenience and they both liked it that way, Allison was too focussed on her carer to entertain anything serious and

Nick just liked causal. There were never any feelings involved and neither expected anything from the other but whenever they got together, they made sweet sweet magic together.So why weren't they making magic now? Nick wondered as he sat watching Allison eat,"What's on your mind?" she asked picking at her plate, the girl barely ate, she was always on some kind of diet or another. But it always amazed him that she had so much stamina in her."What do you mean?" he asked dropping his fork"I mean, we haven't seen each other in almost a year and I've been in town for a week now and you didn't even bother to send me a welcome basket and then you text me today and then you come over and we are having lunch?""What's wrong with lunch? I thought you were hungry?""You were supposed to be lunch" she gave him a coy smileHe smiled back at her,"That can be arranged" he said getting up abandoning his lunch and going around the table to gently pull her up.When he kissed her, he wasn't expecting fireworks or anything, after all they had kissed a hundred times, but what he hadn't expected was this feeling of noth-ingness. It wasn't like this before, he had always been perfect-ly content kissing her, enjoyed it even, so what was different now?He closed his eyes and tried again but this time all he could picture was Samantha."What's wrong?" Allison asked taking a step away from him to look at him better"Nothing. Nothing's wrong" he said too quickly.Everything about this was wrong. This should have finally been his cure, ending this crazy and frustrating desires his brain was making up. This was supposed to prove that him wanting her was just because it had been a long time since he had been with someone. He wasn't supposed to be thinking about her at the very moment he was kissing Allison. He wasn't supposed to be thinking of how intoxicating it was having her in his arms was or how responsive she was. The way she looked up at him whenever he broke off their kiss with eyes so big and brown like she was...Fuck!!! How could this one woman be messing with his head like this?He kissed Allison again, this time putting all his energy into it. She smiled,"That's more like it" she said but it wasn't the same on his part. Everything had changed and, in that moment, Nick knew that this was NOT going to be the answers to his problems. That being with Allison wasn't going to change anything. There was only one person who had the power to curb his perversed urges.

# CHAPTER 10

The decision to go back to his prescription drugs wasn't one Nick made lightly, he decided it was best after he got home from Allison's hotel suite. He knew that though they would make him a feel drowsy, they would let him sleep through the night. And if sleeping through the night meant that he wasn't going to go bang on Samantha Baker's door and beg her to be with him then he was going to take the drugs over and over again because with the way he was feeling now if he as much as laid his eyes on her he wasn't sure he knew what he was capable of doing.The knock on his bedroom door was a distraction he didn't need but he carefully dropped the pill box back on the dresser and went to see who it was.Telling himself to quickly dismiss to whomever it was he opened the door but what he wasn't expecting was to open his bedroom door to see Samantha Baker standing at the other side. And then something that had never happened to him before happened, his heart skipped a beat.He almost laughed, if it hadn't terrified the crap out of him Nick would have laughed at himself. Never in his thirty-one years of existing had that ever happened to him. He wasn't the kind of man that those kinds of things happened to.

"Samantha?" he called as if unsure if it was really her,"Hi" she smiled and his heart did it again. He cursed mentally. "What are you doing here?" he asked her and watched her smile falter."I was... We just got back..." her lips moved but all Nick noticed was that she had done something with her hair, it was now in little curls which made her look chic and somehow more beautiful. She also looked more rested, like she had taken a long nap and had enjoyed it. He didn't know how he swallowed his tongue but it felt like it wasn't there anymore, why was this happening to him?"...I just wanted to thank you" she ended with a smile that wasn't supposed to be as inviting as it was."That's not necessary" he said and began to close the door,"Nick?" she called him and he paused."Did I do something?" she asked,"What do you mean?""I don't know, you seem upset. Is it about the shopping? Because Charlie said that it was your idea, and if it's a problem I could pay you back or maybe return..." "Please stop" he said silencing her. She was nervous, he could tell.He hadn't specifically said shopping, he had just asked his sister in-law to show her a good time. Of course he should have known that shopping was Charlie's definition of good time.He had just felt guilty about running out on her like that but he had little to no other alternative in that moment. The signing of the prenup would have to wait until he was feeling more like himself or until either Jason or his dad came home."I'm not upset with you" which was the truth, he was upset about a lot of things but not at her directly. He was upset at himself because he didn't feel like himself, he was upset that he had taken Chase's advice, he was even upset that he had gone to his wayward brother for advice in the first place and lastly he was upset that he had all these feeling that he couldn't afford to do anything about."But you are upset?" why couldn't the damned girl just leave things alone?"Yes. Yes I am" they was no use to deny it, she would probably find another way to poke."Is that why you left this morning?" No I left so I wouldn't fuck your brains out!"No I remembered I had a prior appointment" he lied"Prior appointment" she repeated and nodded her head in a way that said she didn't believe him."If I did or said something to upset you then I'm sorry"Nick sighed, of course she'd apologise."Samantha you did nothing wrong!" the words weren't supposed to be as harsh as they came out to be."Then why are you speaking to me this way? Why are you being like this? I thought we agreed to be friends?"Nick inhaled deeply and rubbed his hands over his face in frustration.Friends? He almost laughed if not for the frustration. Friends didn't know the way the other tasted, a friend didn't have such dirty thoughts for his friend and a friend sure as hell wouldn't want to do all the things he wanted to do to her.Fuck!"We are friends""Okay" she did the whole nodding thing again before turning around and beginning to leave,"Samantha" the name left his mouth before he could think about it. That was always the case with her, he couldn't think anytime he was around her."I'm gonna go get some rest" she turned around to say"I shouldn't've snapped at you. I'm sorry" he watched her exhale deeply."If you're upset about the money..." "It's not about the money"They stood staring at each other for about ten seconds before she said,"Do you want to make me dinner, I'm starving" she said it lightly and he knew it was to give him room to refuse if he wanted to but the funny thing was, as much he knew he should stay away from her, as much as he told himself that he was going to, he just didn't want to. So Nick took a deep breath and surrendered to himself,"Okay"

Sammy laughed, it wasn't like her but she was determined to break Nick out of the foul mood he was in. He had agreed to cook for her not knowing she wasn't as hungry as she was pretending to be, Alex had treated them to lunch at a restaurant she had said was owned by her special friend, she and Charlie had shared an inside joke about it but that didn't bother Samantha. It was something she was beginning to get used to because she barely knew them and they didn't know her very well either so she tried not to let it bother her every time they left her out on conversations."It's not funny" he said dryly as he chopped his onions skilfully. "It kinda is" she replied and laughed again, he frowned creasing his handsome face only a little which made Samantha want to laugh harder."I think I should put you to work" he said handing her bowl of freshly washed mushrooms."Oh no, I'm just gonna make a mess" she said throwing her hands up in the air in surrender, Nick had never in the few times he had cooked for her included her,"Then we'll eat a mess" or ever eaten with her. She tried to hide the grin on her face and tried to silence the little voice reminding her of how cozy all this felt."Okay" she collected the mushrooms staring at them like they were alien creatures"What am I supposed to do with this?" she asked him."You can dump them in there" he pointed to the pot of  water that was already simmering on the cooker."And then you can cut the parsley" he said with a wicked grin on his face when she was done haphazardly dumping the mushrooms to let them boil."What are you even making?" she asked as she reluctantly collected the vegetable from him,"Bucatini with mushrooms. It's an Italian dish, have you ever had it?" he asked moving to the garlic.Sammy chuckled, the only Italian dish she had ever had was lasanga and that was just when Vicky's mom made it."How do I even cut this?""However you like, it doesn't need to look nice"

"We made this?" Sammy asked surprised when she had the first taste of the pasta an hour later. It tasted great like something you would only find in a five-star restaurant Nick laughed which made Sammy thrill that he was out of his earlier mood, he was more relaxed now and had even laughed a couple of times. Maybe he had forgotten who he was with because he hadn't even frowned once, not even when he had gone to get the wine from the cellar and she had forgotten to take out the mushrooms."I made this" he corrected as he settled with his own plate next to her."You cut one vegetable and then let the mushrooms burn, so instead of Bucatini with mushrooms we are just having Bucatini""Which is delicious. How can you cook like this?" she asked genuinely curiou s.He thought about it for a moment,"This particular dish I learnt to impress this woman.""Oh" her heart sank. It wasn't like she thought she was the only woman Niklaus McCarthy had ever cooked for, if she was being honest she had never thought about it until now but it still left a sour taste in her mouth to think about it and she had to remind herself it was none of her business. The fact that he was being nice to her now didn't mean anything other than that."Yes, Shreya Wong. She was this chef we wanted to hire for the Luxury in Milan, the five figures salary didn't convince her to leave the restaurant she worked for to come work in our hotel but this dish did. Except there were mushrooms in those" he was teasing her.Sammy chuckled, relieved. A chef and not a woman friend, that sounded good to hear. "I almost forgot" he said getting up and going to get one of the wines he had fetched earlier from the cellar, the other one he had used to cook the meal. Getting two champagne flutes he settled back down and began to pour."Nick I can't drink that" she resisted the urge to rub her belly"Oh no, it's not champagne. It's called Tost, it looks like champagne but it's a non-alcoholic blend of white tea, white cranberry and ginger. Charlie's obsessed with it""Okay then, let's toast with Tost." She said raising her glass, Nick chuckled but still clicked his glass with hers and they settled to their meal.

Sammy was happy, happier than she had been in a very long time. Everything was working out better than they ever had for her. She tried to remind herself that her baby daddy was still missing but even that couldn't get her down from her last night's high. There was no going back now at least she hoped not because it would suck if Nick decided he didn't want to be friends anymore.It felt like she was floating as she glided down the stairs, she heard him laugh, she almost laughed too, she now knew what his laugh sounded like so well and that made her a little giddy. She was barely in the room when Charlie half raced to her ignoring the shouts of her husband to be careful."Hi" Sammy greeted with a smile,"There you are" she said as if she had been missing before now,"we were just talking about you"About her? Sammy looked around the room from Charlie to her husband and then to Nick who had done nothing to indicate he had even noticed her presence since she walked into the room. Why had she been a topic for discussion and what had the discussion been about?She smiled nervously and glanced over to Nick again but he seemed to be so engrossed in something he was doing on his phone. Why wouldn't he just look at her?"You were talking about me?" she asked nervously and Charlie nodded"Yes, Nick said you were dying to go back to New York"Dying wasn't exactly the word. Yes she had had a bunch of reasons for wanting to go back but all of a sudden they didn't seem that important anymore."I wanted to go pack up my things and give up my apartment since I'll be staying here now" she looked at Nick again but still nothing, was he mad at her as per usual?"Good! How does tomorrow sound?" Charlie asked,"Tomorrow? Like tomorrow, tomorrow?" were they trying to get rid of her for some reason?"Yes, tomorrow. There's this gala that I'm supposed to be in attendance tomorrow but due to unforeseen circumstances I can't make it" she said the last part while rubbing her ever growing belly and giving her husband the stink eye."Okay, there are no unforeseen circumstances, he won't let me go. That man won't let me go anywhere" Sammy chuckled at the same time Luca did."Babyyy" he called her,"What? I'm not complaining, it's fine. I've come to terms with the fact that I'm trapped in this house for all eternity" "What my wife is trying to say is that she has this charity gala tomorrow, and since you were already planning on going to New York you could maybe stand in for her and then you can do all your stuff afterwards"What? They wanted her to attend a gala! No. No. No. She couldn't possibly do that."That sounds great but I don't think I can, I've never been to a gala before. I don't even think I own the proper attire for such an event." What did people even wear to such events anyway? Definitely not anything in her closet. Vicky would know what to wear to such an event. Vicky would die to attend such an event." You don't have to worry about that, my stylist will fly out with you and Nick""Nick?" all objections she was about to give forgotten, she asked."Yes, Nick's standing in for me" Luca said"He'll be your date" Charlie put in.Date? Her tummy did an uncomfortable summersault and she prayed that her cheeks heating up was only on the inside."It's for charity" for the first time since she walked into the room Nick said and Sammy wasn't sure if he was referring to the gala or going with her but she honestly didn't mind at this point."And you can use the opportunity to clear you apartment and say your final goodbye to New York" Charlie told her.Vicky would be so happy to see her. It had nothing to do with the fact that Nick was going. "Fine, I'll do it"Cheers from both Charlie and Luca filed the room but nothing from Nick and as if that wasn't enough, he got up and he walked out, leaving a very bitter taste in Sammy's mouth. Maybe she should have said no after all.

# CHAPTER 11

The flight from Texas to New York was the longest Sammy had ever been in, it didn't help that Nick wasn't talking to her. It had been radio silence since breakfast yesterday and she marvelled at how he was able to always switch off and on, one minute they were best of friends and the next he couldn't even stand to be in the same room with her. It was exhausting trying to keep up with him.She threw a glance his way and saw he was in a deep conversation with the hostess that was waiting on them and then they laughed and Sammy felt like someone was stomping on her heart. It wasn't jealousy, she told herself, it was just a rightful reaction when a 'your friend' was almost flirting with a girl that looked like that. No it wasn't, she was deluding herself with the idea that she had just platonic feelings for Nick because honestly, it had just been platonic until they had kissed. It had been platonic until she started noticing the things that she wasn't supposed to, until she began thinking about him day and night and not in a platonic way.The hostess laughed again and Sammy watched her pull at her neatly packed hair, she rolled her eyes and threw her face out the window, if Nick was just going to pretend like she didn't exist then she was going to let him, as a matter of fact she already made up her mind that she didn't want to be his friend anymore. Vicky was her friend, Charlie was her friend  even Alex was her friend and all these people didn't leave her feeling like a crazy person, they didn't make her question all her life decisions and they certainly didn't make her feel like a fool at every opportunity.They had had a great time the other day, at least a great time in Sammy's book. They'd talked, laughed and even enjoyed each other's company but then all she got afterwards was the silent treatment and she couldn't understand why.

Their plane landed five hours before the time to the gala and Nick dumped her in five-star hotel suite, he introduced her to Charlie's stylist, Laura and said he would send a car to pick her up later. A car, he wasn't coming. She tried to remember why she had been so excited that they were going to this thing together but nothing came to her mind. Laura brought in her team that consisted of two more people that were going to be helping with the transition and Sammy thought that was a bit of an exaggeration, she didn't need this much people just to put on a dress and tidy herself up a bit but at the end it turned out she did.When Joe, the only guy in the team had said he was going to be styling her hair Sammy almost laughed, she wore her hair really short for the exact reason to avoid having to style it.There was a lot of waxing and probing and a lot of shiny things that made Sammy's heart flutter and it took all of the five hours they had to turn her into someone she couldn't recognize and then she understood how Cinderella felt after the fairy godmother was done with her. It was more like magic because the person she was staring at in the mirror even had cleavage and a feminine figure in the dress they put her in. The shoe was a whole other thing, it took more than a few tries to be able to stand in it and a lot more than that to be able to walk in them. It was a good thing that Laura and her team were really patient and nice.

Nick laughed at something the Russian heiress had said it wasn't particularly funny but he was hoping that her family would do business with Luxury in the near future and since he was planning on going back to work soon it wouldn't hurt to be very acquainted with her. He couldn't stop his eyes from wondering to the entrance every now and again, she was late. He should have gone ahead to pick her up himself, he should call make sure everything was going according to plan. He wrapped his hand around the phone in his pocket and then decided against calling, he didn't want to seem too eager even though the wait was killing him for reasons he barely understood.He hadn't spoken to her since after their Wednesday night escapade but it wasn't from lack of trying , it was just that how they ended things that night left him tongue tied whenever they were in a room together.She had given him a peck on the cheek when he told her to head on up that he would clean everything up, just to show gratitude he assumed but as soon as she was close enough his hand automatically wrapped itself around her waist and his nostrils had opened twice their normal size and was filled with her scent. She didn't wear any perfume but she smelled as nice as if she did and he found himself inhaling deeply. But that wasn't the worst part of it all, the worst part was that he had spent the first half of the night dreaming about her and the next half thinking about all the things he wanted to do with her. She drove him wild without even trying and that was what worried him because lord only knew what would happen when she tried.

It was almost time to start the auction when he saw her, she strutted in looking like a fish out of water, she was nervous but he almost missed it because she looked divine. The dark blue dress she wore accentuated her thin waist, the long length of the dress somehow made her look taller than she actually was or was it the shoes? He let his eyes wonder and his mouth water, was this woman trying to drive him insane? How was he supposed to concentrate on anything else tonight?She saw him and then she smiled in what Nick recognised to be relief and walked briskly towards him."Hi" she said with a smile and it took him two tries  before he got the words out,"You look nice" nice was an understatement but anything else he would say now would just sound as crass as it did in his head.She blushed deeply,"Thank you, but it's all thanks to Laura and her team. They're amazing""Shall we find our seats?" he asked and she nodded and it was right when they began to walk  that he noticed that the dress wasn't finished, it was open from her shoulders all the way down to the beginning of the arc of her bottom, it was basically backless and Nick knew he was in for a long, long night.

Even though Nick had told her to bid for whatever she liked, Sammy recoiled back to watch when the first item sold for five hundred thousand dollars."Charlotte McCarthy? Andrew Silverton" the introduction was made right when the auctioneer closed the bid on a lovely neck piece.She took the shake he offered with a smile,"I'm not Charlie"He frowned,"My apologies, I thought I was supposed to be seated with the McCarthys""I'm just standing in for Charlie, something came up so she asked me""Oh... I'm sorry for the mix up. I'm Andrew Silverton" "You said that already" Sammy told him with a smile as she took the hand he offered again and shook itHe laughed,"I'm sorry, I'm just nervous" "Nervous?" he didn't look nervous until he tugged at his tie."My father is the one who usually comes to these things but he got married last week, to my ex-girlfriend if I might add but it's good now, I'm over it. Well almost. But what I'm worried about is the painting my family's donating, it sold for five hundred thousand dollars and if it doesn't do well in the auction Elena is going kill me. Elena's my sister, she's also the painter"Okay! He was nervous which somehow made her feel more at ease in his company."I'm sure the painting's going to do well and if doesn't? Elena killing you wouldn't hurt as much as your dad marrying your ex-girlfriend" she joked and smiled as she watched his lips coil into a smile and then he chuckled.He placed his hand on his chest,"Ouch! You're a terrible person miss...""Sammy, just call me Sammy""Okay, Sammy, you are a friend of Charlie McCarthy?"

NICK SWALLOWED THE uncomfortable bile that sat in his throat. He kept trying not to pay attention but this was the third time Samantha was laughing at something the gentleman sitting at her other side had told her – more like whispered to her. Andrew Silverton, was no gentleman. Nick only knew that because his father was a major client of Luxury enterprises and a very noisy one might he add. And his sister was a hotshot artist, Luca owned one or two of her works. Andrew on the other hand was rarely out at events like this, he ran more in Chase's circle, with the womanizing and the partying they both could be the same person. And now he had his eyes set on Samantha.An uncomfortable bile rose in Nick's throat, which made him shift restlessly in his chair. It wasn't jealousy he told himself, it was just that Samantha was by definition here with him and that meant that she should be laughing with him and not some other guy that she didn't know.He tried to follow their conversation when she laughed again, except he was a comedian, there was no reason Samantha should be laughing this much."...you could stash it under your bed she'd never know you paid for it" he caught the end of her sentence and the bile that had been rising in throat now tasted terribly as confirmed what he already suspected, they were talking about his bed. Already. Barely twenty minutes since they met, they had somehow graduated to bedroom discussions. Nick felt the sudden urge to punch something, or maybe someone.

WHEN ANDREW ASKED her to dance with him Sammy couldn't help but say yes, his sister's painting which had been the last auction item had done better than he had expected and that had excited him. Plus, the minute the auction was done a very friendly red-haired lady had come and dragged Nick away with no acknowledgement of Sammy – his supposed date who he had completely ignored all night.

Andrew was the only reason she had had a nice time today, he had kept her in the loop explaining auction terms she didn't understand and making jest of all the items that were up for auction and Sammy had found herself relaxing and enjoying the event she had been so afraid to come to. Andrew was good companyThey were already in the middle of the nicely decorated dance floor before Sammy remembered she didn't know how to dance at a ball, she looked around and a few couples were already on the dance floor swaying to the very genteel music. She looked up at Andrew who was already noticing her hesitations,"I can't... I don't know..." he smiled at her which eased her nerves and gently drew her into his arms."Follow my lead" he said taking her hand and keeping it on his chest and without warning taking her waist. Samantha couldn't remember if she had ever been in this position with a man before, or if she had ever been in this position before, period. She tried to follow his lead like he'd suggested as they began to sway to the music like all the other couple."Is this okay?" she asked with a smile she hoped didn't give away how nervous she felt."Better than okay" he said inching a bit closer.

SHE WAS FILRTING, shamelessly if he might add. Nick would have indulged her on an average day, not because she was as irresistible as she thought but just because. He would have asked her to dance and maybe even taken her on the offer he knew was going to come to head up to her room. She already mentioned her suite twice for no particular reason and laughed more times than that at things he said that weren't even remotely funny. Isabella Nettov was beautiful there was no denying it, she was the kind of woman Nick would have no problem going to bed with. She was almost as tall as him and curved in the all right places but it was the hair that gave her character. The fiery red hair made her look more wild than Nick knew she was and she had this smoky voice that would be perfect for phone sex and more importantly she looked like a woman who wouldn't attach too much importance to a night of fun with a man like him, but it was hard to find her attractive when Nick had other things on his mind and by other things he meant what the heck Samantha was doing with that rascal. Andrew Silverton was as shameless as he was brazen, he had stolen Samantha's attention all night. Flirted openly with her like Nick's presence didn't matter, she barely noticed he was in the room, ignoring him like they didn't come here together. Anyone would think she had come with Andrew instead of with him and worse she had enjoyed it, eating up everything he was serving like a child in need of attention.He would have given her all the attention she wanted if only someone had warned him how horrible it would be to watch her enjoy the company of another man especially if that man was as blatant as Silverton.As if just suddenly realising that he had left Samantha alone with the wolf he turned around and scanned the room, she was gone from where they had been sitting before and so was Andrew, the panic rose before he could comprehend what was happening. Samantha was gone, with Andrew? How could she have possibly gone with a man she just met? But why did that surprise him? Was she not the woman that had showed up to their home to announce that she was pregnant with Jason's baby another man she had just met and had jumped into bed with?If she was planning to jump into... his eyes fell on her on the dance floor. Has she always been this pretty? He couldn't remember, right now all he knew was how stunning she was on that dance floor, in another man's arms. The jealousy rippled through him and he could almost feel himself vibrating. She laughed and threw her head back in a manner that was almost seductive. From the little he knew about her, Samantha wasn't a woman that would seduce a man but without trying seduction was all she was giving off. Even from across the room Nick knew that it would take one more laugh like that from her to have him on his knees. He watched Andrew inch his hand lower and the decided he had had enough, "Excuse me" he said carelessly to Isabella and was off before he got a response from her.

Samantha was having fun, all thanks to Andrew she was actually enjoying herself – enjoying his company. Who would have thought that all it took to look like you knew what you were doing on the dance floor was to have a partner that knew what they were doing and Andrew did know what he was doing. She liked Andrew, she would probably never see him again after today but she would also never forget him. It would be nice to think of him as her friend since she barely had any. Eyes like a cat's, a typical Mr tall, dark and handsome he was Samantha hoped he would remember her when tonight was over. It was highly unlikely, she wasn't the type of woman a man would remember but that was okay."You know, you don't have to look down every five seconds, I promise I won't step on your foot" she looked up to see he was smiling, she laughed. He was obviously saying that because he noticed how unease she was."Well, I can't promise you the same thing" she replied and impulsively looked down again, she cringed when she felt him smile."We could just both look at the ground and pretend there's something so interesting happening down there" she laughed loving how at ease she felt with him but before she could figure out something to say to that they were interrupted. By Nick.When he came and stood beside them the smile on Sammy's face turned upside down, she had managed to not think about him for a few minutes and now it was over. Now the hand Andrew had on her waist felt wrong so she took a couple of steps back and let his hand fall gently away.They all stood in silence staring at each other, Samantha wanted to say something, anything just to fill the awkward silence but nothing came to mind."Hi," Nick was the one who spoke but to Andrew"I'd like to have my date back please" oh so he remembered?"Your date?" Andrew asked looking at Samantha who at the moment didn't know if to admit or just to tell Nick to go away. The second option sounded better in her head so why didn't her mouth move when Andrew nodded and began to walk away? Or when Nick said, "Shall we?" just as the next song was starting. Instead she obliged him by taking the hand he had stretched out.Samantha had forgotten that her dress was backless until Niklaus placed his hand on her bare back, that was exactly where Andrew's hand had been merely seconds ago so why did she suddenly feel so aware? He moved her closer to him in one swift move and wrapped his hand around his waist making her jump a little. Why was she suddenly feeling so hot? It was a well-ventilated room, she was practically naked in the dress she was wearing, so where was the heat coming from? She looked up at Nick and was unable to look down, she didn't care what her feet were doing anymore because she somehow was now gliding, moving as if she had danced this same dance with this same man a thousand and one times. She wasn't even hearing the music anymore, she felt completely oblivious to other guest or anything else that was happening in the room. The room could've easily been on fire and she wouldn't have noticed. Eyes locked it was as if neither could take their eyes away she watched Nick, what was he thinking? Was he thinking at all? Because all Sammy found that she could think about was the hand on her back, the man in front of her and the feelings he somehow manged to generate in her. It wasn't fair that he had that kind of power over her. It wasn't fair at all. Her heart felt like it was going to beat out of her chest just because the man was dancing with her, she felt dizzy but like in a good way. Was there any good way when one was dizzy? But with Nick there was, it was more like a heady sensation, like she was high on codeine, like she was high on Niklaus.

The moment Nick placed his hand on Samantha's back he knew what a bad idea this was. But there was no going back once he saw her breath quicken and her mouth fall slightly open before she did that lip biting thing she always did. She was nervous, he made her nervous and that thrilled him. As if to test his theory, he wrapped his arms around her waist and watched her squirm a little.Conversation. He should start a conversation.But that was a bit hard to do when she was looking at him with those big beautiful eyes, as if expecting something from him, only he was not aware of what she was expecting.How could he start a conversation when her soft delicate hands were touching him and she was this close to him swaying to the music like she belonged nowhere but in his arms?How could he start a conversation when all he could think about were those lips and what he wanted to do with them. The side she had chewed on was now void of the light red colour that covered the other part which made him long to run his fingers over her lips. But he didn't, mostly because he knew he wouldn't just stop with the fingers. It wasn't just his fingers that craved to connect with those lips. He made the mistake of letting his eyes fall to her lips just as she bit them again and he knew he could die if he didn't get a taste of those lips. Except he knew what they tasted like, which only made the craving worse. Now he understood what addicts felt like, knowing that something was bad for you but not having any power to resist it. Samantha Baker was not only bad for him but also catastrophic, problem was he didn't care.

"Do you want to go back to the hotel?" that was the first thing Nick had said to her since he had practically dragged her off the dance floor in the middle of their dance and into the car. One minute she had been floating in his arms and the next he was halting and telling her they needed to leave immediately, no explanations, nothing else. And now he was asking her if she wanted to be dropped off at the hotel, seriously?She wanted to ask him where things had gone wrong, they had been having fun, she knew it wasn't just her so why then did he suddenly shut it down. Shut her down. He was the one who had asked for the dance, she had been content having a pleasant time with Andrew and he had interrupted and as usual made promises without uttering a single word only to later break them and make her feel like she was crazy.

"My apartment. I'd like to go home now" she said instead and then threw her face out the window to enjoy the comfort of the night while making up her mind, she was done with Niklaus McCarthy. She was done waiting for him, she was done wanting him, she was done letting him mess with her head, she was done, period.

WHEN SHE GOT back to her studio apartment Sammy found that it didn't feel like home anymore, she felt like a stranger in her own home because now home was the McCarthy manor. She had left all the stuff she'd come back with at the hotel, thankfully her key was always under the mat. That was mostly so Vicky would have access to it whenever she wanted, giving her a spare had been a waste of time because the girl was as terrible with keys as she was with watches, you'd think not because one was specifically designed to be attached to the wrist but she would always find that she was missing it at the end of the day.The apartment was dusty so she immediately got to cleaning, it was past midnight but Sammy found that she still had a lot of energy probably pent up from the anger she felt.It had been a while since she scrubbed and she found that she missed it, not just the cleaning part but also the feeling useful. She had done nothing in the McCarthy house but to just exist.After the vigorous scrubbing and cleaning, she took a long soak in the tub before deciding to call it a night. She was going to decide what her next step would be tomorrow once she had spoken to Vicky whom she explicitly avoided telling that she was already in New York. The girl would have a fit once she discovered she had been left in the dark about a lot of things.

Sammy had barely gone to sleep when the pounding on the door started, it sounded distance at first then it grew louder jolting her from sleep.She knew it was obviously Vicky before she got to the door, the girl had somehow found out she was in New York and was furious that she didn't tell her. Typical Vicky, she couldn't wait till morning for the inevitable confrontation.  "I'm coming! I'm coming" Sammy yelled back hoping the girl wouldn't knock her door down before she had the chance to open up.Sammy spotted the single key sitting on the tiny centre table and grabbed it only to remember that she had just bolted the door, she half raced to the door struggling with her falling robe because she hadn't bothered to wear anything underneath and then unbolted the door expecting Vicky's furious face and mentally preparing herself for the earful she knew was coming. Except it wasn't Vicky's angry face, it was Niklaus'sStill in his tux, the bow tie he had worn earlier was gone and a few top buttons were undone but Niklaus nonetheless. His hair was in a mess, like something that had been ruffled so many times and his eyes looked scary.What was he doing here?Her first thought had been to race back inside and lock him out but instead she stood her ground, there was not much more he could do to her after today's humiliation.

Nick drove around in circles, he was in a heated battle with himself which he was already losing. He should return to his hotel suite and go to bed, he should also purge Samantha from his mind but that was next to impossible. Not when the cool night breeze still carried her scent long after she was gone, that girl was going to be the death of him and there was little he could do to stop it. And by the second time he started to head to her apartment building, Nick knew he had lost the battle with himself, he wanted Samantha Baker like he had never wanted any woman ever. He had tried to fight it, he had denied it and even tried to bury it but neither of those things were working, the only thing left to do was face it and he was ready to face it consequences be damned.It took Samantha all of three minutes to open the door and the more time passed, the more anxious he became. He didn't think things through rushing over here, he wanted her but who was to say she felt the same way. What if she rejected him? She seemed pretty pissed when they had left the gala.She finally opened the door, the look on her face showed she didn't expect him to be on that side of the door, for a minute she looked like she was going to run and then she didn't, instead she sighed like someone who was tired and then asked,  "What are you doing here?"She was putting on a purple bath robe which was a couple sizes bigger than her, it made her look smaller and somehow cuter at the same time. Her face was scrubbed clean of the makeup she wore earlier but she was still beautiful.

"Nick, it's the middle of the night. Is there something you want?" she asked again when he said nothing.Yes. There was something he wanted. No, needed. He brushed past her and entered into the apartment before his sensible side would take over and remind him that he had no business being here.She sighed loudly again before she shut the door, Nick waited while she bolted it and then turned around to face him,"I'm really not in the mood..." he silenced her with his mouth, whatever she had been about forgotten, she clung unto him like she was holding on for her dear life."Samant ha?" he broke the kiss, just to look at her. She looked up at him, her eyes had somehow manged to get bigger and make her more desirable."I want you" he whispered, he left out the desperately part so as not to spook her.It almost shocked him when she dragged his mouth back to hers and continued the kiss.This was how he remembered it and at the same time better, she wrapped both hands around his neck and then slipped her tongue into his mouth. Nick lifted her off the ground and she in turn wrapped her legs around his waist, that was when he realised, she was wearing just the robe and nothing else. He felt her sex rub against him through his pants and he felt his erection grow, wanting nothing more than to just be let out.She weighed next to nothing as he carried her to the bed at the other end of the room all the while not breaking the kiss. He not so gently dropped her on the bed but only because there was nothing like the word gentle in his vocabulary anymore, not with the way he felt when he had Samantha spread out in bed like this.He looked at her, really looked at her since this whole madness started, he kissed her again, quickly but softly. Her bed wasn't very big but she still looked really small laying there. She was waiting for him, he knew she was.Nick caressed her face,"You are so beautiful" he hadn't meant to say it out loud but it was still true.She closed her eyes and smiled,"That's not true. I like hearing it though, but it's not true" Why in God's name did Samantha not think she was beautiful? He wasn't going to argue with her right now, instead he was going to show her.He kissed her again, this time putting his heart into it, she helped him shake off his jacket and she began unbuttoning his shirt. She had already undone two buttons before he began to notice that her fingers where shaking, she was nervous. He covered her hands with his,"Allow me" he said locking his eyes with hers,he had never been with a nervous woman in bed but that only added to Samantha's allure and made him want her more.He began to undo the buttons himself before realising that his hands too were shaking, she laughed and then he looked at her and right there and then Samantha Baker was the most beautiful woman in the planet.He laughed too, it was truly laughable that he was nervous in bed. He had been with a considerable number of women and not once had he been this nervous if at all. If anything, he had always been confident, cocky even, he knew his way around a woman's body, he knew how to enjoy it and most importantly he knew how to make them enjoy him. But with Samantha it was different, he was obviously going to enjoy himself, so why then did his confidence fly out the window?She lay back on the bed and then on her side supporting her head with her hand and then stared at him, he in turn mimicked her. She laughed,"Hi" she said with a smile on her face"Hi" he replied and smiled back.They hadn't bothered with the basic greeting before but it just felt right as they lay staring at each other."Kiss me" Samantha requested making Nick's pulse jump a bit.He shifted closer to her and then took her mouth in his, at first slowly and then suddenly he got greedy, it was Samantha how could he not.Their positions changed and then suddenly she was lying beneath him, he could feel her getting bolder as her hands reached inside his shirt to caress him. This time she did succeed in getting all the buttons undone and discarding the shirt. Her hand reached into his pants and grabbed his member, Nick jerked when the heady sensation hit him and he thought his head was going to explode right there and then. He threw his head back and swore when she began to stroke him, slowly at first and then faster. Nick closed his eyes, he knew he was close and he was just about to tell her to slow down when he convulsed and then his orgasm hit. He gritted his teeth as he was hit with a sensation he had never felt before.He slowly opened his eyes, just to make sure he was still alive he found Samantha looking expectantly at him. Her hand was already out from his pants and she had a small victorious smile on her face.He kissed her, long and hard. He could easily kiss those lips forever.Time to repay the favour, he thought loosening the belt of her robe, the clothing parted to revel like he suspected, everything.He thought about how easy it would be to plunge into her and selfishly take his own satisfaction. But wouldn't do that, he couldn't. He wanted it to be good for her, more than he wanted it to be for him.He smiled when he noticed the blush that crept into her face so he kissed her. He slowly cupped her breasts with both his hands easily swallowing them. Her breathing deepened the same time her pupils started dilating and Nick was glad he didn't miss any of it, he couldn't help but be a little proud he was responsible for that.He moved his hand, tracing it down to her abdomen and then to her thighs, her legs parted instinctively. He traced upward now, as she writhed beneath him and then he found her arousal, he pressed two fingers just to see and then she gasped which gave him pleasure. Then with his index and middle finger he began to massage her, forming a rhythm. She spread her legs wider as if hoping for more and Nick obliged her, he quickly began to finger fuck her not taking his eyes off her for once. She looked divine like that, the flush on her face, her eyes closed he discovered the lip biting thing wasn't something she did only when she was nervous."Nick" she called lowly at first and then screamed it again just as she came. She limply fell back to bed, eyes still closed and a wide smile spread on her face she looked divine.Samantha Baker was the most beautiful woman in the world, Nick decided in that moment.He was going to give her a couple of minutes to recover before he continued to show her all the pleasure she deserved, Nick had decided but then she sat up with that ridiculous smile on her face, she kissed him, long and hard,"I want you now" she whispered reaching for his belt buckle. Nick pulled away,"Not yet" he told her before gently shoving her back into bed.If she had been about to protest he wouldn't know because he covered her mouth with his, kissed her and then letting his mouth take the same path his hands had, Nick found his way to her breast, suckling on them like his life depended on it. She was back to moaning, tightly clutching unto the bedspread. He took deliberately slow nibbles down her belly and then to her thighs and when he found her moist heat he was very aware of her nails digging into his back. It would probably bruise tomorrow and sting like hell but in the moment they felt really good.He used his tongue at first and then he suckled, making her writhe on the bed and dig her nails deeper into his back. Forget bruising, those were definitely going to scar.By the time she screamed out in orgasm again Nick knew he was going to lose his mind if he didn't take her there and then. So he did, he didn't wait for her to come down from the high before entering her. His resolve to go slow was broken once his tip found her entrance, all the blood in his body rushed to his head once he entered her and Nick hoped he didn't have a heart attack making love to Samantha Baker.She gasped and not in pleasure and Nick suddenly remembered how small she was, he had somehow forgotten the girl was tiny that he might have crushed her."Did I hurt you?" he asked gritting his teeth because being still inside her was torture"No. No" she shook her head but her eyes were still closed"Samantha?" he called, sharper than he had intended and she slowly opened her eye"Are you alright?""Fuck me" she looked him dead in the eyes and demanded shattering the last of her resolve.He smiled, that he could do.He withdrew and slowly advanced, sex had never felt like this for him before, everything with Samantha felt dialled to a hundred.His pace increased without warning, filling her over and over and just when he felt himself getting close to the edge she wrapped herself around him and then exploded with a sharp cry of his name and then he let himself go.Nick managed to roll over before he collapsed the last thing he wanted was to crush Samantha or the baby.They both lay in silence, the room filled with only the sound of their breathing. Nick caught himself wishing that Samantha would roll over into his arms but she just lay there and in two minutes her breathing evened out and Nick knew she was asleep.

NICK SAT ON the only side stool in the room and watched Samantha sleep. He had no idea how long he had slept for or how long he had sat watching her, all he knew was that after they had had sex Samantha had immediately fallen asleep and he had joined soon after.He had woken up a few minutes ago, at least he thought it was a few minutes ago to realise he was butt naked in bed with Samantha in her New York studio apartment.How could he have let this happen? Richard would definitely kill him when he finds out about this?She had stirred and turned around to face the other side, Nick had lain beside her for only ten seconds before realising that he hated not being able to see her face so he had gotten out of bed, fetched his earlier discarded pants and then for the first time took a proper look around the room, he moved the only stool in the room so it sat next to the bed where she slept.Samantha Baker wasn't the kind of woman he usually shared a bed with, Nick reminded himself. Yes she was beautiful but until now, he had almost always been into exotic women and she was everything but exotic.It was stupid, what they had done but he knew that in the next fifty or so years he would still remember what her skin felt like and how it felt to be inside her.She scratched her jaw and coiled into a ball making the bedspread fall slightly off her shoulder giving Nick a flash of her left boob.Forget fifty years, Nick wanted her now. He wanted to have the feel of those breasts again, he wanted her period.He swore under his breath and got up, he needed a drink. He had thought that once he had had Samantha in his bed, he would get her out of his system, Chase had told him that and Chase was an expert on these types of things. But this was worse, now that he got a taste how the hell was he supposed to walk away from this? How could he allow her to be with someone else when he knew what being with her was like?He rummaged through her kitchen cupboards and cabinet but came up empty, apparently Samantha didn't store liquor in the house, or she hid it well enough."Nick?" he heard from behind, he spun around so fast to find Samantha awake and sitting up on the bed."What are you doing?" she asked rubbing her eyes lightly,Nick didn't expect the ball of anger that rose to his throat, how could this one woman have this much control over him?Without meaning to he slammed the cabinet door, hard."What are you doing?" she asked again climbing out of bed and getting into her earlier discarded robe.Her brief display of nakedness made Nick's cock twitched. Hard.She turned on her bedside lamp and it illuminated the room a little, she started walking towards him and then stopped."Y ou're angry?" it was more of an observation than a question. He took a deep breath and then started walking to her,"I have a few errands to run tomorrow but I think it will be con-venient for us to leave the day after tomorrow"She blinked several times, still waking up Nick presumed"Leave? Where are we leaving to?" she asked in utter confusion. Maybe he should have given her a minute or two to properly wake up before springing this on her but if he had waited Lord knew he would have probably jumped her."Texas, my father thinks he has spoken some sense into Jason" he watched her frown in confusion,"Jason?" she asked as if it was a foreign name to her."Yes"She bit her lips and then nodded before turning around to head back to bed,"Samantha?" his lips moved on their own accord.

"Please don't" she said turning back to face him,"I know what you're about to say, you're going to say this was a mistake" she gestured to the rumpled bed that now looked like a wrestling match had happened there."you're going to come up with a perfectly good reason why you should be mad at me and I won't see you for days. Nick, I know the drill"Why did she have to say it like that?"I'm not mad at you" he said shoving his hands into his pockets,"You're not? Well that's a relief" she said sarcastically."For god's sake take a look at your face in the mirror, Nick! You look like you've made the worst mistake of your life" she told him,"Of course I have!" It was like a punch on Sammy's face, at least it hurt like that."You're marrying my brother, Samantha. You're carrying his child. What do you want from me?""Nothing. At this moment I want nothing from you." She said, took a deep breath then turned back around and began to go back to sleep, not that she was going to get anymore sleep but she was going to burst into tears if she kept looking at his face."Samantha, wait" he said tiredly,"No. I'm done waiting Nick" she spun around, willing to give into the anger she felt,"you weren't drunk this time so you can't use that as an excuse now""I'm not looking for an excuse" he denied"No, of course not, you're just looking to let me down easy?""That's not...""Then what do you want Niklaus? What do you want?" she asked cutting him off"in case you've forgotten, you showed up here tonight, you came to me on that dance floor. The night in the kitchen it was you who kissed me.""I know""Do you? Because one minute you want me, the next you don't. One minute I'm in your arms, the next I'm alone in the dark on top of the kitchen counter. One minute I look like a malnourished boy and the next I'm so beautiful. Please make up your mind on what you want, otherwise just leave me alone"What did he want? He obviously already knew the answer to that question,"I want you Samantha. I want you" he said closing the distance between them and not giving her any time to process what he had just said he took her mouth in a kiss. He was going to be honest about what he wanted, even if it was just this once.

# CHAPTER 13

Sammy opened her eyes with a wide smile on her face, her body was still ringing from all the orgasms she had last night and remembering made her blush, deeply.It took her all of five seconds to notice she was in bed alone. She sat up and glanced around the apartment but there was no sign of Nick.He was gone. Her heart sank at the realisation that he was gone.She got up and wrapped herself in the bedspread before checking if he was in the bathroom, as expected he was not.Why was she so disappointed? Sammy wondered. She half knew that he would bail but at the same time she had gotten her hopes up. But for what? It wasn't like anything beyond this could happen between them, not when she was carrying his brother's baby and certainly not when she had agreed to marry Jason.

She knew he would regret getting back in bed with her, but what she hadn't anticipated was that he would leave even before she woke up.They'd made love all night, it was almost five thirty the last time they had gone to sleep and she had never felt closer to anybody in her entire life. But that certainly wasn't the case for him because he had just woken up and brushed everything off like it meant nothing.Maybe it meant nothing to him? The fact that he had confessed he wanted her severally last night didn't mean he felt the same today.S ammy was still in her thoughts when the door jiggled and in walked Nick struggling with a couple of grocery bags."Nick?" she called hesitantly."You're awake. I hope you don't mind I used your keys" he said dropping the bag on the kitchen counter."I thought you left" that just slipped out"I did, there was nothing edible in this house so I went to get a few things" he told her as he began to walk closer to her,he grabbed her gently,"Good morning" he said before taking her mouth in a mind numbing kiss.Sammy melted into the kiss, grabbing on to his now rumpled dress shirt like her life depended on it.How could this one man make her feel all these things at the same time. First was the overwhelming sadness when she realised he was gone and now all her senses were at a halt and all over the place at the same time.Her head was still spinning when he let go of her and smiled,"Good morning" she replied breathlessly, still clutching unto his shirt."You went grocery shopping?" she asked him after catching her breath,"Yes. I figured that since you exhausted yourself last night you'd be very much hungry when you woke up" he told her and she blushed as the images from last night flooded her head."Now go take a shower while I whip us some breakfast" he told her and gave her a kiss on the forehead.Sammy felt like she was dreaming, it was the whole domestic setting that was making her head spin. she tried to tell herself not to make too much of it as she walked to the bathroom but Nick McCarthy was in her kitchen whipping up breakfast after they had spent the entire night in each other's arms there was no making less of it.

There was more than one side to Niklaus McCarthy and Sammy was getting to know all of them. He was smart, nice, playful and even somewhat funny but most of all he was present. He was present when he had taken her to his favourite gallery, Gavin Brown's in the lower east side for an exhibition. She had never been to an art exhibition before but she couldn't deny it was fun pretending she understood how captivated he felt being in there. He ended up buying her a painting from a female artist that had such a long name Sammy couldn't pronounce it but it made her feel good. She knew she was going to cherish it for the rest of her life.Sammy found that no matter how much fun they were having she couldn't stop thinking of the night before. In all honesty she just wanted to jump him again as soon as possible, but they hadn't been alone long enough for her to do anything about it. Even if she could summon enough courage to. She wondered if he thought about it and when it might happen again but he seemed quite content with just being there with her and made no indications of wanting a repeat.That wasn't the case when they ended up in his hotel suite for the night because then he was the one who jumped her, confessing that he had thought of nothing all day which really pleased Sammy. Again, they had stayed up all night alternating between making love and talking and by the time Sammy fell asleep in the early hours of the morning she did so wearing nothing but a wide smile on her face.Saturday started with Sammy waking up to Nick's mouth on hers, they made love yet again and then again in the shower after which they ordered breakfast although it was well past noon. Sammy decided she needed to go back to her apartment to fetch some more clothes and Nick tried to dissuade her, it didn't matter because she wouldn't be wearing them anyway, he had told her in a tone that made her just want to have sex with him again. Truth be told everything just made her want to have sex with him. And the funny thing was, Sammy had never thought herself as a sexual person before, but after a few days with Nick she realised that the problem hadn't been with her at all but with her other lovers.Sammy smiled at the thought of the word lovers, she was now a person that had use of the word in a sentence concerning her. In reality there hadn't been that many lovers and none had mattered like Nick did.

She ended up letting him convince her to shop for clothes from the hotel boutique, which was totally unnecessary she argued because she had perfectly good clothes in her apart-ment but since he was paying she let herself be convinc ed.That evening he surprised her with a picnic, which was actually the sweetest thing anyone had ever done for her. It felt like she was in this amazing dream that she most certainly did not want to wake up from.Sunday, they spent cooped up in Nick's hotel suite. It was amazing not having the outside world distraction. They ate, talked, laughed, made love and started again in no particular order. There was no room to think, not about what exactly it was they were doing or about the fact that she had completely ignored her best friend since coming back to New York.  She also didn't think about what would happen when they finally left the hotel room and she hoped that didn't happen anytime soon.They had just ordered dinner when Nick's phone rang, he excused himself and went into the bathroom to take the call but from the look on his face Sammy already knew. She knew that the bubble they had buried themselves in these past few days was about to burst open. She knew that whomever was on the other end of the line was going to force them back to reality.The dinner they ordered arrived while he was still taking the call, he had been in there for almost thirty minutes which made Sammy worry more. She sat on the bed in nothing but the hotel robe staring at food in the trolley and all she thought of doing was knocking on the door, she advised herself against it. She was going to sit right there and wait.It was another ten minutes before he came out, the food was already cold but it didn't matter because she had already lost her appetite. The usual scowl was back on her face to Sammy's utmost dismay and she could swear that whatever had been said on that phone conversation had something if not everything to do with her.

She waited a whole twenty seconds before asking,"Is every-thing okay?" he looked at her as if noticing for the first time that she was in the room."Yes" he carelessly said.She waited for another ten seconds before asking,"do you wanna eat?" conversation had been so easy before but now with every word she spoke, she feared she might say the wrong thing."No""Something's wrong" no use avoiding the elephant in the room."Nothing's..." he began to deny it,"Please don't say nothing's wrong, Nick. We were having a good time and then your phone rang, you spend almost an hour in there and you come out looking like that"he rubbed his hand over his face clearly in frustration,"Samantha please stop""No. Tell me what happened" she insisted because she knew that despite the outcome of their conversation, their time together would change. She could already tell by the look on Nick's face."Sa mantha," he called in a warning tone but Sammy wasn't ready to back down yet,"Tell me who called you?""That doesn't concern you Samantha. And just because we slept together a few times doesn't give you the right to pry into my business"A slap Sammy was sure would have stung less. It wasn't the words as much as the way he had casually dropped them that made Sammy feel little. Slept together a few times? As in past tense? Done and over with. She had let herself get carried away by a version of him she knew wouldn't last that she thought this something it wasn't."No, it doesn't. I'm sorry I asked" she plastered a smile on her face because the alternative wasn't something she could handle.Sammy was grateful when he went to the living area, picking herself up in front of him wasn't something she could handle now.It took her less than a minute to get dressed in the dress she had come in, she thought about leaving the dresses they had purchased from the hotel boutique  but on a second thought she decided to take them, he had paid for them but she had picked them afterall plus she really liked the three of them very much. She neatly folded them and then packed them up in the bag they had come with. She quickly took a glance at herself in the mirror just to make sure she looked okay because she really wanted to look okay before making her way out to face him, she wished there was another exit but the only way out of the room was through the living area where he now was. She knew that because she didn't hear him leave.

NICK WAS STILL pacing back and forth when Samantha came out, he paused when he saw her. She was already dressed in the clothes she had worn when they had gone to the gallery, not the shoes though, she was wearing one of the sandals they bought together yesterday. He remembered because that one made her foot look sexy as hell with the rope straps tied all the way above her ankles. She was carrying the bags from the boutique and Nick didn't have to guess what was inside them."What's going on?" he asked cautiously"I think it's time to go" she told him, it was the gentility in the way she spoke that made him frown."What do you mean?" he asked"I mean, I had an amazing weekend thank you very much," she was thanking him, which was never a good sign"I'm really grateful for it all but let's be realistic, that call you got changed things and I think it's best I go back to my apartment before things spiral out of control"she waited for him to say something, a goodbye, anything but he just stood there. As if conflicted by things Sammy was totally unsure off."Okay then" she nodded, no need to let him see how much his silence was hurting. She began to leave, she was already almost at the door when he spoke,"Samantha wait," she paused without turning knowing very well that if he said something like 'let me drive you home' or 'let me call you a cab' she was going to lose all her composure and break down in tears. There would be a lot of time for that later, when she was alone.She turned back around really slowly, the panic on his face was something she hadn't been expecting."don't go" he said coming to stand in front of her"Nick I don't know" she told him,"I'm sorry okay? I shouldn't have spoken to you like that""Are you going to tell me what happened?" he took a couple of steps back and then ran his fingers through his hair, he was frustrated."It was Richard on the phone," he began and then he rested himself on the back of one of the armchairs in the room and then folded his arms."Your dad?" Sammy asked,"Yes, he's furious. Apparently there was a reporter at the gala the other night and they took a photo of us and now they want to run a story""What?" why would anyone want to run a story on her?"I didn't confirm or deny anything but according to him the picture didn't look so good. He wants us home tomorrow"wow. Sammy took a deep breath, things were just getting more and more complicated.She dropped the bags she was carrying, Nick looked so agitated and sad at the same time and she just wanted to hug him. She had no idea how he would react to that so she held herself."And you? What do you want?" she asked instead"Samantha you are marrying Jason, like it or not you are carrying his child. This whole weekend was selfish, we were selfishly deluding ourselves."Sammy swallowed the lump that formed in her throat,"So you regret it?" she asked expecting the worst, it was always the worst with him."I don't know. This whole thing was a mistake"So definitely a yes, he was definitely regretting it. She did ask, why did she?"So what now?" she asked,"We can't... I can't..."she nodded, except that they had, he had. Of course she had known that this came with an expiry date, but she didn't expect it to be so soon or for it to hurt this much."Okay" she said picking up the bags she had gently dropped before"I don't want you to leave tonight""No. I want to go. I want to go sort myself out and tomorrow, I'll pretend all this never happened"

So this was what heartbreak felt like? It felt like she couldn't breathe at the same time like someone was wringing her heart. How did people survive this? She was in an excruciating pain and it hurt all over. She felt like she had no right to feel that way. Three days. That was how long Nick had belonged to her and how long he had taken to turn her world upside down.She had rushed back home to her apartment to find solace but it was worse being in there, he was everywhere and not there at the same time. She laid on her bed but all it felt was empty, she couldn't look at her kitchen because all she saw was him standing there like he belonged there. Cooking for her like that was what he existed to do.Niklaus McCarthy had ruined her home, he had been here for just one night and everything suddenly reminded her of him.There was only one thing left to do and she did it, she called her person. Vicky would be mad angry but she still wouldn't let her deal with this alone. She hated that it was her voicemail but Sammy still left her a message telling her she was in New York,"come when you can" she didn't want to get into it in a voice message or have her friend charging in thinking it was an emergency.It was over an hour later when Sammy was crying in the shower that her friend came, she didn't hear her knock but she heard when the door opened and closed. Vicky called her name once and immediately barged into the bathroom,"Oh my God, you're alive" she said coming in and giving her a hug not minding that she was getting herself wet."Why haven't you called me?""Vicky I'm in the shower""I see that" she said reaching over to shut the water off,Sammy shook her head at her friend before reaching for a towel to cover herself up,"Why haven't you called me?" Vicky asked again"I called you today" "You left a very cryptic voicemail, I left a date because of you""You were on a date?" Sammy asked noticing for the first time that her friend was very dressed up. And now she was feeling a little guilty."Yes, this guy named Mike. He's super sweet and he has this... that's not important right now. Where have you been? When did you get back? You look so beautiful" Sammy smiled. She had really missed her friend so much."can we get out of the shower atleast?" Sammy asked right before her friend engulfed her in a hug. Nakedness, wetness and all."You have no idea how much I've missed you"

"THURSDAY? YOU'VE BEEN here since Thursday?" Vicky made her disappointed face which was basically squinting her eyes at you and then shaking her head. It was kinda hilarious how she thought that was intimidating."I was going to call you but things got out of control and then...""You slept with the other brother!" Vicky finished for her. She said it like it was something to be excited about."Who are you and what have you done with my friend?" "Vicky""And then he kicked you out?" "He didn't kick me out, he regrets it. Which is somehow worse because...""Because you love him" Vicky finished."No. No" Sammy almost laughed, that wasn't what she was going to say. She didn't... it wasn't... She barely knew the man so there was no way she could love him."He's rude, and condescending. He makes me feel bad half the time we are together. I don't even think he likes me" Sammy explained"He liked you enough to jump into bed with you""Vicky it wasn't even like that""You were crying when I got here""I wasn't crying, crying. The shampoo got in my eyes and…" Lie. A horrible one at that"You're an idiot if you think I'm buying that""I don't know what you want me to tell you""I want you to tell the truth!""What truth? That my heart feels like it's been stumped on? Or that the thought of marrying someone else makes me want to break in hives. I can't imagine… I don't want to imagine…" she felt her chest start to tighten and she felt like she was going to puke. She began to hyperventilate, was this what dying felt like?"Hey, hey. Calm down. Come, come sit" Vicky said gesturing for her friend to join her where sitting down on the floor, resting on the sofa. Sammy sat down and rested on her and Vicky began to cradle her. How did people survive this?

Vicky watched her friend sleep, she couldn't help but worry. What had she gotten herself into? And this was all her fault. Everything was her fault. She had let her friend go into the lion's den alone and now she was in way over her head. She shouldn't have made Sammy go to those people, she should have stepped up for her friend. The two of them would have made amazing coparents and Sammy wouldn't be in so much pain right now. Love? Samantha baker was in love. It was almost laughable because the girl was sure she was cursed and would never find love. Not that she had ever put in the time or the energy to look, she was too much of a coward to actually do that. Well according to her, the feelings weren't reciprocated but it was still a marvel that she even came that far.Vicky didn't know him but she was sure she already hated Nick McCarthy, playing with her friend like that he should pray they never meet because she had a few things she wanted to tell him that just wouldn't sit right with him. She carefully lifted the duvet that was now loosely hanging by Sammy's waist so it covered her better. Vicky still didn't understand why her friend had insisted on laying on the sofa, that thing was uncomfortable as hell. The bed was small but they both managed to fit in it anytime she slept over.She gave her hair one final stroke before deciding to head to bed, she was going to sleep now and tomorrow she was going to be all her friend needed. And if she decided that it was not going back to those people then Vicky was going to be by her side, she was done pushing and pretending she knew what was best.

# CHAPTER 14

RICHARD MCCARTHY DIDN'T get to where he was by trusting people, he had inherited a small fortune and the McCarthy name and then he singlehandedly turned it into ten times what it had been and then made a name for himself. And that was before he had any of his boys. So when he summoned Nick to discuss the Samantha Baker issue, Nick didn't know what to expect. He knew he wasn't his father's favourite but he was the most efficient, the most reliable so his father had turned him into the fixer, the handler. Any problems that needed taking care of, Nick was his man to call.So it didn't surprise him when his father had ordered him home when the Chinese had bailed on the Sea-world project, he had fixed that  without complaints even though that had pulled him away from his life. But when Samantha had come into their lives and his father had put him in charge of everything Baker, that meant he was taxed with her welfare, the medical tests, the legal part of her marriage to Jason and everything else. Not the man who had knocked her up, the man who she was going to marry but Nick.He had been a little sceptical about the issue at first, especially after everything that had happened with Jason's first wife, he didn't think it was right for his father to put him in charge but he had said yes anyway and then he had gone ahead to screw thing up. Knowing Richard, he knew that this wouldn't be a pleasant conversation and it wasn't one he wanted to have.

Nick got back home even before Richard and Jason left Miami, apparently Jason was partying it up on a beach there. The only reason he had was found out was because he had drunkenly swiped one of Luxury's card when he paid for a speedboat he bought. Richard was still mad but he had bothered to keep Nick updated. He had insisted on going down to Miami to fetch Jay but that was a surprise to no one because it had been clear for a long time who Richard's favourites were.Nick left Samantha in New York only because he was sure that if he saw her again he would lose his resolve. The hardest thing he had done in his life was easily not following her last night, it had taken everything in him and more to show the level of restraint letting her leave him like that. It had been awful the feeling of overwhelming sadness he felt after she had left, staying awake all night because his dreams haunted him. He left her in New York because he hoped that by the time she got back he would be long gone, he couldn't possibly imagine how he could exist in a world where Samantha Baker wasn't his. What if he had met her first? What if they had met under different circumstances? What then would have happened. He would have loved to pretend that things would have been different, that they could have stood a chance but that would just be lying to himself. He probably wouldn't have noticed her or given her a second thought. He probably wouldn't have noticed her big brown eyes that screamed her innocence or her tiny body that was made to be caressed, he probably wouldn't have noticed the slouched shoulders like she was carrying the weight of the world or how she always got excited by little things. Or her laugh that didn't come as often as he wished but brought joy when it did. He wouldn't have noticed how her go to emotion was nervousness or how she would often bite her lips because of it.Damn it! He definitely would have noticed.There was no not noticing Samantha Baker for him, he would have noticed her even if he was asleep.

The house felt devastatingly empty when Nick got home, Lu and his wife weren't back from that wellness retreat weekend at Luxury Atlanta. It was funny because he had insisted his wife couldn't travel for the gala in New York. And Alex, she had decided that it was the best time to fly to Paris with her latest fling, a Baron if Nick was remembering correctly or was he an Earl? It didn't matter, knowing his sister she was going to fall heads over hill in love with him, allow him to spoil her silly and then find an excuse that made absolutely no sense to dump him and then unto the next. She was more like Chase in that regard even if she would never admit it, at least she had the curtsy of actually dating them before dropping them.

It well past noon before Richard returned home, a tired looking Jason with him. This was exactly how he had looked the last time he came home after that awful bender after the whole Sophia incident. Okay maybe this was a mild mimicry given that a pregnant girl had followed two weeks later but no one knew what would happen this time, there might be more pregnant women coming.Nick tried to pretend he was still in control when Richard summoned him, slapping him in the face with the said pictures of him and Samantha. It was just as bad as Richard had said, he hadn't exaggerated when he said they were having eye sex, whatever that meant. It had been the moment when he had wanted Samantha the most, on the dance floor after he had cut into her dance with that guy, both were clutching unto each other and Nick couldn't understand how a single picture could capture all that essence. What was the saying about a picture being better than a thousand words?

"Do you mind explaining this?" Richard asked as he tossed the photo to him"We were just dancing, dad" and maybe imagining all the ways to rip into each other."Just dancing" Richard repeatedNick wished he was having any other conversation right now, business related, politics. He would take literally any other thing."Dad I don't know what you want me to tell you""I want you to tell me why I paid a lot of money to have this buried. Laura from Chances called me to inform me that one of her reporters covered the event and that they caught you and your girlfriend leaving the gala on Thursday. The next thing she was saying they even have a couple of photos coming out in their tabloid and then she sends me these. Jesus Nick!""Dad we were just dancing" he said again for lack of nothing better to say."Dancing? That girl was looking at you like someone who's madly in love and you are looking at her like you couldn't wait to ravish her. I put you on this because I thought I could trust you, I thought I could rely on you and then you go and do this?

Your brother needed this, our entire family needed this and you selfishly go and ruin it""Nothing's ruined dad, she's still going to marry Jason. She still going to have he's child" Nick said bitterly"We have been through this before," Richard said tiredly, he massaged his temples in a way that showed he was frustrated,"need I remind you it ended with you almost dying and Sophia actually dying""It's not the same thing, Sophia was sick and she refused help" Nick said, he wished that what he had with Samantha wouldn't be compared with the thing with Sophia."And this Samantha girl? You barely know the girl and you want to tank our chance to fix your brother, to make him whole again"So that was why he was being insistent on this marriage thing? Because he thought that Samantha was his chance to fix Jason? What did he even mean by make him whole again?"I won't cause any trouble anymore""No you won't." Richard said and then took a deep breath, Nick already knew that he wouldn't like whatever it was his father was going to say next"Luxury Milan needs a renovation and I have decided to move the winery down to Palermo to be closer to the vineyards. You will oversee all of that"that would take up to a year or even more, Nick thought. He was sixteen all over again been thrust away from his family, only difference this time was that he wasn't so keen to leave, he actually had a reason for wanting not to leave. But knowing Richard this was non-negotiable but it was also the best plan right now, for everyone involved."And how soon is this happening?" Nick asked "As soon as possible but I still need to talk to Dr Brenda, she needs to clear you for work. You've been neglecting your check-ups with her. I need to make sure you are fit to work."

"I am fit to work" not that he didn't trust their company doctor, he just didn't want to give Richard more reason to get upset."Then go get ready" Richard said and once Nick turned to leave he said,"Once again you have disappointed me"

It was on Tuesday evening that Luca called, Sammy didn't know whether that was a good thing or a bad thing. Nick left without her. How could he do that? She had been here suffering, thinking about him and letting the sadness consume her and he just packed his bags and left. Left her. She had expected it, predicted it even but she was still an idiot to hold out hope. She had lied to Vicky about it but she had been waiting for him to show up at her apartment like he had that night and tell her that he wanted to be with her. That didn't happen and by the looks of it never would d.Luca explained that his brother had pressing issues that needed his attention back in Texas, Sammy didn't buy that obviously but there was really little she could do about it.She wondered if Luca knew, if Nick had told him of everything that happened but she doubted it, she didn't think he'd be asking her if tomorrow or next would be more convenient for her to travel. She almost laughed through the phone. How about the fact that she was contemplating going to the clinic tomorrow or next to have an abortion, how about that?She had even gone as far as calling the clinic a couple of times but each time she had gone ahead to lose her nerve. But that didn't mean she didn't want to do it or that she wasn't still going to do it, it just meant that she hadn't made up her mind yet and so she told Luca. She told Luca that she didn't know if she was ready to go back because she still had a lot to do here in New York. He had ended the call by saying "okay, you can take the week" like she was an employee asking for time off work. Apparently the arrogance ran in the family, Sammy thought bitterly. Was this really the type of people she wanted to be tied to the rest of her life? Was this really the kind of life she wanted for herself? Being controlled and told what to do all the time? They were being nice about it now but only because they still wanted something from her. What would happen when she was married to Jason and they didn't have to walk on eggshells around her in fear that she might leave? What would happen when she collected the first pay check making her a proper employee? How then would they treat her?

IT WAS THE call with Luca that had been the nudge Sammy needed to make her decision. She called the clinic and made an appointment for tomorrow, she didn't want to wait because she feared she would change her mind. She feared that waiting any longer would remind her of the reasons she had wanted to keep the child and remind her that the only reason she wanted to do this was because she was selfish.

Vicky went with her obviously, not just because one of the requirements was that she came with someone that would take her home but because she knew that she wouldn't be able to do it without her friend's support.The place was as depressing as she had thought it was going to be with everyone looking like they would rather be anywhere else. She hated that she felt like she was doing something wrong, something she was definitely going to regret Sammy read all the pamphlets and pretended she listened when the doctor explained the procedure. She hoped Vicky paid attention though. She chose the local anaesthetic because she wanted to be very participatory in the termination of her child. She cringed at the thought of it, she was never going to meet her child, never going to see them walk or talk. Would never know if they had her boring looks or their father's good genes. All of those things made her really very sad.She didn't understand why there was going to be an ultrasound since she was already getting an abortion. An ultrasound was one of those things she hadn't gotten around to doing and now she never would, Sammy thought sadly.She had felt numb to the whole procedure until the blurry image appeared on the screen, that was her baby, she thought. And she almost jumped out of the examination table when they started to hear the heartbeat, it sounded like galloping horses. She looked at Vicky and her friend was equally as excited to hear them as she was. Her baby had a heartbeat, she thought with a smile."Is that?" Vicky was the one who asked,"The baby's heartbeat" the doctor confirmed."I can't. I can't, I just can't" she said climbing out of the examination table. This was her child, hers. Shouldn't she be doing everything in her power to keep them safe? Shouldn't she be fighting to protect them? And somehow she was the one who was about to hurt them? No. There was no chance in hell that she was letting them do anything to her baby.

SAMANTHA WAS GRATEFUL for Levi taking his sweet time to get back to the house, he may have seen it on her face but she was in no hurry to get back. It took almost thirty minutes to get her back from the airport to the house and she was mostly grateful for it. Thirty minutes she had done nothing but worry. Nick had said back in New York that Richard thought he might have succeeded in convincing Jason to marry her. So all the while she had been waiting for him to come home, he still wasn't convinced whether he wants to marry her or not. Even that other time he came home, kissed her and took off, he hadn't been convinced then? And now she was heading back to him again, but for what exactly? She didn't see herself marrying Jason McCarthy no matter how many times she tried to picture it. At least not after the weekend she had had with his brother. The silence was what was mostly killing her, why didn't Nick call her? A whole week had passed and he couldn't even be bothered to know if she was dead or alive. Or how she was doing.

Charlie was the first person to rush out to greet her, she was standing outside when they drove up to the house. Her excitement was so contagious that Sammy forgot how un-happy she had been about coming back here. She embraced her in a long hug and Sammy felt right at home again, "Where have you been? You've been gone forever" Charlie said "I had a lot of things I needed to sort out" she told her "You all left me here to die of boredom, imagine Alex had the nerve to travel to France, she's been touring Paris with this Earl she met at..." she paused and frowned, "Are you okay?" Charlie asked noticing Sammy's glumness "Yes, of course. It was just a long flight and I'm a bit tired" "Of course. I wanted to go with Levi to pick you up from the airport but Luca wouldn't hear it. He's a psycho. Let's get you inside, I made you dinner" "You did? Sammy asked and she smiled genuinely, Charlie was the only person that made her stay here worth it.“Yes. Meatloaf, I know it doesn't sound exciting but trust me it's delicious”“It sounds really exciting and thank you” she told her as they made their way inside.They just got through the front door when Charlie jumped,“How could I forget, Jason's back!” she announced it like it was something to be excited about.“He is?” Sammy asked as her heart sank,“Yes. He came home same day Nick got in”“Nick's here?” she hadn't known if she was going to see him again, not hearing from him the past week was more heart wrenching than she thought it would be.“Not at the moment, he's been so busy with Richard that I've barely seen him at all. Italy has stolen him from us” “What do you mean?”“He's moving to Milan” Charlie said it like it was public knowledge and was surprised that she didn't know.

Sammy didn't expect the overwhelming feeling of nausea that hit her,“What do you mean moving? Like permanently?” she asked trying to steady her knees which now felt too weak to carry her.“Maybe not but he prefers staying in Europe, once he gets to Italy he's going to forget us all. But I forgive him because Italy is such a...”“I... I have to... I need to lay down... I gotta go” Sammy said and without waiting to hear what Charlie had to say she hurriedly made her way up to her room.

Sammy threw up, twice for that matter. Before now she had never gotten sick, it was a part of being pregnant but the only symptom she had experienced was the constant hit to her bladder so she wasn't even going to pretend that the throwing up was about the pregnancy. He was leaving for Europe and she knew it was all her fault, he couldn't stand being in the same country with her, not after what they had done. She had had no idea what would happen with her coming back here, how he would react seeing her after everything but she didn't imagine that his first reaction was moving to a whole other continent.The pain in her chest just kept growing until she thought she just couldn't take it anymore. But then she took it, and then some more because what was the alternative? The alternative had been getting rid of the pregnancy and not coming back here but that wasn't an alternative she could live with.

Sammy was still coiled under the duvet when the door opened,"Hey Sam, are you okay?" Charlie asked with the most caring voice Sammy had ever heard her use."Yes." Sammy replied hopping that would get her to leave but highly doubting it would. There was no way to hide that she had been crying and so she remained under the duvet."Are you sure?" Sammy didn't see but she already knew that Charlie was standing right in front of her face, she should have locked the door."Yes Charlie, I just felt a little sick but I'm good now" she lied. She wasn't good, she probably never will be."Okay. But can you come out from under the sheets now because I brought you a slice of my very famous meatloaf. I promise one taste will change your taste buds forever." Sammy smiled and sniffled. She had a friend in Charlie no matter what happened in the future, at least she hoped so. She wiped her face the best she could before raising the cover and sitting up. She was met with one of Charlie's luxury smile and in her hands was a plate with a huge slice of meatloaf, it didn't look very appetizing but Sammy was grateful regardless because

she had offloaded the contents of her stomach into the toilet
earlier.

# CHAPTER 15

S ammy was barely done dressing up when the knock on the door came, she already knew it would be Charlie coming in to complain about something Luca might have done or coming to pretend she needed advice on something she had the perfect solution to. Sammy guessed that she came in most times just to keep her company and truth be told she did enjoy it anytime she came in. It surprised Sammy when the knock came again, it wasn't in Charlie's habit to knock twice, one knock was all the girl needed and she wouldn't even wait for a response before barging in.Sammy quickly did the button of her jeans, which now hung to her waist so tightly. It wasn't that obvious to the eyes but Sammy knew she was putting on weight. It was kinda exciting and made her drop a hand to her belly. She was having a baby, she smiled. She remembered the picture of her tiny black and white baby that was now sitting in her dresser drawer and she almost squealed.The knock came again and Sammy concluded it wasn't Charlie, there was no way Charlie would knock three times and still wait for a response, the girl would have pulled the door off its hinges by now. She would just have to find another time to get excited about her baby, Sammy thought before running a hand through her hair and going to see who it was.Sammy stumbled back in shock, she would have maybe fallen if he didn't catch her by her waist. The last person she had expected to see on the other end of that door was Jason McCarthy and he was the one holding unto her like his life depended on it."Jason?" she called as if to make sure he was really the one"Hi" he said balancing her and then letting go of her.He was smiling, which somehow was creeping Samantha out way more than it should."You're here" not the smartest thing she could have said in the moment but her brain decided it was time to go on a vacation."Yes. Can we talk?" he asked her and she nodded because opening her mouth would just be asking for trouble."I asked Mrs. J to make us some breakfast I hope you don't mind" she shook her head even though she knew that settling down to share a meal with him was going to be very difficult after everything she had done.

They ate in silence, not because Sammy was hungry as a matter of fact, she didn't have any appetite at all but she ate so she wouldn't look him. She ate to fill the hole the guilt was chipping at.Sammy realised that this was the longest they had been alone in a room together, well except for the night they had met. But that didn't count because she barely remembered that night."I'd like to apologise for the last time we saw each other, I was drinking and my friends weren't helping matters at all. I shouldn't have kissed you like that"an apology, just what Sammy needed to make her feel more guilty than she was already feeling."It's fine" she said, but it wasn't fine. She didn't want him to think it was okay to grab her and kiss her like that anytime he wanted but given that a week ago she was wrapped in bed with his brother what he did wasn't so bad in comparison."No, it's not. I'm not that person and I don't want you to think I am""I didn't think you were" didn't she?"I went through a lot last year. I lost my wife and when I found out she was pregnant before she died, I spiralled and I did a lot of things that I now regret. That was when we met. I wasn't in a good place then and I wasn't in a good place when I came home before but I'm going to try to do better now. For you, for our baby. I want us to be a real family all three of us"It was more the sincerity than it was the words that tore Sammy's heart into pieces. What had she done? This man had been through so much already and she had done the unforgivable by getting involved with his brother, how could she be a real family with him after that?"I want you to just think about it, but I'm all in. I spoke to my dad, I think we should get married next month, I want us to be married before you start showing and I want us to get comfortable with each other before the baby comes.""Wow" that was all Sammy could say. He had obviously thought this through when she was busy in falalaland with his brother.She had agreed to this, hadn't she? So why then did the thought of it make her almost want to puke?"You don't have to give me an answer now but I just want you to know that I'm not going anywhere"Jason McCarthy really wasn't who Samantha had thought he was and that really made her feel worse, she wished he had literally said anything else. It felt better when he had almost physically thrown her out on her ass, when he had been so rude that she wished never to see him again it hadn't felt this bad. This was the worst feeling ever.

CHARLIE WAS GENERALLY a really smart person, it helped that people underestimated her a lot and she liked it. But sometimes her brain was often a burden, it didn't help that she noticed things that was better left unnoticed and that her brain would gnaw at it like it was a maths equation that needed to be solved until it ended up getting her in trouble .Like when she met her best friend in middle school, she had noticed that the boy was always sneaking away during lunch and came back wearing a wide smile on his face so on the fourth day she then decided to follow him, mostly because her curiosity would have killed her otherwise. It had led to her discovering the underground boys fight club, which was lame. Why only boy? Not that she would have wanted to fight but she knew a bunch of girls that would have liked to claw each other's eyes out but she still would have enjoyed watching them do that.Nick didn't fight, he had been too scrawny a kid to actually fight anyone. But he had been the one to call the loser or the winner and everyone listened to him. That was why she had gotten away with spying on them after they caught her, some of the guys had wanted to punch her and some wanted to kick her, one even suggested they tied her to the chair to make her talk, Charlie suspected he just wanted to try out the stupid things he had seen on TV because they didn't need to 'make her talk' she talked just fine. As a matter of fact, talking was one of Charlie's strongest suit, she could talk herself out of any situation which was what she had intended on doing except there hadn't been a need to. Someone came to her rescue, Nick came to her rescue. He went ahead to tell the other boys that he had brought her and that she could be trusted, apparently all the other girls couldn't. So, they then allowed her to be a part of their fight club only if she promised to tell no one. And she stuck to Nick like glue after that because that wasn't the only time he helped her get out of trouble since then.And trouble was what Charlie suspected was coming when her brain started feeding her another puzzle. She tried to ignore it when Joanna James suddenly started actively avoiding Samantha the same time Nick had gone to stay with Chase, which had been weird because the brothers called that place a whorehouse and tried not to visit unless it was absolutely necessary. And Nick had stayed there for more than a couple of nights which was really suspicious because there had been no reasons given.It had sounded off when he had almost begged her to give Sam her place at the gala instead of Alex but Charlie didn't want to read too much meaning into it, they were all trying to make the girl feel at home after all. But last night, after she had walked in on Samantha crying everything clicked. The girl almost literally run out on the conversation when she had told her that Nick was moving to Sicily and then she had cried over it. Charlie loved Nick a lot but even she didn't cry when she heard he was leaving, not now, not all those years ago.And that got her thinking about other events that have happened, like Nick staying back in New York days after the gala. At the time it hadn't seemed suspicious but now thinking back on it and how Richard had been since he got home, the sudden move to Italy and how sad Nick was being, none of it was making any sense. They were obviously keeping something from the rest of the family.Even as a boy he had been so eager to leave everything behind, and now he had on several occasion spoken about how much he hoped to heal fast so he could get away. He had based his whole life in Europe, enjoyed his freedom and made no commitments, everyone used to think he liked living that way but just yesterday Luca was told his wife that he was thinking of speaking to his father about finding someone else to help with the winery stuff because he didn't think Nick was ready to get back to work. Not the renovation though, Luxury Milan was Nick's baby and everyone knew it, there didn't need to be a will to know that that was his by default.And so as Charlie knocked on Nick's door, she was also mentally preparing herself for what to say.

NICK LAY ON the bed wide awake staring at his ceiling, his thoughts were not his own anymore. He knew she was back, he knew she was back yesterday that was why he had worked himself to the bone hoping that once he got home and hit his pillow that that would be it but that hadn't been it, there had been no peace for him knowing that she was a floor beneath him. There had been no peace for him even before she had come back but last night had been the worst, he had almost had to physically restrain himself from going to her. He wanted to see her so badly, it physically hurt. His stomach hurt, his throat felt constricted and he really wanted to drink. But he didn't, he didn't because he knew that if he so much as took a glass of anything, he would convince himself it was the liquor guiding him when he went to her.The knock came swiftly and Charlie came in carrying a plate of what he now saw was her infamous meatloaf, she had promised him a slice yesterday but he had stayed out so late that neither had remembered it.Nick smiled as he watched his sister in-law waddle in sticking her tongue out at him, he forgot this sometimes but they had been friends first, before Luca, Alex and everyone else, she had been his friend first. His best friend. It was actually through him that she met Luca and then everything else happened."If you didn't look like a pregnant penguin, this would have been a tad less cute" he told he as he came out of bed.She laughed,"Here" she said handing him the plate. This was what happens when his sister in law cooked, everyone was obligated to eat it. She had even gone as far as sending some to Chase's house.Nick took the plate without complaining, Charlie wasn't an amazing cook but no one could accuse her of being a terrible one either."You missed dinner" she told him climbing into his bed"My meeting ran late, I was going to catch a bite on my way home" but he couldn't go to his favourite café anymore because since he had had the bright idea of taking Samantha there and now he couldn't go there anymore because he just couldn't handle one more thing that reminded him of their time together."Joanna is worried about you," Charlie was the only one who dared call Mrs. James by her first name"she thinks Richard is overworking you""Richard's not overworking me. I've just been out of the game for almost a year so I have to work twice as hard to get things done" he explained, plus he didn't want to disappoint his father anymore than he already have."You know you don't have to go. You can say no to him, I'm sure he'd find one of his other employees to do it" Charlie knew Nick struggled with refusing his father, as a matter of fact he had never told the man no in his entire life and he wasn't about to start now."I want to go" he said in a not very convincing tone.Charlie narrowed her eyes at him and then shook her head,"You don't sound very convincing. Even as a teenager you couldn't wait to leave here, you were so excited""I am excited, I'm just..." wiser for it now"I am excited" he repeated"I feel like I'm just getting you back and you are leaving again" she sounded genuinely sad. Nick took a deep breath, dropped the meatloaf on his dresser and then joined his friend in bed, she made room for him to lay down and then she laid on top of his chest and he wrapped his hands around her. Well barely."I'm gonna come back more often than I did last time, I'll come for birthdays and Christmas, Thanksgiving, I'll even come back for the birth of my goddaughter""She's not your goddaughter" she said immediately"Okay, I had to try" Nick said with a chuckle"Wait, is she...?""Nope, we still don't know the gender""How can your curiosity let you indulge this?" he asked her knowing how curious his sister in law could be."I know right? It's killing me but your brother just won't budge" she said and they both chuckled."Point is," Nick said stirring back to conversation,"I'll try to show up for important stuff""That is the same promise you made me before and then you abandoned me here with Luca and Alex" she said with a pout"And then you married Luca" she chuckled and then raised her face with a play frown"My points exactly. I would have done so much better if you didn't leave me alone here to fend for myself" Nick smiled, he knew she was joking because he knew just how much she loved Luca. For her there had been no one else."I'll show up more, I promise. I just don't want to stay here and watch..." he bit his tongue, he had gotten so comfortable that he had almost said..."a nd watch Sam marry Jason?" she finished.The silence was deafening, Nick was almost certain he had misheard Charlie, there was no way she could have said what he thought she said. She was laying on his chest so she could definitely hear his heartbeat start to go haywire."What?" he asked in a shy of a whisper.Only two people knew about the affair with Samantha, minus Samantha and himself. Charlie and Richard were very close but Nick doubted the man would reveal such secret to her. And Mrs. James? The woman had promised she wouldn't say anything, but she was on a first name bases with Charlie so maybe she had let something slip.She sat up,"Nick I notice things, you know I notice things" she looked him in the eyes and said."And you noticed that I don't want Samantha to marry Jason?" he faked a chuckle so she'd believe he thought they were still joking aroundShe looked at him like he was stupid,"C'mon Nick.""I don't know what you want me to tell you" Nick told her and sat up, there was no way he was having this conversation laying down."Why did you ask me to ask her to the ball?" she asked folding her arms above her belly"She was bored here and she wanted to go back to New York, I told you that" Lie."So it had nothing to do with you wanting to spend time with her? Alone?""Of course not" maybe at the time he hadn't realised that so that wasn't exactly a lie."And you stayed back because?""I had things..." he couldn't even complete the lie"And why does Richard want Luca to take over everything Samantha?" She didn't wait for an answer before asking again, probably because she already knew the answer."I'm moving to Italy, someone is going to have to take care of things" Lie."Seriously Nick? We don't lie to each other" she reminded him."I don't know what you want me to tell you" he said again before getting out of bed."Tell me what is going on between you two""Charlie please..." he said and he ran his fingers through his hair."So you slept with her" why wouldn't the girl just stop pushing.Nick didn't say anything, there was really nothing he could say right now, Charlie had already figured everything out. At least she thought that she had."And Richard knows this?" he still said nothing, just standing there like a fool."That is why he is sending you away""Charlie please stop. Please" he couldn't take it anymore.Charlie got out of bed and walked past him and then took the late of meatloaf he had kept there,"Sit down" she gestured to the bed and when he did she handed it to him,"Eat" only Charlie would offer you food after she had called you out on sleeping with your brother's baby mamaNick took the plate from her but there was no way he could eat, his entire stomach was in an upheaval.She came and she sat next to him,"She was crying last night""Samantha?" he asked"Yes. When I told her you were home she fled to her room and when I came to check-up on her, she was coiled under her duvet in tears""Why?" she was crying because of him, here he was thinking about his guilt and how things made him feel and he had neglected to think about how she was dealing with everything."I didn't ask but I suspect it's for the same reason you've been sulking all week" Nick resisted the urge to deny he had been sulking.Nick picked up the fork, he cut out a piece of the meatloaf and then toyed with it,"Did you tell Luca?" he asked her"Not yet" which was a miracle because those two didn't keep anything from each other"Could you wait until I leave?" he asked. He didn't want to ask her to keep secrets from her husband but he also didn't want to be here when she told him. Nick didn't think he could handle also disappointing Luca."Are you going to eat?" she asked him when it was obvious that he was just playing with the food."I'm not very hungry" or hungry at allThey fell into an uncomfortable silence,"I don't want to judge you on this, I really don't but I have to know, does this have anything to do with Sophia?" Charlie broke the silence. But not to say what Nick was expecting?"Sophia?" he asked,"I know she's a discussion we've never had but is this some petty revenge thing for Sophia?""Jesus Christ! Charlotte" how could she even ask that?"I had to ask. Sammy's carrying Jason's baby, Richard is currently speaking to a wedding planner about their wedding" that was information Nick didn't have. A wedding planner? Seriously? All this was becoming too real."It's not some revenge thing okay? After Sophia, I didn't think I'd ever recover. Not because I still cared for her but because the guilt was eating me alive. I was the reason she drove off that cliff, my rejection is the reason she's dead. But believe me when I tell you that the thing with Samantha just happened, it caught me off guard but it's done now. I promise"Done. The finality of the word made Nick's heart ache. Was this what he really wanted? For it to be done. More importantly, could he keep that promise? What would happen when he ran into Samantha anywhere in the house? What would happen when she married Jason? These were questions he honestly didn't want to think about but he knew that whatever the answers were, he wasn't going to like them.

"What do you mean it just happened?" Charlie asked"I don't know what to tell you" he said in frustration, why wouldn't she just let this go?He ran his hand through his hair, he wanted a drink badly, this wasn't a conversation he wanted to be having sober.He took a deep breath and then he began,"I tried to fight it, I tried to stop it but I couldn't. I mean since the accident the first time I got a solid five hours of sleep was the first time I kissed her. It had been unplanned but it was glorious." He got up and dropped the plate he had been carrying on the bed and then he began to pace."I left the house, I stayed with Chase because I thought being away from her for a while would put things back into perspective" he laughed, a dry humourless laugh."but being away from her just made me want her more. I'd never enjoyed cooking until I started cooking for Samantha, watching her eat something I made her just gives me so much pleasure. I can't describe how I feel when I'm with her, it's just..." he paced again and then rub his hands over his face,"...being with her is so easy, yet so complicated. She just makes everything feel good, she makes me feel good and bad at the same time. Being with her gives me the most complex feelings ever" he really, really wanted that drink now."So you love her?" Nick felt his heart jump out of his body"What?!""Nick, calm down""No. Why would you even say that?" he asked"Because it's the truth"Nick would have laughed if he didn't head straight to panic. Charlie had no idea what she was talking about. The notion of him being in love was a laughable one."Samantha is marrying Jason, you know that. You just told me that Richard was speaking to a wedding planner" the room suddenly felt so hot and Nick wanted to be any place else."Nick calm down" Charlie told him again coming to stand with him and gently rubbing his back."I am calm" he said and shrugged her hands of before walking a couple paces away from her, he really didn't want to be touched right now.She looked at him and smiled, really smiled. Nick was about to have a nervous breakdown and she somehow found it funny."You know you're only freaking out because you know I'm right""Can you please stop saying that"She wasn't right, he told himself. If he loved Samantha then he'd know, he didn't need Charlie to tell him what he felt.Charlie bit her tongue, she was going to back off now not because she was wrong, she was never wrong about these things but because she knew Nick wasn't ready to hear it. In time he was going to discover it himself, all she hoped was that it wouldn't be too late by the time he did."Okay. Come here" she said, engulfing him in a hug, he himself wrapped his hands around her and held on tightly and in that moment, Charlie knew that this was just what her brother in law needed.

# CHAPTER 16

Niklaus McCarthy had never been in love before in his entire life, not because he avoided it or because he didn't want it but simply because it just didn't happen for him. He had always pegged himself as that kind of person that just wasn't capable of having those feelings. His siblings thought it was as a result of their mom leaving, he just assumed that he was just built that way.So hours after Charlie had gone he lay on his bed thinking, frankly he was still a bit shaken up, that had been the last thing he had expected to hear. True he had very complicated feelings about her, but love? He barely knew the girl. Well that wasn't entirely true, he knew her well enough. He knew the details, the very fascinating details about her, he knew that she bit her lower lip when she nervous, he knew that she hated being complimented, he knew her laugh sounded like breathless giggles. She hated being tickled, she had a sensitive spot behind her ears and she faked a pout anytime she didn't want to be amused but got amused anyway. He knew how she looked when she was excited and how she looked when she cried, he knew what her crossed face looked like and he knew what her happy face was. He knew the important stuff, the stuff that made him lie awake at night thinking of her. The stuff that made her so desirable. That was the stuff he knew.So as much as he told himself Charlie didn't know what she was saying, or that she was just wrong he couldn't help but give it a second thought.

IT HAD BEEN easy for Sammy to forget she was pregnant sometimes, her symptoms had mostly been the frequent urination and then the insomnia most nights but that hadn't been the case the week that followed her returning to the McCarthy manor. The tiredness was now a constant and the nausea wasn't stopping. She literally couldn't keep a meal down when she found the appetite to eat which was rarely and everything just made her want to cry now. It was a lot to deal with, existing feeling like a stranger in her own body, not just because her feet were now almost twice their normal size but also because she didn't know how to handle all the emotions attached to everything she was feeling.The other day, Jason had brought her breakfast and then held her hair while she hauled the whole thing into the toilet and all she did after he left was to lay down and cry. She cried again after he had brought up the wedding plans the day after that and yesterday, she had cried because he decided to show her the family photo album and again after he left because she realised how much wrong she had been about him. He was sweet in a way that made her want to cry and caring in a way that made her feel guilty. He seemed genuine in a way that worried her and she couldn't help but worry what would happen when the truth came to light, the truth about her weekend with his brother, truth about her feelings for Niklaus and most of all the truth about the fact that marrying him was the last thing she wanted to do.She tried hard not to think of Nick, she tried to fill her days, spending most of the time with Jason getting to know him better. She watched the news and spoke to Vicky for hours on the phone.But at night? When everyone and everything was asleep, when there was nothing to keep her from thinking, that was when she thought of him. That was when the thought of him didn't stop coming, painful thoughts of him and their time together and most times it just felt like her heart would fall out of her chest and other times she just closed her eyes and begged for sleep.

She knew he was in the house, at least she knew he slept here. She knew this because everyone spoke about how busy he was planning his escape. But she somehow had never actually seen him. He clearly was avoiding her, she was sure of it but somehow also glad about it. She didn't want to see him, wasn't ready to. She didn't even know what she'd say to him if they somehow managed to run into each other and quite frankly, she was still pissed at him. Pissed at him for being the reason for so much hurt and also pissed at herself for giving him that much power over her.

IT WAS LATE Thursday evening that Jason came and asked her out on a date, he said it was the least he could do since they were already having a baby together. It was a nice gesture and Sammy couldn't understand why it didn't excite her, she hadn't been on a date in so long that she already lost count. The last time she had been in a public place with a guy was the gala with Nick and even that hadn't been a date.He took her to a fancy restaurant, the kind that people like her could only dream of serving in. One glance at the menu told her that this was way out of her league, she knew he wouldn't honestly expect her to pay but she still felt mighty guilty eating at a place like this. She regretted the yellow romper she threw on, he had told her she looked good but had skipped out on the fact that she was so under-dressed for where he was taking her."Are you okay?" he asked after the waiter gave them a minute to decide what they were having"This place is so fancy" she told him nervously,"Is it?" he asked absentmindedly,how could he not notice how bougie the place was."Luca is looking to purchase it as a side project but he's holding off until the baby's born. Their baby, not ours" he smiled at her. Sammy almost cringed at the way he said 'ours' but instead she smiled back. It had always been 'her' baby but things were different now."Oh shit. I wasn't supposed to tell anyone that. But it doesn't matter since technically you are my wife" again with the familiar tone that made Sammy just want to puke."The place looks great" she said for lack of nothing better to say."Yeah. And their food's even better. Do you want me to order for you?""Yes, please" she said thankful that he asked"Okay then, let's have our starter with the soup of the day is that okay?" he asked already motioning for their waiter.Sammy was glad she trusted him because the soup wasn't only delicious but it also went down unlike most things she'd had all week. Unlike the macaroni carbonara, their main, the smell alone had made her nauseous and they had to send it back and although Jason told her it was all good, Sammy couldn't help but feel really bad. He had been so excited for her to try it and then because of her he didn't even get to have his own plate.It was when they started dessert which was a triple chocolate cake that she began to feel less bad, that was also when she almost choked on a piece of cake when Jason decided it was time to talk wedding dates,"I think it's best we do it before Nicky leaves and once Lu and Charlie have their baby they are going to London for a while to stay with her parents so I think now is the best time" he explained, Sammy cleared her throat,"And by now you mean?" she asked hoping that now meant never."I'm thinking next weekend, Alex thinks she can plan something by then""So you've spoken to Alex?" the cake forgotten, Sammy wished something would pull her out of this conversation."Yes but it's your wedding so you'll obviously have the final say and everything will be your decision"Sammy nodded, could she also decide she didn't want to marry him?"I didn't think we were going to have a wedding" she told him, Niklaus had said it was signing some papers so she thought they'd just go to a court house or something."Why wouldn't we?"'because you have been married before, because this is not a real marriage and also because I barely know you.'"I just think next weekend is too soon""It's not Sam. I want to marry you, I really do" why did he have to sound so certain? So sure"Okay" Sammy said with a nod even though everything in her screamed no. She had already agreed before, already slept with him and is having his baby so what else was there to do?"Good," he said with a smile,"do you want to finish your cake?" he asked,"I'm not really hungry anymore" more like, 'I don't really have the appetite anymore'Sammy took a sip of her juice and then watched Jason continue eating his dessert, what had she gotten herself into? She didn't know who her father was, it could have totally been the same way with her daughter but she had gone ahead to get greedy and now she was in an impossible situation."I was thinking, you could start staying in my bedroom. It's big enough for the both of us and then after the wedding we could buy a house in town"so he had plans? Plans that sounded super scary to Sammy.

IT WAS ALMOST midnight by the time Nick got home, he was home earlier than usual today because the conference call to the investors in Japan had been cancelled. He organised his schedule in a way that he was busy from the wee hours of the morning till so late at night that he had no time for nothing other than to rest his head for a few minutes. He worked his body and mind to exhaustion because the alternative was torture. Because the alternative was being in constant pain, having thoughts that were literally driving him crazy and the overwhelming sadness that came with it. The sadness was still there, it was a feeling that wasn't going away but the other ones were curbed by his exhaustion and his focus on work. It felt good to be working again, but it wasn't as satisfying as he had remembered it to be.

Nick was on his way to the kitchen to fix himself a sandwich, he hadn't eaten since... he honestly didn't remember the last time he had had something to eat. He was at the base of the stairs when he heard Jason's voice coming in, Nick had actively avoided his brother. He turned around and started to head back upstairs and then he heard her voice,"Can I think about it?" she asked,Nick froze at the sound of her voice. He knew he should leave but he didn't want to, he wanted to see her, he just didn't realise how much until she was this close to him."You can, if you let me kiss you" Nick heard his brother say and for some reason he felt his blood begin to boil."Kiss me?" Samantha asked. Nick hated that he wasn't seeing her face, he hated that he just stood there in the shadows like some kind of creep."Yes. The last time I kissed you I was drunk, heck the time before that I was wasted. I really want to kiss you Samantha" Jason said inching closer to her,"Why?" Samantha asked nervously."Because you're beautiful, because you're sexy as hell and because that's all I thought about at dinner"Nick cringed, sexy as hell? What did that even mean? He knew Samantha was sexy but she was wearing an oversized romper that did nothing to accentuate her sexiness. His brother was working Samantha and worse she was falling for it. Why didn't she disagree when he called her beautiful? She didn't believe Nick when he told her but she somehow managed to trust that Jason was telling her the truth."You have?" Samantha asked and in response he locked his lips with hers and Nick thought he might pass out with rage but instead he stood there in the dark and watched his brother make out with his Samantha.

SAMMY HAD BARELY closed her eyes when the incessant knocking on her door began, she was so tired that she had almost fallen asleep in the shower.She considered ignoring whomever it was but they were quite persistent, not loud just persistent. She glanced at the clock hanging above her, it was almost twelve AM. She dragged herself out of bed hoping it wasn't Jason, she honestly couldn't handle seeing him at the moment after their horribly awkward kiss. He had kissed her in the hopes of making up for their past awful kisses but this one managed to be worse than the others even though they were both sober now.She opened the door and thankful it wasn't Jason but instead it was Nick. He brushed past her and made his way inside of her bedroom before she could say anything.She closed the door and turned to him, he looked angry, furious even. Both his hands were in his pocket and he was glowering at her like he wanted to strangle her.Wasn't she the one who was supposed to be angry with him? Wasn't she the one he had dumped and left back in New York?"What are you doing here?" she asked folding her hands tiredly. She was trying to pretend that she wasn't flipping out by the mere nearness of him. Like her tired body wasn't suddenly becoming aware.

"How was dinner?" he asked"Wow" Sammy whispered to herself, so that was why he'd come? Because she went to dinner with Jason? And she had foolishly thought it was maybe he missed her as much as she had missed him."N ick, I'm really exhausted and I wanna go to bed" she told him"Exhausted? From what? Your dinner or the event that followed afterwards?"Sammy narrowed her eyes and shook her head, this guy was really unbelievable. Was this why he was here? To question her?"And what do you mean exactly when you say events that followed afterwards?""I saw you kiss him" was that jealousy she was detecting?"And?""So you two kiss now?""We are getting married and that is what married couples do. Isn't that what you wanted?""What I wanted?" he asked with a frown"Is it not? You left me in New York, alone, sad and..." heartbroken. She didn't want to say the last part out loud because she didn't want him to know."You left me first. At the hotel, I asked you to stay and you refused and the next time I'm seeing you is with Jason's tongue down your throat"did he really just say that to her?"You asked me to stay right after you told me that you couldn't have anything with me. what did you expect me to do?""What I didn't expect was to find my brother's tongue in your mouth a week after you had been in bed with me"Sammy mentally counted to ten and then bit her upper lip not because she was nervous but because she was furious, how dare he say that to her? Who gave him the right to judge her like that?"Well don't worry about it, soon enough I'll be in bed with him too" she carelessly said and then decided she was done with this conversation. She made to move past him and get back into bed and then he grabbed her by her upper arm and then drew her closer to him in a not so gentle manner."Don't test me Samantha" he said in a dangerously low voice that somehow made goosebumps run down her spine.Sammy shrugged away from him in an angry jerk,"What exactly do you want from me, Niklaus? What? I know what your brother wants. He wants to try, he wants to be there for my child and I. He wants to have a family with me, he wants me to move into his bedroom. He wants to have a wedding, he wants to buy a house, he wants everything that I should want" so why did she not want them? Why did the mere idea of those things make her want to flee? Easy. Because of the man standing right in front of her.Sammy rubbed her face in exhaustion, this is not the way she thought her night was heading. She went ahead to sit down at the edge of her bed. Nick stood staring at her the anger that had been on his face earlier was now replaced with something Sammy couldn't place."And I'm trying to want those things, I swear I'm trying" she continued tiredly"and you show up here angry that I kissed him. Do you know what I thought about when he kissed me? You. I thought about you. I thought about you atdinner, I thought about you before we left for dinner, I think about you all the time and it is exhausting. Having to pretend is exhausting and missing you is worse""You miss me?" he asked the voice that had been filled with so much rage when he was warning her not to test him was now filled with so much warmth.Sammy scoffed,"I miss you so much it's driving me insane"He came and squatted in front of her so they were at an eye level,"I miss you too" he told her"Do you? Then why are you leaving me? You are moving to Europe" she said half hoping he'd tell her Charlie was wrong. She couldn't imagine staying in this house without him, she didn't want to."Do you think I want to? But I can't stay here and watch you marry Jason, watch you kiss him, watch you move into his bedroom, become his" he sounded pained"He wants us to get married next week" she didn't know why she was telling him that but she just wanted him to know."Next week?" he asked standing up and taking two steps back like he had been sucker punched."And he wants you to move into his bedroom, and he kisses you now" he was getting angry again, Sammy could see that. She didn't understand why, did he expect that the thing with Jason would never actually be practicalized? Truth be told she had never seen it happening until he started saying all those things at dinner."Yes" she replied"And you are just fine with it?""Of course I'm not fine with it but I already agreed""And now you're agreeing to fuck him" so they were back to fighting,"No one said anything about that""What do you think is going happen when you move into his bedroom Samantha?""Or when I marry him?" she watched the rage crawl back into his eyes and he frowned, deeply."So you do want to fuck him?""It's honestly none of your business okay? You barging into my room in the middle of the night to tell me all these is totally unacceptable.""I think we have crossed the bounds of what is acceptable or not where we are concerned. You barely knew my brother when slept with him and got yourself knocked up, you agree to take money from my family in exchange to marry him but you just had to sleep with me too and now you intend to crawl back into bed with him. How acceptable do you think that is?"it was the condescending way he said it that almost drove Sammy to tears. Accusing her like she was some kind of gold digger? Looking at her with that disgusted look on his face."It's not. You're right, it was inappropriate to sleep with you but that is never going to happen again. And I'm sorry"his demeanour faltered and the frown was replaced with an apologetic look not that Sammy cared anymore."Samantha, I didn't..." she didn't want to hear anything from him right now,"I'd like to get some sleep now" she told him and got up and made her way to the door and gestured for him to leave, the conversation was over as far as she was concerned so was her thing with Nick.

SAMMY LOOKED AT the wall clock for what felt like the hundredth time, it was seven on the dot. She just couldn't wait anymore, if she did she might just explode.She didn't get any sleep last night, not because of the horror show that had happened but because she had lain awake thinking. She had made a few decisions last night after that awful talk with Nick. He had made her realise a few things about what she wanted out of this, out of the whole situation.She got out of bed, contemplated showering and then decided she couldn't wait. She'll shower when she got back. She was going to speak with Jason and knowing herself she might lose her nerve if she waited a bit longer.She discarded the large t-shirt she was wearing for a pair of sweatpants and then made her way to find Jason.It didn't take her long to get to his bedroom, by the look on his face he was surprised when he opened the door to find her on the other side,"Samantha?" he said in a worried tone"Good morning" she greeted with a smile, not because she was very cheerful but to ease his worry."Good morning" he replied and engulfed her in a hug and then he gave her a peck on the lips. Sammy tried her best not to cringe although she was cringing hard on the inside."Is everything okay?" he askedShe nodded,"Yes, I just wanted to talk to you""Are you okay?" he asked"Yes, I have a few things I wanted to get off my chest if that's okay" she told him."Okay then, but let's go grab breakfast and then we can talk there" he said and Sammy nodded, she honestly was already starving.He excused himself and went back into his bedroom to grab his phone.***Sammy sat and waited while Jason fried the eggs, he didn't have his brother's cooking skills and definitely not his finesse. He was, for lack of a better word rather clumsy. He dropped things and made a bunch of noise while he worked and it didn't surprise Sammy that her first bite of the egg was met with a piece of shell. She smiled through it and swallowed so she wouldn't hurt his feelings. It was the gesture that counted after all and cooking for her was a rather nice one.He sat after he poured her a glass of juice and himself a cup of coffee,"You said you wanted to talk?" he asked as he wrapped up some eggs in a slice of bread and took a generous bite.Where to begin, Sammy wondered. She cleared her throat,"Yes," she began"I thought about it and I have decided that we should maybe wait a while for the wedding" she watched him frown,"Why?" he asked'definitely not because your brother almost chewed my head off when he heard about it'"Because I think we should get to know one another better first. I have agreed to marry you and I don't intend to change my mind so I don't think we need to rush it"he sighed, deeply and then took a sip from his cup of coffee."I'm sorry" she added because she felt like she had maybe upset him.He nodded,"Okay. I agree" he said.That was it? He was just agreeing? Sammy had thought it would have been a more difficult conversation that would have made him more upset."You do?" she asked"Yes. Samantha this is a partnership, if you want to wait then I want to wait" he smiled which made Sammy smile too. He was such a nice guy and that made Sammy more regretful of the fact that she had gotten entangled with his brother. Maybe if he had been around things would have been different."Is there anything else?" he asked taking a bit from his food,"Yes" a couple more things actually."Go ahead but first eat up and drink you juice" he suggested with a smile. Nick would have ordered. No thinking about Nick today, she reminded herself.She returned his smile before taking a long sip from her glass, just to please him."Your father offered to pay me a million dollars for every year that I am married to you, did you know that?" she asked.he nodded,"Yes, it's in the prenup. I thought my brother had you look at the initial draftings?""He did" she told him,"You'll get the first half of the payment once we are married but if you want money for anything before then I could...""No, no. I don't want the money.""Come again?""I am rejecting your father's offer, of course I'll still marry you and I'll still sign the prenup but I want the payment clause removed""Sam, maybe you should take some time to think this through" he said"I have and that is what I want""My family can afford to pay you more than that""I know and I'm not saying that they can't, I'm just saying that I don't want people thinking that the reason I am marrying you is cause of your money""No one thinks that" he was obviously just saying that. Sammy remembered vividly how he had acted after she had first told him, he was the one who had insinuated that she had come for the money but she was not going to bring it up now. She didn't want the money anymore, never did. She only accepted it because they had offered but the fact that Nick had insinuated she was a gold digger last night was the only eye opener she needed."I know no one thinks that but I still wouldn't feel right taking the money" because she was sure last night wasn't the last time it would be used against her, it would always be there hanging over her head and probably that of her child's if anything happened. That wasn't a risk she was eager to take anymore. She obviously would never be equals with them but she didn't need to begin her relationship with them this way not after she had had a glimpse of what was going on inside of Nick's head."could you talk to your father about it?" she asked"Okay, sure" he said with a nod."Lastly,""Lastly" he repeated"Yes, lastly. I want to go into town to look for a job" he was shaking his head even before she finished the statement."No, Sam, I don't think that's a good idea""I can't just stay locked up in your father's house, I'll go crazy. I need to do something and I need to earn some money too" she explained"Samantha you're pregnant," he said as if she needed any reminders."you don't have to do anything my family and I will take care of you""I know I'm pregnant but that doesn't make me an invalid. I'm not even showing yet. And I don't doubt that your family will take care of me but Jason I can't stay locked up in here."Jason took a deep breath and then pouted his lips in a way that showed he was thinking,"Okay, but..." he said raising his index finger, stifling the gratitude that was about to come from her"but, if I notice that it's stressing you in anyway then you must stop. And once you get to the third semester of the pregnancy then you must also stop. If you agree to these terms then I'm sure we can find you a job"She didn't need to consider it, she already agreed to it. What was the alternative, to argue further with him? An argument she wasn't even sure she was going to win."Okay, I agree" she said"and thank you""Can we now please eat?" he asked and she smiled"Yes" she was actually starving but she needed to get the conversation over with.

# CHAPTER 17

"You turned down the money?" a very angry looking Nick asked Samantha barely two hours after her conversation with Jason."I don't think it's any of your business but yes, I decided I don't want to be the gold digger your family decided I am. You decided I am" she didn't care how angry he was or what his opinions on her decision were. She shouldn't even be talking to him right now, not after the way he had spoken to her last night, the things he had said."I never called you a gold digger" he denied"You didn't need to say the words aloud, to you I am the girl who deliberately got knocked up by your brother and just to get my claws into your family fortune""So you are going to punish me by punishing yourself?" how he could still make her feel so stupid with just that one look was beyond her."I'm not punishing myself, I don't need the money. I have never seen a million dollars in my life before, never had need for it and never will" she told him."The money is not for now, it is for when my brother finally realises and I'm sure he will and then he'll leave you""When he realises what exactly? That I'm not good enough?" how could one person make her feel all these emotions? A week ago, she was sure that she was almost in love with him, yesterday she had been so angry with him and then today? Today, she was sure she had never hated anyone more than she hated Niklaus McCarthy at this moment.A man who berates her this way, time and time again."I didn't say that""It doesn't matter, I got it" she took a deep breath,"But I wonder why you came to me, since I'm not good enough, why would you sleep with me?"

"What!"They both turned simultaneously to find Alex standing by Sammy's door."Alex" Nick called going to her immediately,"What did she just say right now?" Alex asked coming in properly into the room."You don't understand," Nick began"I understand that she said that you two slept together, can you please explain"That was the last thing Sammy heard from Alex before the pain started, she was sure Nick said something else but she could barely make it out, it sounded distant, faint and she couldn't concentrate on anything but the overwhelming cramping pain from her stomach.She clutched the lower part of her belly when it felt like the pain was coming from there and then it was every-where, intensifying by the second.'The baby' she thought as she closed her eyes. She wanted to scream, she thought she was going to but nothing came out.She bit her lips hard, hard enough she drew blood, her legs became wobbly she couldn't stand anymore, she tried to reach for anything to hold on to but she was in the middle of the bedroom."Nick?" she called at the same time she felt the liquid trickle down her thigh.Nick turned around to look at her, she was there half standing, she looked pale and like she was in physical pain."Samantha are you okay?" he asked, he was already by her side.His eyes followed hers to the blood on the floor in droplets,"I don't think so" he was hauling her into his arms before she was done talking.

Sammy woke up with a slight headache and a little confusion, she was in a hospital bed, in a hospital gown. She sat up and placed a hand to her head as if that would do anything to ease her pain.She took herself to the last thing she remembered which was the gut-wrenching pain in her belly and the blood!Her hands immediately flew to her stomach, headache forgotten.'oh God' she hoped her child was okay.She had barely finished sending the thought out before a nurse strode in,"Oh, you're awake" she said coming to stand by the bed."I was just going to check your vitals" she informed Sammy before picking up what Sammy made out to be a notepad."What happened?" Sammy asked her while she wrote"We have managed to get the bleeding under control but the dosage of the drug you took was a bit off"the confusion was back, what did she mean by the drugs you took? Sammy wondered."I'll go get the doctor" she said and was gone before Sammy could even ask her to explain what she was saying.The stubby looking doctor came in exactly two minutes after the nurse left, it was hard not to notice how it looked like the buttons on the belly part of his shirt were working overtime just to stay in place and that one deep breath might just send them flying."Hi, I'm doctor Pitcher" he said with a weird smile on his face,"how are you feeling?" he askedSammy took a deep breath,"Confused" tired and a little sore"the nurse said something about a drug, I don't understand""The toxicology report shows there are traces of mifepristone in your system" the doctor explained."I don't understand" she told the doctorMifepristone. Sammy only knew the drug because after she got pregnant, she and Vicky had explored multiple options on how to deal with it, said drug was one of the options they had explored at the time. Not that she had ever taken it or intended to, so what was it doing in her system."We managed to get the bleeding under control but I would still like to keep you for supervision overnight" the doctor continued."What do you mean mifepristone?" she asked"It's a drug that is usually used to stop a pregnancy in the first ten weeks" basically an abortion drug"I know what it means but why do you say there are traces in my system?" she askedDr Pitcher looked almost as confused as she was,"It means you ingested it in the last twenty four hours""What? I didn't... I did not... what?"the baby!"How is my baby?" and why was he looking at her like she was crazy."The cramps you felt earlier was the foetus leaving"Sammy let out a strangled cry, the only thing she was understanding from what the doctor was saying was that she lost her baby."My baby is gone?" she said more to herself as the tightening in her chest began, she was having another panic attack.

NICK HELD HER hand as he watched her sleep, her palm was callus and rough. A worker's hand. He had held her hands before. On multiple occasions he had done exactly what he was doing now, rubbing the scar in her palmar flexion creases gently, he knew the scar was from a wine opener a while back, when she had worked with a manager who overworked her. She had shared that story with him the second night they had lain together after he told her about the scar on his knee.He hadn't decided if he was more angry or scared. Maybe more scared. She looked so fragile lying there with the needles and machines connected to her, her eyes were closed and his mind went back to her passing out in his arms, she had looked so lifeless, scaring him half to death. For a moment he had thought he would lose her, for actions she herself had taken.What was she thinking? What did she intend to archive? To prove? Maybe she had done it to hurt him, probably because of what he had said to her last night when he had been so angry, not at her but at the situation.Maybe more angry, he decided. How could she do that? Hurting her baby like that, Jason's baby. Putting herself at risk. She had been haemorrhaging when they got to the hospital, haemorrhaging!Nick couldn't shake the nagging feeling that this happened because of him, because of something he had said to her last night.She stirred and then tightened her grip on the hand that held hers, Nick sighed, he was both mentally and emotionally drained, but he was thankful too. Thankful for the first sign of life in her besides the breathing.Charlie strolled in, Luca behind her and Nick pulled his hand from Samantha's, he tried to be subtle about it but Charlie already caught it before he could."She's not awake yet?" she asked"No. The doctor said it might take awhile, they had to sedate her, she was freaking out" he told them"Have you been able to reach Jason?" it was Luca that asked. Nick shook his head. For the first time ever, he was thankful that his brother wasn't taking his calls. How would he even break the news to him? The plan had been to invite him to the hospital first and then maybe let the doctors tell him themselves."And Richard?" Nick asked his brother, it had been Luca's job to tell their father. Nick was thankful because the man was still mighty mad at him."He's threatening to take legal actions against Samantha" Luca told him.good thing the man was in Hong kung"She really killed her baby?" Charlie asked and Samantha stirred again, she gave this tiny throaty noise, like she was in pain and then she opened her eyes.She blinked severally and Nick watched the look of confusion clear with each blink,"You're awake" Charlie said coming to stand next to her"Charlie" she called tiredly"How are you feeling?" Charlie asked taking the hand that Nick had been holding."I'll get back to you when I'm sure what I'm feeling""Okay" Charlie said with a nod as she caressed the hand she held"You're going to be fine" she reassured her as if she knew anything.She might start bleeding again or worse, die in the middle of the night they didn't know what would happen."Luca and I are going to take off now but I'll be back first thing in the morning" she told her"but if you need me at anytime call me, no matter the time" Sammy nodded and Charlie gave her a kiss on her forehead, Nick watched her eyes fill with unshed tears.Charlie started to leave and then she turned back around and said,"Sam, I'm really glad you're okay""Thank you" she replied and then watched Charlie and her husband leave.Sammy felt Nick's eyes even before she looked at him, she wasn't done processing the events of the day and all she wanted was for him to hold her while she cried her eyes out. She lost her baby, after everything she had done, sacrificed, she was just gone.She waited patiently for Nick to say something, hopefully something comforting to her but he just stood there staring at her. She looked him in the face and was met with the disgusted expression that was all over his face, she opened her mouth to call out his name and then she closed it again. What would she even say to him?"How could you do that?" he asked after a while of silence."Do what?" she asked hoping by God he wasn't asking what she knew he was asking"So the plan is to lay there and lie to me" he said nodding his head"I didn't do anything, the doctor is mistaken""The doctor is mistaken. The doctor is mistaken" he repeated in his scary voice,"did you visit a clinic back in New York after I left?" the question caught her off guard"How did you...?""You went to have an abortion""But then I didn't, I changed my mind and then I came home""You came home" he chuckled dryly"You killed your child Samantha, my brother's child""Is that what you think of me?" she asked her heart aching. Did he really think that low of her? She thought as the hot bout of tears started to roll down her face."Don't try to play the victim with me. All I really want to know is why. Why did you come here, why did you say yes, give us hope, give my brother hope, just to take it away?""Nick I didn't do this. I promise" she sat up to look him better in the eyes. Did he really not know her at all? Or even trust her a little bit."And am I supposed to believe you? Someone who was willing to sleep with me while carrying my brother's child, after agreeing to marry him"Sammy placed a hand to her cheeks, like she had been slapped she held onto her face. Maybe he should have just slapped her, she was sure it would have stung less. Why was he putting all this on her?"I can't believe I ever thought there was anything beautiful about you. You are disgusting and you make me sick. I hope I never ever see you again in my life" with that he turned around and left the same way Charlie and Luca had.He didn't even give her the chance to defend herself, to explain. He just decided that since she was a person capable of having an affair with him, she was also capable of killing her child. A child that was growing inside of her.Sammy turned around dipped her face into her pillow and then let her tears out. She cried and cried, even when she felt light headed she still cried, when she was sure she had no more liquid in her body she still cried and even when she thought she would pass out from the pain in her chest she still cried. She cried until she couldn't produce tears and even then, she still sobbed because the pain wasn't going away.

NICK GOT HOME, tired and exhausted. He sat down to process the events of the day knowing that it was maybe partially his fault.His bedroom door opened and Alex came in. He sighed in exhaustion he had totally forgotten about that part. Ofcourse his sister would want some explanations after what she heard but he wasn't sure he was up to having that conversation right now. Or ever."Did you two plan this?" Alex asked placing her hands akimbo and giving him the stink eyes."What are you saying?""Did you tell Sam to kill Jason's baby?" Nick knew his sister was probably angry with him but for her to suggest such a thing was sickening."What! Ofcourse not! Why would you even suggest that?""Because you are a terrible human being. How could you do this to our brother? Again" she shook her head in disappointment."even if you didn't ask her, that girl took those drugs because of you. She killed her baby because she has it in her warped mind that that baby was somehow preventing you from being with her""That is not true, the thing with Samantha was over immediately it started""And still I found you in her bedroom today""We were just talking""You broke our brother the last time, you tore our family apart, how could you do this again? Jason's never going to recover from this"it was more shame that kept him quiet but in all honesty there was very little he could say. He made a mistake, a selfish mistake that was now going to cost him. Cost his entire family."You shouldn't have come home. I wish you never did because everything was fine, everyone was fine when you were in another continent" it surprised Nick, the way his sister was speaking to him. It was something she'd never done before. No matter how angry she had been there was always some affection when she spoke, except for now, all affection was gone and now replaced with what Nick prayed wasn't hatred."You don't mean that" he told her hoping to God he was right."You should leave, go back to Europe but this time don't ever come back" with that she left him, with a bitter taste in his mouth.

TRUE TO HER words Charlie was at the hospital before Sammy woke up, she brought some chicken soup that smelled delicious but Sammy didn't have any appetite to eat."I should have brought something else" Charlie said regretfully when Sammy was refusing to eat,"here, I'm going to call Luca and he'll bring something else. Maybe a bowl of chili" Charlie said bringing out for her phone."Please don't do that" Sammy said placing her hand on Charlie's to stop her, the last thing she wanted was to be any more trouble to the McCarthy household right now. She wasn't even sure she should be laying in this hospital bed racking up a bill she wasn't sure who was going to be responsible for."I'm not hungry right now but when I am, the soup smells amazing" she tried to feign a smile, it was a bit difficult at the moment. Charlie nodded.They fell into an uncomfortable silence, uncomfortable because Sam kept waiting for her to ask her about the baby."Why are you here?" she asked when she couldn't take the silence anymore"Because you are here and that's what you do for family"Sammy felt herself tear up so she blinked severally.They weren't family, not anymore. Her only family was miles away and still had no idea what had happened to her. She still couldn't summon the courage to call Vicky, she almost did severally last night but each time she lost her nerve and didn't make the call"We are not family" she whispered, she wasn't going to delude herself anymore .Charlie smiled, as if she was somehow amused by the statement,"Then atleast we are friends and this is what you do for your friends too"Yes, they were friends, Charlie was the only one who had done the most to make her feel comfortable since she had come to Texas"I'm sorry about your baby" Charlie said after they sat in silence for awhile"You don't think I killed her""I can't say I honestly know what happened but all I know is that on more than one occasion I've seen you rub your belly without even know you're doing it and there's always this tiny smile on your face. I don't think that someone would take out something that makes them smile like that. At least not on purpose"Sammy didn't realise that she did that"You just have to get better now. And to do that you need to eat something" she said opening up the bowl of chicken soup and urging her friend to eat.

It was exactly six thirty seven when they got back to the manor and Sammy was sure she knew everything about Charlie McCarthy- who was previously Charlie Augustine, she hadn't wanted to go to college but had graduated two years early from high school just so she could follow Luca to Princeton because her mother had told her that as brilliant as Luca McCarthy was he would never go for a girl who dropped out from school. 'it's kind of an unwritten rule' she had said. So, Charlie had worked twice as hard to graduate with his class even when everyone had tried to talk her out of it. There was no point in going to college if she wasn't going with him. She applied to the same schools he did and followed her man across country to a place she knew absolutely no one.She was sixteen, right at the time Nick had left for Europe.But what had sucked the most was when he had gone ahead to tell everyone that she was his little sister. An awful thing to say when all she thought about was jumping his bones. She had stopped being his little sister when she had started dating one of his best friends at the time, Jeff. Another brilliant advice from her mother. According to Charlie, Luca had almost died of jealousy and after that she then became a friend of the family. And after she and Jeff had broken up, Luca had been dating this girl, a law major, she recalled but didn't remember her name but after that it was just one bad timing after another but then their first year out of college they had gotten together and it had been epic and worth the wait according to Charlie. But after seven months of dating Luca broke her heart when his high school girlfriend had returned and he claimed he was confused.That was the year the Augustines moved to London and it took two years before they ran into each other in a bar in Lond on.There was a lot more to the story and although Sammy was really grateful for the company and the distraction she had had all day she still knew what she was about to face once she stepped into the McCarthy manor. She wished the hospital had released her earlier so she could head back, she had still considered it but Charlie then convinced her to stay the night and wait for tomorrow.Luca met them downstairs with a huge smile on his face that was obviously for his wife. He enveloped her in a hug and then bit her ear, Charlie squealed and then took a step away from him but only so she could make a fist and punch his stomach. He groaned and then placed a hand to his belly and then used the other one to draw his wife closer to him."Hi Samantha" he said like he was just noticing her. She spared him a smile and then a small wave."My feet are killing me" Charlie told her husband,"so carry me upstairs" she said and then threw her arms up in the air, he chuckled but still lifted her off the floor and into his arms"You are so fat... and heavy" he told her as he made his way upstairs with her in his arms. She hit his shoulder,"You are the only reason I'm fat" she told him and then turned back to Sammy,"call me if you need anything" she told herAnd Sammy watched as Charlie wrap her arms around her husband's neck and she placed her head on his shoulder, he whispered something in her ear that made her laugh, she realised that was something she would never have. Someone who would love her as much as Luca loved Charlie and vice versa. Someone who would get as excited at the sight of her, who would wear that kind of smile Luca wore just because she was in the same room.

SAMANTHA BAKER HAD only been with four men in the course of her entire life, four men. First was her boyfriend senior of high school, Kenny, he dumped her the night after she had lost her virginity to him. He had said that Taylor Omega had asked him to prom so he had to break up with her. But he had waited till after he had given her the world's clumsiest sex to say something.Samantha had cried for a whole week, she had missed prom but she didn't blame him, Taylor Omega was kind of a big deal back then.Second was George, he had been the manager in a diner she worked in, she only went out with him because she didn't know how to say no. They had gone on one date and had ended up having sex in the back of his truck, super uncomfortable experience and she had gotten a condom stuck inside of her. He didn't bother to follow her to the hospital because his dad had the flu and he needed to check up on him.Samantha had spent a lot of hours in the ER but she didn't blame him, of course he should check on his sick dad.And then there was Jason, she wished she could remember more from that night but she had woken up alone in a very fancy hotel room that quite frankly scared her but she also didn't blame him because they barely knew each other and were probably never going to see each other again.But then six weeks after that she had found out she was pregnant so she with the help of her friend, Vicky had come to the conclusion that she was cursed. So she had decided that having sex wasn't an option for her anymore because not only did the curse prevent her from having good sex, it also made for grievous aftermaths.It hadn't been like that with Nick, the curse didn't-couldn't interfere, the sex had been so good she forgot about it. Except that it did, taken worse than she was willing to give and now she was all alone. So as she lay staring at the ceiling, Sammy decided that she was done with sex, forever. Yes she was only twenty four and still had a long way to go but she would get through it, as a matter of fact before Nick she didn't know there was much she was missing.She would have maybe joined a convent if she was more religious, her mother had been religious, the woman prayed the rosary every morning to start her day but after she died Sammy just didn't have the time or the patience to believe anymore.Maybe if she believed she would have maybe prayed herself out of this mess.Grabbing her phone, she decided to send Vicky a text. She hoped she was asleep because she didn't know if she had it in her to deal with her friend's worry.'it didn't work out, on my way home tomorrow' she turned off her phone just in case Vicky tried to call her back. Better they did this face to face.

# CHAPTER 18

Joanna James was twenty-five when Richard McCarthy hired her, his wife had been having post -partum depression because she didn't feel any connection with the child she just popped out.Joanna was great with children and it helped a great deal that Luca was a sweet boy and she couldn't help but to fall in love with him.June, their mother never formed any connections with her kid but she went ahead to pop out four more but that was only because her husband had paid her a stated sum every time she had a baby and promised to double it if it turned out to be a girl. He called it 'the child birth allowance' but he knew and she knew that it was just plain and simple payment for allowing him use her body as an incubator for nine months – well Chase had stayed for eight but that was beside the point.Richard had once told Joanna that his wife felt like a surrogate with no emotional connection to her children. So Joanna had done her best to love and care for them the best she could.And it didn't come as a surprise to anyone when June had asked her husband for a settlement to sign over her parental rights to him, Luca was thirteen and Alex three when she left and never looked back.At first, Richard had said it was just a phase and that she'd come back and when a month turned into two and two into a year, it became obvious that June had moved on with her life. And then Richard resented his children, they had caused him the love of his life. He didn't need them and having them was a mistake. When that was over, he then began to throw money at them, keeping his distance but still making sure they had everything they wanted.Joanna had watched him spoil his children because that was the only way he knew to love. Some of his children had leaned into it and the other two, Luca and Nick. Luca forced himself to take charge where his father couldn't, he was the only reason his siblings didn't get buried in their father's wealth. Richard had expected them to know right from wrong, rewarding them when they did right and icing them out when they didn't but Luca had actually taken the time to teach them, even when he wasn't sure what it was, he tried to make sure his siblings were raised right. Even if that meant beating the crap out of Chase the time he found out he was using cocaine in high school or tracking Alex down and dragging her home by the hair the year she ran away with her boyfriend at fifteen, Luca did his best to make sure everything turned out alright and Joanna did her best to guide and teach him.And Nick, Nick just leaned away from everyone and everything. Joanna suspected he didn't know he did that but the more his father threw money at him the more he withdrew into himself. And that hadn't entirely been a bad thing, he didn't wait to be raised or taught by anyone he just did that himself. It made him smarter, wiser and more resourceful than the rest of his siblings. So, no one had worried when he decided at sixteen that he wanted to go and explore the world, no one actually understood what he meant by 'explore the world' but everyone had supported him. Even Richard had waited two full years before putting him in charge of his oversee estates, which gave him the flexibility to travel how he wanted.'if he wants to travel, he should at least make himself useful while at it' Richard had told Joanna.So when his peers were being children, still learning and growing, Nick was forced to become an adult. To grow apart from his siblings and family.It did break Joanna's heart but she reminded herself that that was what the child wanted.

He did come home for Christmas, thanksgiving and most special occasions but it wasn't enough time to be as close to his siblings as they were with one another. So it came as no surprise when his brother had brought Sophia Jamieson, the only woman he had ever had a committed relationship with home and his siblings didn't think it was a problem."It's been a whole year since you two broke up" Luca had said and Chase had made a joke about it.Alex had come to him begging and crying, it was something she always did to put her brothers on the spot and it had worked that time too.So Nick had let his brother marry his ex, whom apparently his entire family had known he was dating and then kept it from him.It wasn't like Nick had wanted to marry Sophia or anything like that, he didn't love her or care about her like he knew he should but they had understood each other- at least he thought they had until the day she had called him an emotionally crippled person who didn't have the ability to love anyone but himself.

She packed up and left him in Brazil that evening and he didn't see her again until the next Christmas in his father's house.So Nick had skipped out on his brother's wedding and didn't come home again until his father had asked him for help on a project he was working on. And the minor problem that was supposed to keep him in Texas for a week or two turned into a night mere when Sophia had decided she didn't like the way her bipolar meds made her feel, she stopped taking them and no one noticed until she began to act a bit crazy.That was why she decided she was ready to take Nick back even when he wasn't asking. So, on one Sunday afternoon she had jumped into his car just as he was about to leave and had asked him to tell her he loved her. Nick could not because he didn't feel it when they were together and he certainly didn't feel it then. So she had started to physically assault him because her scrambled brain had told her that he came back for her- he didn't.Nick was still trying to calm her down when the car swerved off the road and before he could do anything about it they were headed down a cliff.It ended with major broken bones for him and a crushed windpipe for her. She died and his family blamed him for it, his brother hated him for it.

Nick sat in one of the smaller kitchen stools as Mrs. James gave him the first aid he needed. She tilted his head backwards because his nose wouldn't stop bleeding before shoving oversized cotton swabs in his nostrils. She was probably trying to suffocate him, Nick thought, and it would have been well deserved.She returned to the cut on his lips and Nick closed his eyes.Jason was in the living room getting the same treatment from Charlie. Nick couldn't remember who had thrown the first punch but he sure as hell knew his brother had an amazing left hook. You wouldn't know by just looking at him but Jason sure knew how to pack a punch.He couldn't remember the last time he had gone physical with any of his siblings, maybe with Luca but never with the other ones. But it had been inevitable today. Inevitable because Alex had decided to open her big mouth to tell her brother what she knew had happened with Samantha, Jason had come charging. He said a bunch of stuff that Nick had taken and some that he just couldn't. Jason had brought up Sophia, Nick didn't remember if he had lost it when he had said the things about that or when he had called Samantha a slut- well cheap slut- but that didn't matter.Nick winced when Mrs. James switched to the cut under his eye, she rolled her eyes and dabbed harder. If he couldn't handle the heat then maybe he shouldn't have gone into the kitchen.Nick moved his head away and then looked at her, ready to snap but didn't when he saw the look on her face. She was pissed-scratch that- she was furious.He knew that because when-ever she was angry there were these hot-angry unshed tears in her eyes. She wouldn't cry but they would hang there until she calmed herself.Nick hated that he was the reason those tears were there. Joanna James was someone he didn't like disappointing and he rarely did but from the look on her face he had tonight."I'm sorry" he saidshe closed her eyes and took a deep breath,"You said you didn't sleep with her""I hadn't at the time""So you continued""It's more complicated than that"Mrs James shook her head before going to fetch an ice pack, she placed it on his hand, his punching hand that was already beginning to swell."You are an idiot, you know that?" he knew that, Nick was sure that if he wasn't battered enough already, she would have smacked his head"We made a mistake... I made a mistake""And you fight your brother over a mistake?""I didn't fight Jason because..." he sighed, he would have run a hand over his face in frustration if he wasn't sore all over. He was tired too."Jason and I fought because I'm tired. Samantha wasn't his, he didn't even want her here""You did something wrong to him" Mrs James accused, like he did not know that."I know that, but I'm not the reason Samantha did what she did. She did that all by herself" his ribs were back to hurting, the damned things were already almost healed and now the pain was back. He placed the ice pack Mrs James had given him on his side underneath his t-shirt and huffed when they touched his aching ribs."Your siblings are not happy with you""I don't care what they think" he said stubbornly, but only because he was angry now. He would care later, especially if Luca had something to say about what he had done. Luca was another person he hated disappointing."You do care, if not now then later" she told him as she removed the gloves she had put on only to tend to his wounds, she was done now."Jason was actually the first person I introduced Sophia to, he was the only person I called when she dumped me. He brought her here as his fiancé and they all stood by his side, so no I do not care if they are happy or not with me"Mrs James adjusted the plaster on his forehead,"Your brother is a spoilt brat in every sense of the word and your siblings knew that. They saw a woman that you didn't care for but wouldn't let go off because you were jealous. they saw your brother filled with love and would do anything to get his way. They didn't stand by him to hurt you" Joanna explained,"Chase called me emotionally inept" he hated that he still thought about that phrase from time to time."Oh honey, you are not inept. Just because you find it harder than the rest of us to express your feelings doesn't mean you can't" she told him with such affection that he immediately wanted to be hugged."Do you really think so?" he asked"Yes" she said and then gave him a gentle stroke on the head that he immediately leaned into."Now about Samantha..."

JOANNA JAMES HAD no children, at least not biologically anyway, she had no husband and made no other family. All these was because she had loved the McCarthy children like she had birthed them herself and she knew that making another family would imply leaving them so she did not.It hurt her deeply when one of them were in pain and after speaking with Niklaus she found that he was in a great deal of pain and had been for more than a while now. The boy was dealing with things that he didn't know how to deal with and most of those feelings had to do with Samantha. He was angry, sad, ashamed and Joanna was sure, in love.She didn't say anything to him about it because she knew he wouldn't admit it, at least not yet anyway. He wasn't ready. She hated that all these feelings were wasted on the wrong person but she knew it was good that he was feeling them because the boy never lets himself feel anything.She also hated that she was wrong about the girl, she had prided herself on being able to read people until Samantha Baker. She had definitely misjudged her, thinking her a sweet and innocent girl when she was the worst kind of person. Joanna had learnt her mistake that first night she had caught her offering herself up to Nick like that, that was when she began to suspect how awful the girl was. But she didn't think her awful enough to kill her own child. And now everyone was suffering because of that.Joanna was on her way to Jason, she would talk some sense into him, maybe scold him a little and then listen if he wanted to talk. She knew he too would be hurting after losing his child like that and from the fight with his brother too but his behaviour was still unacceptable.She was a little disappointed when she met his room empty, but as usual his room was a mess. He was the messiest of his siblings even as a boy.The tossed around clothes she decided to pick up first, dropping the jean trouser and the tank top that was rolled up with it on the floor into the laundry basket. The sweat pants next but before she could drop it into the basket she felt something in the pocket, she reached inside hoping it wasn't a used up condom, on more than one occasion she had found those in the boys rooms, mostly Chase's the boy was as shameless as he was brazen. It wasn't any used condoms thank God but what she didn't expect to find was an empty packet of drug. She read out the name, she didn't know why but she knew she had recently been in contact with the medication or heard about it somewhere.She shoved it into her dress pocket and then continued tiding up, she would definitely figure it out later but for now she was going to make this room more conducive.

The house was silent and it had been that way for a couple of days now, everyone avoided coming downstairs and one other. Alex took off after Charlie had given her an earful for the fight she had caused. Although she was adamant that she had done the right thing and was upset that Charlie had even suggested she kept it a secret from her brother.Richard was in Brazil, no one knew when he was coming back or if he was coming back.It took Joanna two whole days before she got around to calling her physician concerning the medication she found in Jason's bedroom. It would have been easier to just google it but Joanna was a bit old fashioned like that and she trusted her doctor of twenty years more than she trusted what some crappy internet page would tell her. If Jason had some serious illness she would rather Dr Diaz told her.But it wasn't a cancer medication or a drug for some chronic illness, Jason was keeping an abortion drug in his pants. That was why it sounded so damn familiar because that was the drug everyone was accusing Samantha of taking, she hoped to God that this was some kind of misunderstanding because she didn't want to believe what she knew in her gut to be true.

NICK WAS PACKING, he had already over stayed his welcome here, Italy was waiting and truth be told this place didn't feel like home anymore. After the fight with Jason nothing felt right anymore, Alex told him to leave and Charlie and Luca had been a little preoccupied with their pregnancy.When the knock came, he hoped it wasn't Charlie, it probably was because he didn't think any of his siblings still wanted to have anything to do with him at the moment and quite frankly with the way he was feeling he didn't know if he wanted to have anything to do with them either.He just wasn't ready to face her or anyone else.The knock came again in shorter louder rasps and Nick sighed in frustration, he could probably spare a few minutes he thought before abandoning his suitcase and then heading to the door. It wasn't Charlie, instead Mrs James came in with a worried expression on her face. Why hadn't he considered it would be her?"You're packing" she stated when she saw the boxes on his bed all half empty. By habit she picked up the shirt on the top and refolded it."This is all wrong" she said referring to the way he had folded all the other clothes. She placed the shirt she had folded on the bed and then emptied all the other content of the box on the bed and then got to work.Nick sighed internally, he doubted this was the reason Mrs James had come in here but as he watched her fold his clothes he could tell that something was bothering her"You know if I needed help with folding my clothes I would have asked Alice" Alice was the girl who was now in charge of laundry. Mrs James threw him a glance,"I was folding laundry before you or that girl was born" she told him and then went back to the folding"I'll be fine" Nick waited for a few seconds before saying, maybe she was worried about him leaving so he decided to reassure her. She was the only one who had tried to convince him not to go the other time"I know you'll be fine" she said without even looking at him"It's not you I'm worried about" she told him and Nick sighed again. He felt like he already knew what this what about and he was sure he didn't want to hear it."If this is about Jason then I really don't want to hear it" he knew she was probably here to ask him to apologise to his brother."It's about Samantha"That was unexpected. For two days he had done his darn hardest to stop himself from thinking about her, from worrying about her, but the more he tried, the harder it was. And now all of a sudden Mrs James wanted to talk about her. He had already told her all he had to say about that issue."Samantha" he repeated"Yes. I found this" she told him handing him an empty packet of a combo kit of mifepristone"What is this?" he asked before taking a look at it"you found it in Samantha's bedroom" he reminded himself that it wasn't Samantha's room, it was the third guest bedroom and she had only stayed there because Charlie had suggested the bath would be more suitable for a pregnant woman."I don't understand why you are showing this to me, we already know what she did""I found it in your brother's bedroom"Nick paused but only because he needed a moment to think. Nick had never considered himself slow but he also knew that he was missing the information behind the thing Mrs James was saying."Why would this be in my brother's bedroom?" he asked feeling more stupid than ever."It was in Jason's pants" the look on her face said what he didn't want to believe."So you're saying Jason knew about the abortion?" he seriously didn't want to believe that. Not after all the things Jason had said to him, he had even gone as far as to accuse him of being the one who instigated Samantha to do the abortion.Mrs James was looking at him like an idiot,"I'm saying, the girl denied taking those pills, did she not?""Yes but..." traces were found in her system. Nick's brain was going into overdrive as he began to realise"Jason wouldn't... I mean he was willing to start a family with her, he talked to her about buying a house, he wanted to marry her next week" he told Mrs James.Someone who was willing to do all these wouldn't go ahead to kill his child."Jason and Samantha had breakfast together that morning, I remember because he had ordered everyone out of the kitchen and decided to do the cooking. That surprised me because you know how your brother wouldn't cook to save his life but I just thought he wanted to impress her" more like wanted to drug her"Jason wouldn't" Nick repeated again stubbornly even though he now knew in his gut that that was exactly what had happened, Jason drugged that poor girl. His head went back to all the awful things he had told Samantha at the hospital, she must have been in so much pain after losing her child and he had gone ahead to pile on her like that.How could Jason do that? How could he kill his own child? Samantha's child?Nick ran his fingers through his hair in frustration, packing forgotten,"I gotta to talk to him" he said and then went to find his brother.

Jason wasn't home as usual and Nick decided he was going to go meet him at whatever dingy club he was in, Levi would know or security could track him down in less than an hour. He was still contemplating when Jason walked in, he had been drinking obviously but not quite drink."Jason, heads up" he called before tossing him the drug packet.He instinctively caught it mid-air,"What is..." he stopped once he took a look at what he had caught. The look on his face said everything Nick wanted to know and more."You drugged her?" It was more a statement than a question but he still hoped his brother would deny it."I did not..." he paused and ran his hand through his hair, in frustration that he had been caught obviously."I did the right thing" he said stubbornly his entire tone changing. Nick was just now realising what his brother was capable of doing. How was it that you could know someone your whole life and still not know them at all?"That girl was a gold digger and she came here to cart all our money away" he said accusatorily."she was mum all over again and I wasn't going to let her fool me, fool all of us"Nick felt like his head was about explode, so this was about the money? Money that he had never worked a day in his life for."For all her faults at least mum gave us all a chance to be born, she let us live" Nick watched his brother's demeanour falter, he had obviously thought that bringing up their mother would bring Nick to his side."I don't owe you an explanations, I put that baby in her and I took it out"Wow. Just wow"...and hey, it's not like you didn't have your fun with her"Something in Nick's head snapped and before he knew what he was doing he was pinning his brother to the floor and feeding him with punches. It wasn't like their fight the other day, this time Nick didn't let his brother return any of his punches.It was Mrs James that found them first but it took Luca and Chase put together to separate them. But Nick wasn't done, he didn't know where the urge came from but he just wanted to kill his brother, with his fist. And he probably would have if he wasn't stopped, he was blinded with so much rage and something else he couldn't place."You son of a bitch!" Jason said as he spat out a mouthful of blood.Everyone was there now, everyone except Alex and

Richard"I'm going to kill you" Nick said in a quiet voice that sent chills down everyone's back."You screwed her a couple of times and that gives you the right to fight for her? I did you a favour, I did her a favour" Jason said and that only pissed Nick off some more. He wriggled hard to get out of his brothers grip but both boys weren't letting down."You need to stop talking" Mrs James told Jason and then to Nick,"You need to calm down""How can you tell me that? You know what he did""What the hell is going on in my house?!" forgetting the ruckus in front everyone turned around to find Richard standing at the door."Could someone start talking?" he said when no one made an attempt to explain"Dad we got this under control, you can go upstairs" it was Luca who said. He honestly didn't know what else to tell his father because he barely understood why his brothers were having another round of boxing match, they were barely getting over the other one."By under control you mean bodily restraining your brother? If no one starts talking so help me God I'll...""Tell him Jay," Nick began and then shrugged out of his brother's hold"Nick shut up" for the first time since this whole thing began Jason looked terrified"Why? So dad doesn't find out the kind of person you are?" Nick asked him"I mean it Nick, stop talking""Okay. I won't tell dad how you drugged Samantha with Mifepristone and blamed her for the abortion you induced" everyone gasped including Richard who prided himself on not being easily surprised."You did what?" it was Charlie who took the question from everyone's mouth.Jason turned to their father,"I did what you asked me to do""What?" this time everyone looked back at Richard for some sort of explanation and even him seemed surprised by the accusation."Dad told me to come back and handle it the best way I know, he said that whatever choice I made no one would blame me""And your choice was to kill that poor girl's child? To put her at risk like that?" Charlie didn't bother to hide the disgust on her face"I did what was best for me" Jason said stubbornly.No one realised Charlie had moved until they heard the smack on Jason's face, it was a bit inconsequential given that his face had already began to bruise and swell from the punches Nick had given him earlier."I watched that girl fall apart, I held her cry and listened to her beat herself up over something you did" she wiped the angry tears that had rolled down her face"I can't even look at you right now" she said and then turned around and headed upstairs. Luca immediately followed his wife, whatever he was dying to say to his brother could wait until his wife calmed down.No one said anything, not Chase, not Nick and not even Jason, they were all waiting for Richard to go first, but he didn't say a thing, instead he turned around and headed to his study. Nick immediately followed, how was it that his father wouldn't say anything on the matter now it was Jason but had been on the verge of disowning him when everyone thought it was his fault."So you are not even going to say anything?" Nick asked when they got into the study"What would you rather I said?" he asked lazily"Did you not hear what Jason did?""Your brother had been through a lot this past year, he did what he thought was best"wow. Just wow. Was his father seriously making excuse for what Jason did?"And what he thought was best was killing that girl's child?" Nick felt like he was losing his mind"That girl wasn't right for him or this family and you of all people should know that""So that justifies what he did" yep, he was definitely losing his mind."You had a sordid affair with that girl, if I'm to say anything, you ruined your brother's chances of ever having something tangible with her" his father accused"The only reason anything ever happened with Samantha was because you forced her down my throat and because your precious Jason was too much of a coward to take responsibility for his actions""I sent you to fix something that you broke but instead you made it worse""Jason was broken long before Sophia and that is your fault. I was ready to walk away from Samantha, despite the things I felt about her I would have let Jason marry her and he goes and does this and you don't see how messed up it is? Cause nothing's ever Jason's fault" Nick couldn't remember a time if any that he had ever spoken to his father like this, Richard McCarthy wasn't someone you lost your temper with or yelled at but at the moment all Nick wanted to do was to punch him in the face."What's done is done" Richard said with finality, a tone he used to end conversations when he was done listening to what the other person had to say. A tone Nick knew all too well since he was a child and usually, he would have let his father have the last word but he was too angry right now to."I am the one who's done" he said calmly, Richard wouldn't hear him if he yelled, they would just get into another round of pissing contest that Richard would probably win."I'm done with you, I'm done with Jason and I'm done with the entirety of this stupid family" he said and began to leave, he was almost out the door when Richard said,"If you leave this house...""What dad? What?" he knew what his father was going to say, he had heard so many versions of the same threat that he knew it by heart and quite frankly he was tired of hearing it"you'll cut me off? Freeze my accounts? You wouldn't do that"Richard was shocked to the core, never in his life had anyone spoken to him with such blatant disrespect, least of all his very own son."I wouldn't?" he asked. His children knew he had fangs and quiet often he had used it on them. So why then, he wondered did his boy think he wouldn't bite now?"Unlike Jason, Chase and Alex, every single penny in my account I have worked my butt off to earn, I manage more than fifty percent of all your assets. I have brought in more business and closed more deals than any of your other employees put together. So cut me off, freeze my accounts, there's a lot of companies that will give an limb just for me to consult for them. Then we'll see how fast the Luxury estates crumble after that" with that he didn't wait to hear what his father had to say, he stormed out. He headed to his room closed off his suitcase and then headed out.

Richard McCarthy was a man of his words and all of his children knew that, so after Nick left the manor and called the airport, he was half expecting to be told that his privileges had been cancelled. Same with when he got to Luxury Milan and every time he used his cards anywhere he wondered if this was it.But that wasn't the case, Richard didn't go through with his threats. At least not yet but knowing his father, the man still might. So instead of letting himself worry about that, he decided not to think about anything and everything. So, for two months, he found himself hopping from city to city in Italy with only a single thought in his head.Although he tried not to, Samantha was all he thought about. He thought about her crappy neighbourhood and her tiny apartment. He was there for only one night but every corner of the placed was crammed into his head.He remembered her tiny bed and her cheap sheets, it was purple. He remembered because the purple was the only bright colour in that apartment. So, every time he saw the colour purple all he could think about was Samantha spread out on the bed beneath him.The more he tried not to think about it, the more it was all he could think about. The only time he wasn't thinking about her was when he was sleeping and even then, he was dreaming of her.He thought of going down to New York so many times but each time he reminded himself how much of a terrible idea that was. He was probably the last person she'd want to see, after the things he had said to her it'd be better if she never laid eyes on him again.He wouldn't even know what to say to her. Both were excuses and the truth was that he was a coward and he couldn't face her. He was so ashamed of how he had treated her that sometimes he just wanted to punch himself in the face.So, for two months he just floated from place to place because nothing in his life made sense anymore. It was stupid because he had been contented with his life before, liked it even, but now everything felt wrong and he felt quite so miserable.His siblings wouldn't stop calling, mostly Alex, to make sure he was alive. He didn't answer her obviously but she did leave messages. He just wasn't ready to speak to her, not until he got a handle on the turmoil going on in his head. He did speak to Charlie, just once, but only to tell her he was okay even though he was not. That was a month ago, she stopped calling which was a bit surprising because the usual Charlie would persist until he gave in and came home.

WHEN ROOM SERVICE knocked, Nick just wanted to scream at them to go away. But he couldn't, firstly because he knew his head was probably going to fall off if he attempted to and also because he was still hungry, tired and so hung over. He wasn't sure if it was Wednesday or Thursday, but he hoped it was Wednesday because he had a flight to Florence set for Wednesday. What was happening in Florence again? he couldn't focus enough to remember. The last day he had been sure of was Monday, he had followed a couple of friends on their cruise boat and they had partied till they dropped him off here yesterday.He groaned and crawled out of bed when the knock came again, it felt like they were banging right on his head."I'm coming" he managed to mutter as he walked to the door in nothing but his boxer briefs and it was just at the moment before he opened the door that he remembered he didn't order any room service. He had been passed out since he got here that he hadn't had time to.He opened the door and there stood his brother, Luca, wearing that stiff look he always wore."Woah... you look like something the cat dragged in" he said shoving him aside and making his way into the hotel suite."Luca?" he would have had a better reaction if he wasn't so hung over"At least you are alive" Luca said sarcastically, taking a seat."Your wife knows I'm alive" he said and then winced at his own voice. He needed an aspirin and he needed it now."You're drunk, it's barely 8:am""First of all, keep it down I'm dying over here. And secondly, I'm not drunk, I'm hung over""And what's the difference?" Luca asked"One enjoys the noise and the other loathes it" that was a phrase he learnt from Chase, but he was now observing it was true. He crawled back into bed because even standing felt like a tedious chore.Luca got up, dragged the covers off him and dropped them on the foot of the bed."Go take a shower you reek of alcohol and whatever you're on""Go away" Nick told his brother and then turned around to face the other side of the room."I will go down to reception to find you some aspirin, you better be out of bed and in that shower before I get back" with that Nick was left alone once again. He wanted to ignore what Luca had said, close his eyes and go back to sleep but he knew his brother. He knew that as quiet and as reserved as Luca may be, he wasn't someone you wanted to mess with. He also knew that Luca was probably going to drag him into that shower by the hair if he had to and he was already feeling a lot sore so he wouldn't risk it. So, he forced his aching muscles up and headed to the shower.

The white tablet was waiting along with a tall glass of water when Nick came out of the shower. And so was Luca. Nick sighed, he had almost forgotten he still had to face his brother. He picked up pill, swallowed and took a generous gulp of water."How did you get in here?" he asked heading to the closet"I'm a part owner of the hotel" Luca told him waving a key card at him.Nick groaned, he just wanted to lay down but he knew that probably wouldn't happen until his brother had said whatever he had come to say and knowing Luca it was a lot for him to drag himself away from his pregnant wife. And important too because he wouldn't get involved otherwise."I feel like crap" Nick said as he struggled to get dressed"You look like crap" Luca told him with a frown on his face,"don't worry, the pill will soon kick in""I hope so because I feel like a large animal trampled on me" he said taking a look at himself in the mirror, today wasn't the day to wear red, the colour was too bright for his mood."What are you doing?" Luca asked him"Changing into something else" he said, as if it wasn't obvious"That's not what I meant," Luca said and he looked up at him"what are you doing?" Luca asked again. Nick understood what his brother was asking but he didn't know what to answer because he honestly didn't know what he was doing."Six hundred thousand dollars in Milan, four hundred in Rome, I don't even want to think about Turin and you bought a bar in Genoa?" the disappointment on Luca's face was almost embarrassing."The bouncers tried to kick my friends and I out" Nick said with a smile but with one glance at his brother's face he tucked it back into his face."And these your 'friends' where are they now?" Luca asked"I don't know. I met them in Genoa, one recognised me and we hung out for a couple of days until I left for Palermo""You mean, you partied for a couple of days" Luca corrected. Nick shrugged and then decided the blue turtle neck would look better."Is this what you do now? Party until you drop and on to the next city?" Luca asked"Jason did it for almost a year and I didn't hear anyone complaining""So Jason, that's who you wanna be like now?""I have a plane to catch, so maybe you could check out when you are done" Nick said deciding he was done with this conversation, he began to put on his shoes.He had meant to cancel his plans for Florence but he didn't feel like sitting around and listening to Luca all day."Your flying privileges have been suspended""Richard can't do that. I bought that plane myself""It's a Luxury jet and dad didn't suspend your privileges, I did. And you are no longer welcomed in any of Luxury's hotels, I did that too""You can't do that, I manage more of Luxury's assets and oversee more hotels than you do""You used to buddy, now you are like any other employee on sick leave""So what? You of all people is shutting me out?""Dad wouldn't do it. I let this go on for long enough but not anymore. You are here embarrassing yourself and the entire family" his brother told him"I'm not listening to this" he said and made to leave,"You will sit down and you will listen to everything I have to say" scary Luca was out, he didn't come out often and never had with Nick."I will not""So help me God, if you leave this room I will tackle you in front of all the guest and the employees" Nick stopped at the door, he knew his brother wasn't playing around, so he walked right back and sat down with little if any finesse"I have never had to worry about you," Luca began,"you were the sibling who never gave me cause to worry. Jason's spoilt, Chase's a mess and Alex was the baby- is the baby. But you have always had your shit under control, sometimes better than even I have, so I let myself believe I didn't need to worry about you and I neglected you. For that I'm sorry"Nick groaned, an apology, really? As if being called an embarrassment wasn't making him feel awful enough, now there was an apology too"You have nothing to be sorry about" it would have been easier if his brother had said something awful or had been angry at it. He didn't want anyone to worry about him."On the contrary. I am your big brother, it's my job to worry about you""It's not your job" he argued"This is what I'm saying, you don't let anyone take care of you, but you do know that you can always count on me right?""I know"they fell into a comfortable silence and Nick closed his eyes for a bit, he didn't realise when but the aspirin he took had already began taking effect, which felt good in more ways than one."So," Luca said after a while and waited for his brother to open his eyes, sleep was going to have to wait"have you been on the internet? Or seen the tabloids?" he asked"I've been a little busy" Nick replied and even if he hadn't been tabloids wasn't something he indulged in quite often"Yep. Busy being in the tabloids""You're kidding""I wish I were. How do you think we found out about the bar in Genoa? That was when we started to worry""Fuck! Fuck! Fuck!" this was something he had never had to worry about before, when he made the headlines it had always been something work related, except for that time with that Spanish heiress and a few speculations about whom he was seeing from time to time but that had always been gossip, never facts. But this time was different he realised as Luca pulled out his tablet and handed it to him."Billionaire baby severing ties with family" Nick read aloud and then swore"are you kidding me?""Four gossip outlets have written about you in the past two months, here let me..." Luca took the tablet from him and pulled up another site"Business tycoon parties his way around Europe" Nick read again, he slapped a hand to his forehead. He didn't know which was worse"at least this one recognises... Billionaire baby? What does that even mean?"Luca laughed,"I think they thought you were Chase" it was more of a Chase thing to do"And the crap titles. I haven't even left Italy yet" he groaned, he felt like throwing up.Luca chuckled again, it was good to know that his brother somehow found his misery amusing."You've been spotted in more than four different cities, no one knows when or if you'll stop" Luca said"I'm glad you are enjoying this""Oh I am" he was unapologeticNick went back to the articles,"And what's with the awful pictures?" he asked gliding through the screen. He wasn't going to waste his time reading the body of the articles because he didn't want to feel worse than he already was. Maybe he deserved to feel worse."TMZ said we were taking turns going through midlife crisis""Midlife crisis? I'm barely thirty""Quarter life crisis?" Luca joked. He was enjoying the look on his brother's face at the moment, at least the next time he decided he wanted to skip to another continent on a drinking spree, he'd think twice about it."I hate you right now" Nick told his brother"I didn't do this, you did""I hate this" he said and then ran his hands through his face in embarrassment."I knew you would, why do you think I left my very pregnant wife to be here?""And you guys couldn't bother with damage control?" Nick asked"You should have bothered with controlling your damage" Luca replied. He had been drunk for two months, he hadn't been thinking about how humiliating it would be when he sobered up. His stomach growled and he realised how hungry he had been."Let's go downstairs for breakfast" Luca suggested.

"Are you going to tell me what you are doing hiding out in Italy?" Luca asked as soon as their food came and they began to eat."It's a beautiful country and their dishes are to die for. In Millan, I had this ossobuco alla Milanese and I wanted to move there. And there was this food critique I met in Rome, we went to a different restaurant every-day and ordered the spaghetti alla carbonara for a whole week. The meat dish in Millan was good but the pasta was way better and in Genoa...""Nick" Luca called cutting him off, he knew that wasn't what he was asking."What? You asked" Luca sighed, his brother obviously wasn't ready for the serious conversation so he decided to oblige him for a bit"So you're saying that you've spent your entire adulthood bouncing around Europe and you've never had the ossobuco alla Milanese in Millan?"I'd always been working, I've never been a tourist""You didn't stay because of the food""You don't know that""I didn't come because of the bar. Charlie was going to hop on a plane to come smack you on the head" Nick chuckled, knowing Charlie he knew his brother wasn't joking."I can travel if I want to travel""You didn't travel Nick, you left. And it's not the first time""Are you going to ask me about it?" Nick asked. His brother never did ask about it, not even after the explosive fight with Jason did Luca ask about the thing with Samantha. Nick guessed Charlie probably spoke to him about it."So you slept with Samantha" it was more of a statement than a question"Yes. We made a mistake. I made a mistake, she was alone, pregnant and vulnerable and I took advantage of her" he said ashamed."Alex says she seduced you""She seduced me?" it was laughable the notion of Samantha seducing him, he was the one who had done the seducing if anything."Samantha didn't seduce me, at least not on purpose. I took advantage of her innocence and gave her grief in return" he said bitterly."Do you want to know what Charlie thinks?" Luca asked and Nick said nothing, he knew already what Charlie had to say on that topic. But Luca continued anyway"She thinks that you are in love with her"Nick gave a weak scoff and shook his head,"I don't... I do not... it was just sex. Samantha didn't make me do anything and I wasn't trying to hurt Jason"Luca didn't say anything for the longest time, he just sat there eating which made Nick all the more anxious. He wanted – no needed to know what his brother was thinking and Luca was absolutely enjoying making his brother nervous."You are generally a mean person," Luca began after he was sure his brother had suffered enough with the uncomfortable silence"you are rude and most of the time arrogant. Let's not forget how condescending you can be" Nick hoped his brother was going somewhere with this"but you have the biggest heart of anyone I know. So I know for a fact that you wouldn't take advantage of Samantha or do what you did to hurt our brother""That's what I did""Because you love her""It's more complicated than that""I thought you said it was just sex?" Luca asked"Can we just drop it? Let's just go back upstairs" he didn't have the appetite anymore.Luca reached across the thumped him on the head, hard."Ouch! What are you doing?" he asked rubbing his head were he had been hit"My wife said to do that if you tried to avoid"Nick rolled his eyes, only Charlie would send her husband with a message to thump him"I don't know what it was with Samantha but it's done now. It's over""She also said to thump you again if you said it was done. But I'm not gonna do that""You better not" he warned rubbing still were he had been hit earlier."Look, I've been in love before – I am in love now. And I know how scary it can be sometimes" Luca told him"I was in a car crash, that was scary. This is just annoying and nagging. It never goes away, never shuts off. It doesn't even take a break" he said and sighed tiredly."So you love her?" Luca asked in excitem ent."Luca" Nick called"What? You are the one who's out here making a fool of yourself instead of going to New York and actually talking with the woman you love"Nick cringed, that sounded so weird 'the woman he loves'."I am the last person that girl wants to see""So you're a coward now too"he knew his brother was just goading him but that didn't stop him,"I'm no coward. I said some awful things that I don't think she'd be able to forget""My ex-girlfriend came back and I let the love of my life leave because I was a coward, just like you. Charlie forgave me and I think Samantha will if she loves you back" Luca told him and right there was the problem,"What if she doesn't" he whispered almost ashamed"Oh Nick. I told you it was scary. But at least then you'd know. You are not doing yourself any good by hiding out here and partying your life away" Luca told him."Does she know? Did anyone tell her what Jason did?" Nick asked"Charlie was going to, but she said it needed to be face to face and she can't travel at this stage of the pregnancy. Richard sent her a cheque a month ago but she wouldn't cash it, we don't know why. So I told my wife I was going to come get you, you're the one who's in love with the girl""Gee! And I thought you came because you missed me" Nick said sarcastically"I came because I felt sorry for you. You've embarrassed yourself too long and too hard" Luca said and then chuckled"so go down to New York and try to get your girl, drinking won't help, she's the only thing that will" Luca said getting up"What are you doing?" Nick asked when he came around and hugged him"Going back home. My wife's due in a few weeks and I'm not wasting any of that time here with you"Nick nodded, he understood his brother's rush. He knew it was a miracle that he had left his wife to come talk to him."Go to New York. And no more drinking because if I have to haul myself down to Sicily or Florence or where ever you decide to stop next, I won't be this cordial" Luca told him and then kissed him on his head."I love you" he said and then turned to leave"I can't get to New York if I can't fly" Nick told him"I'll call the airline""And the hotels?" he asked"Luxury doesn't have any hotels in New York and that's where you are headed""And after that?""Come back home then we'll talk" Luca said and then began to walk away, he turned back abruptly,"And please pick up when our sister calls you, she's miserable"

# CHAPTER 20

S ammy sat with her legs folded staring at the cheque laying on the table, it had been laying there for six weeks untouched because she couldn't decide what to do about it.She obviously wasn't going to cash it but she also didn't think that sending it back was the better idea so she just left it there collecting dust on top of her centre table.It was now a habit, to sit and stare at it for an hour everyday. A habit she now couldn't break.Of course, there was obviously some misunderstanding or an accident because with the way the McCarthys felt about her when she was leaving Texas there was no way there were giving her anything let alone a check of half a million dollars.She got up and took the envelope, she walked to the waste basket and then tossed it inside and then walked back to the sofa and sat back down. Better to just get rid of the thing, right? There was no use waiting anymore, it had already been more than a month.She waited a minute, then two and by the next she got back up and went to fish out the envelope from the trash. She returned it to the undisturbed corner it had been sitting.She wasn't going to cash it but it felt good just looking at it, knowing it was there.

Good might be a bit of an overstatement because nothing felt good anymore, but it felt okay. It felt like she had a piece of Nick with her, which was mostly repulsive but other times soothing.Her hands absentmindedly rubbed her belly as she let the overwhelming sadness engulf her. This was a feeling she didn't know if she would ever escape, the sadness. It felt like it was going to swallow her whole. She had thought the pain she had felt back when Nick had dumped her had been excruciating, this was worse. Her heart most of the time felt like it had been ripped out of her chest and then replaced with one that wasn't working, one that could feel nothing but pain. She wanted to crawl into a ball and cry but she knew that Vicky was getting off work soon and then she'd be here with food Sammy didn't want or need and then only leave once she was satisfied that Sammy was okay or spend the night if she wasn't. Sammy hated it but it was their normal now, not because she was sick or invalid but because she was cursed. Her life was one big curse with no reprieve because no matter how far she ran, the bad things always caught up to her.

"WE ARE STILL wearing the sweatpants from yesterday I see" Vicky said setting the bags she came in with on Sammy's kitchen counter.Sammy sighed and then rolled over on the sofa so she'd face away. Vicky's eyes went to the well-made bed and she shook her head, the sofa now had this little depression because the girl barely got up from it."I bought groceries, I thought maybe we could cook together" Vicky told her friend, she knew her evening was going to be spent talking at Sammy, the girl would either ignore her all night or simply just give yes or no answers, which was somehow worse than her silence."You're right I'm exhausted, it's better if we order in" she went ahead to say without waiting for Sammy to reply."Or we could maybe go out and grab something to eat?" more silence followed. Vicky took a deep breath and told herself that this wasn't permanent, her friend would get better and things would go back to normal.She took off her jacket and then her shoes, work had been really exhausting but she didn't have the luxury of being exhausted at the moment because her friend was suffering.She came right around and turned on the TV filling the room with sound before going to grab the mail, nothing important just some utility bills. She put them in her purse, she'd offset them tomorrow if she got the chance."Have you had anything to eat today?" she asked Sammy going to confirm but the leftovers from last night that she had careful packaged was still sitting in the refrigerator so no, her friend hadn't had anything to eat all day. She took a deep breath in frustration, this wasn't working at all, it wasn't working."I can't do this anymore" she turned around and said to Sammy"Then maybe you should leave" Sammy replied from where she lay on the sofa.She could barely answer questions but she could offer suggestions, Vicky thought with a frown."And who's gonna take care of you, pay your bills, clean your apartment?" the list went on and on, but the time for the babying to be over. Vicky knew her friend was hurting but she obviously needed the tough love right now because her way was definitely not working and hasn't been for a long time."I didn't ask you to do any of that" Sammy replied"No you just lay there and say nothing, then you count the minutes till I leave so you can cry your eyes out" Vicky said all the empathy gone."you are hurting, I get that. But you can't just lay in here and waste your life away. You haven't even been outside this apartment since you got back""It's my life to waste"Vicky counted to ten to temper her anger and then said to her friend,"Get up" and as expected she was met with silence"I said get up Samantha" she said and then began to walk to where Sammy was laying stubbornly."Samantha get up" she was done allowing this"Leave me alone" Sammy managed to say"I have and that has only made this worse, so you will get up and go take a shower and then the both of us are going to go out for dinner" again the annoying silence followed"Samantha get up" she said and began to pull on her friend's leg"I said no!" in response Sammy used her other leg to kick her belly, hard.She groaned in pain, but it wasn't just reflex when she got up and gave her a well-deserved slap."I'm sorry, I'm sorry" she said almost immediately realising what she'd done, but Sammy was already out of the sofa and getting away from her"Just leave me alone" Sammy said her hand still placing a hand to the part of her face where she had been slapped."I can't do that," Vicky said her voice breaking,"you're hurting and that means I'm hurting, you're sad, I'm sad. You're stuck in this crappy apartment, then I'm stuck" she was crying now, weeks of frustration all flowing out with the tears"you are my best friend, my sister, so I can't. I can't just leave you" she sat down on the floor and rested her face on her knees and then she cried.Sammy felt sorry, she had never seen her friend fall apart like that and now it was happening because of her and that just made her feel so bad."I'm sorry" she said joining her friend on the floor."I didn't mean to kick you that hard"Vicky chuckled in between her crying, she raised her face to look at her friend,"I'm not crying cause you kicked me, you idiot. I'm crying because you're hurting and I don't know how to help you. And you won't tell me how to help you"Sammy rested Vicky's head on her shoulder and then took her hand in hers,"I don't know how you can help me. I don't even know how to help myself. I am always in pain and I can't describe it" she swallowed the bile that rose to her throat"Why won't you talk to me then?" Vicky asked and then she sniffled"Be cause... because..." she took a deep breath"because talking's hard. Breathing's hard, eating's hard, everything is so hard" she replied as the first drop of tears started to glide down her face."you believe me, right? You believe me when I say I don't know what happened? I didn't do it" she asked"Of course I do" Vicky lifted her face and looked at her in the eyes, her heart was breaking for her friend"Nick didn't" now Sammy was sobbing now,"he said I am disgusting and he never wants to see me again in his life. He hates me"Vicky cradled her friend,"I hate that you're in pain, I hate that all that happened to you and I hate, hate that I wasn't there with you. But I'm here now, and I'm going to help you get through this if you let me, because I love you. Do you love me Sam?""Of course I do" Sammy replied with a sniffle"Then let me help you. That means no more icing me out, no more not eating, no more locking yourself in here all the time. Will you let me?" Vicky asked"Do you really think I can get through this?" she asked"Of course you can and you will. Do you know why?"

Vicky asked and then she shook her head"because you are the strongest person I know, you're the nicest and you're the most honest. You have survived things most people can't even begin to imagine""Now you're just being nice""I'm being honest. Because that's the truth. And if those people can't see it, if Nick can't see that, then it's his loss trust me" Vicky told her and then hugged her tightly.

SAMMY STEPPED OUT of the shower, showering felt good, it was one of the things she had missed enjoying. She wrapped a towel around her body and headed to the kitchen. She was going to eat, but only because she had promised Vicky she would and then after eating she was going to go for a walk, another thing she had missed enjoying was the fresh air. She had gone for a walk yesterday and the day before and she had always come home feeling like a different person.She quickly made a sandwich and then took a generous bite, eating still wasn't as much pleasant but she promised Vicky she'd try to get better and that meant she was going to stop avoiding eating. Her appetite was going to come back soon, she was sure but until then she was going to eat just to get healthy.She abandoned the rest of the sandwich on the kitchen counter and then headed to go and get dressed. She chose the orange sweat suit for no other reason but that it was comfortable, she got dressed, went back to her sandwich and took another generous bite and then decided she was done. She was going to leave the half-eaten sandwich there on the kitchen counter so when Vicky came later in the day, she was going to be super proud. Not that the sandwich was half eaten, but because she had even eaten at all.

An hour later Sammy was walking back to her apartment, the street managed to somehow be busier than it had been when she walked the route earlier. She stopped for a moment to watch a group of street performers but when the crowd started to grow, she went on her way. She stopped again and bought a cup of coffee from a cart a block from her apartment, she gave directions to a lady who looked like she was a tourist and helped a newspaper vendor pick up some of his papers that some trouble causing kids had knocked down and smiled when he offered her his thanks. She was feeling more like her old self again and that was partly being out in the city. But then she decided it was time to head back home and go back to looking up job vacancies, she wasn't going to let Vicky pay for life anymore.She was almost in front of her apartment building when she spotted him and her heart leapt out of her chest. She froze as she watched him just standing there looking rather contemplative.He had grown a beard, which somehow made him look even more handsome. He wore that stupid scowl he always wore as he stood looking at something on his phone but that was beside the point, what was Niklaus McCarthy doing here? Sammy wondered as she contemplated her next move.Every instinct in her told her to run but Sammy realised her legs wouldn't carry her since she could barely feel them anymoreShe was just deciding that turning back around was best, maybe she could hide before... he raised his face and their eyes locked. Turning back was not an option anymore she decided to face it head on, he was the one who had come to her home after all.Maybe she should call Vicky? No doubt the girl was going to drop everything and rush to her rescue, but she wasn't going to do that. If Nick had come all the way from Texas to New York just to give her more grief over what had happened then it was best they got it over with. Vicky didn't need to be here to witness whatever awful thing he had to say and hopeful once he said it, she'd never have to see him again.

NICK STOOD STARING, he could recognise the panic on her face as she stood staring at him. He didn't know how long she had been standing there but she looked like she was contemplating fleeing and he couldn't even blame her because he knew that he obviously wasn't someone she'd ever want to see again.She didn't move and neither did he but none of them looked away. He was going to move to her eventually but he just wanted to take in the sight of her some more. He had missed her so much, more than he even knew.She had lost weight, her hair was grown out, it was still short but not as short as it had been but she was still as beautiful as ever.He watched as she began to bite the corner of her lower lip and then decided it was time to make the first move, he waved. She did nothing but frown and then she began to walk towards him."Hi" he said, before she even reached him. She still said nothing which somehow made him more anxious than he already was.Just when he thought she was going to walk past him and head up to her apartment, she stopped"Hi" he said again even though he was sure she heard him the first time. She nodded slightly and folded her hands in a way that showed she didn't know what to do with it."How are you doing?" he asked again she nodded again. She was being cold in a way that worried him and he wondered if she was doing it on purpose.He cleared his throat, nervously, it was hard to talk to someone when they weren't talking back.He tried again,"Can we talk? Maybe somewhere more private?" he asked and she said nothing for the longest time and just when he was deciding she was going to refuse she again nodded and then began walking to her apartment building, he followed.

Sammy leading Nick back into her apartment was the funniest thing to happen to her in a long time. If someone had told her that this was the direction her day was going when she woke up this morning, she would have surely laughed.Somewhere more private, he had said but Sammy knew that what he meant was somewhere people wouldn't hear whatever awful thing he was going to say to her.They were almost at her apartment when she realised what he had come for, he had come to take back his father's cheque. How many times had she thought of tearing the damned thing in half? Now she was so grateful she didn't because knowing him, he'd probably think she wanted to steal from them. Is that not why he had come all the way here himself when he could simply have sent one of his employees.She let him into her apartment and then regretted that she hadn't done more cleaning today or even arranged at all. The duvet and pillow she had used to sleep on the sofa last night still lay there so she went ahead and picked them up, she gestured for him to sit before taking them to the bed. She regretted that the half-eaten sandwich she had left out to get some accolades from Vicky now made the room look unkempt. She went around and then tossed it into the trash while he sat patiently and waited. She could feel his eyes on her but she took her sweet time only because she was practicing her breathing exercise. This was really happening, Nick was in her apartment, she thought as she went back to face him.She picked up the envelope that was on the table in front of him,"I'm sorry I was going to send it back but I was a little busy" battling depression. Totally a lie though, she wasn't planning on sending it back. She didn't intend to cash it either but she didn't plan to send it back."What?" he asked sounding a bit confused"Your father's cheque. Isn't that why you are here?""Oh no. My father wanted you to have that" he told her which was a total shock to her."Why?" she asked. The last time she had seen these people, they could barely stand her, blaming her for the miscarriage and now their father wanted her to have such a huge amount of money?"Could you maybe sit down?" he asked and Sammy looked around her apartment, the only sitting arrangement in her apart-ment was the sofa he was sitting on and although there was space enough for the two of them she wasn't sure she was ready to be that close to him."I'm good" she told him and then feigned a smile. Whatever he wanted to tell her she could take it standing.He ran his hand through his hair and then took a deep breath, whatever it was he was trying to say Sammy could see he was struggling with it so she folded her hands and she waited."Jason did something," he began"he was the one who drugged you with the drug that killed your baby" he watched as all the colour drained from her face, she stumbled and then lowered herself down to sit on the tabl e."What?" she asked in a whisper, she looked confused"That can't be true," she said with a shake of her head. Her head was spinning and she felt like she was in some sort of dream.Jason was fine, he had come to terms with the pregnancy and he was accepting her. He had wanted to marry her sooner rather than later, he wanted a family with her."that can't be true" she repeated again even though she was coming to the realisation that it was. She needed to throw up.Why would Jason want someone like her when he could easily drug her and get rid of her. He had made her breakfast that morning, she realised. But she had been there the whole time and she didn't see him put any drug in it."Did you know?" she asked Nick, he had said all those awful things to her when he'd known what his brother had done to her. They were probably all laughing behind her back and congratulating him for getting rid of the gold digger in their midst."No. I didn't. We just only found out after you left" he said"When exactly?""About a week after it happened" he told her."So months ago," while she had been here suffering, hurting, blaming herself over something that wasn't even her fault they were just sitting on the truth."and you're just telling me now. Is that why your father sent the cheque? Because his son killed my child?" she asked and he said nothing.This had to be some cruel joke. Or maybe a prank."And you? Why are you here?" why did it have to be him that was bring her this news"I came to apologise" he told her.She laughed, in a dry and humourless way."For what exactly? For your brother killing my child or for you blaming it on me""I'm sorry and I wish I could take it back" he told her"But you can't" she told him"Please leave, I want to be alone" she said turning away from him, she knew she was seconds away from having a breakdown and she didn't want him to be here to see it."Samantha I want to be here for you" he said and she scoffed"Why?" he hadn't been there when she needed him the most, when her life had fallen apart. so why now?"Because I love you" he said it just like that, like that wasn't the most important sentence ever. Like he was talking about something else that wasn't as personal.She frowned as she turned back around to look at him, this was unbelievable. How dare he say that to her? Right at this moment? Sammy could feel the anger growing.If he had said it to her back in Texas when she had been on the hospital bed wishing for him to hold her or their weekend together when she had almost been sure she felt it back then maybe she wouldn't be in so much pain hearing this now.

"Did you love me? Back in Texas when I told you I didn't do this? Did you?" she asked, he didn't say anything for like ten seconds, like he was thinking about it. And then he nodded,"Yes, I think I did""And you couldn't trust me or even give me the benefit of doubt?""I'm sorry" he said againshe then looked him in the eyes,"So trust me when I say this because I mean it from the bottom of my heart. I hate you Niklaus McCarthy. I hate you with every fibre of my being. I hate you more than I thought it was possible to hate another human being and I never want to see you again in my life" she told him and as he sat frozen there on her sofa she got up and went ahead to open the door and motion for him to leave. This chapter of her life was over.

# CHAPTER 21

♥

"So you're just gonna come back home?" it was Luca who asked"I'm going to Milan, dad's renovation project still needs supervision" Nick replied, he hadn't spoken to his dad since he left Texas, he wasn't even sure he was still had employment with Luxury, Richard could've maybe decided to punish him with that. But in all honesty that didn't matter to him anymore."I told you he was going to chicken out" Charlie told her husband and Nick frowned into the computer screen where Charlie was lying on her back with a bowl of grapes resting on her now gigantic belly and Luca was sitting rubbing her feet."I'm not chickening out" maybe calling them was a bad idea after all."Yes you are, you are running away" she said as casually tossed a grape into her mouth."I am not. You said to tell her how I feel and I did and she told me she never wanted to see me again, so I'm leaving" his heart still felt like it was still being stomped on hours later."I did tell you he was a coward now" Luca told his wife and she laughed. They were obviously just goading him, it wasn't hard to see that. He should have just slapped the laptop shut and be done with them but he honestly needed to talk about it even if that meant they were going to rag on him.“She said she hates me” it felt just as awful to say as it had been to hear.“what am I supposed to do with that?” he asked feeling defeated.“She doesn’t hate you” Charlie told Nick and then to her husband,“help me sit up” she wanted to get closer to the tablet so she could see Nick’s face better“You don’t know that” Nick told her“I know Samantha. She might be angry right now but there’s no way that girl hates you”“do my back next” she told Luca who was now done with her feet.“She seemed different, not just because of the hair. She was cold and distant, it was horrible”“What happened to her hair?” Charlie asked“It was grown out, it looked nice”“Are you smiling?” it was Luca that asked“Fuck you!” he replied. Had he really smiled?“So, what are you planning to do now?” Charlie asked“I already told you, I’m going back to Europe. I’m gonna start working again”“You’re not giving up” Charlie told him stubbornly.“What would you rather I did? Force her to be with me? I hurt her and now she hates me”“If you leave New York right now you are going to regret it for the rest of your life. Not fighting for what you want is simply just losing” Luca told him.Nick sighed,“Then what should I do?” he needed someone to tell him what to do and that was why he had called the only two people in the world who could.“She’s hurting and quite frankly it was stupid of you to tell her you loved her the same time you told her what Jason did” Luca told him“It just happened, I didn’t plan it. Just like I didn’t plan to feel this way about her”“Love is the easiest thing in the world when it happens by accident, Nicky. But it doesn’t get real until you do it on purpose. So, fix it”“How?”

he hated that he sounded desperate."By showing and not telling. Show her how much she means to you instead of just saying it and expecting she'd understand""Okay we have to go now, I think I'm in labour" Charlie told them"What?! You're in labour?" Nick asked he could feel himself already starting to panic so he wondered how his brother was feeling. But Luca was as calm as ever."No, she not" Luca said, he rolled his eyes and Charlie smiled, mischievously."she's been lying about it all week. Almost shit my pants the first time she said it" he narrowed his eyes at her and shook his head at her. She kissed him, which earned her a smile from him even though he tried hard not to."We really do have to go, I gotta pee" she said and then hung up before Nick could say anything else.

The moment Vicky stepped into Sammy's apartment she knew something was off. Even before she began to hear her friend sobbing from the sofa, she could already tell that the everything was off. The good news on her lips died as well as the smile she wore."Sam?" she called softly coming to her side. She really thought that the days of finding her friend like this was over."Sammy?" she called again kneeling down next to the sofa. Sammy raised her face, she sniffled."What's wrong honey?" Vicky asked"He came here" she said.Well that was vague,"Who sweety? Who came here?" she asked mentally preparing herself for battle, if someone had come here and hurt her friend then..."Nick""Nick McCarthy?" What the hell?! "Yes""Oh I swear to God, if he said anything to hurt you then I'm...""Jason did it. He killed my baby"wow. That was unexpected news."What?""Nick told me. He said they found out months ago""What a minute, are you saying Jason drugged you?" this was so hard to comprehend, hadn't Jason been the nice one?"He pretended to be my friend so he could get close to me and force me to have an abortion, Vicky I don't know how I'm gonna get over this" Sammy said and then she put her face into the arm of the chair and began to sob again.Vicky rubbed her friend's back, she shocked speechless but she knew her friend needed some encouraging words right now, she wanted to give them to her but nothing came to her head."You are gonna get over this" Vicky said as she rubbed Sammy's back"How Vicky?" Sammy raised her face to ask, she genuinely needed an answer to that question"I feel like someone reached into my chest to rip my heart out but they kept it so they can stomp on it every few minutes." She sniffled,"not someone. Nick" it was breaking Vicky's heart to watch her friend like this and not be able to do anything about it."Come here" Vicky said coming to sit on the sofa so Sammy rested her head on her laps, she stroked her hair softly."You are going to more than recover from this, you are going to thrive" she whispered. Sammy closed her eyes as she enjoyed the hands combing through her hair and the very much needed soft words that accompanied it. She wanted to believe Vicky, she badly did but she couldn't because deep down she knew there was no coming out of this for her, no recovering. Niklaus McCarthy had ruined her forever.How was it that in all of this she still couldn't get the strength to be mad at Jason but somehow hated Nick with every fibre of her being?"I hate him so much" she muttered and sniffled again"I know, baby" Vicky replied as she kept stroking her hair softly. She wasn't sure her friend meant what she was saying but

Sammy needed to hate right now and so she was going to let her."He said he loves me" Sammy said and then scoffed, the hand that had been stroking her hair paused,"What?""When he came over, he said he loves me""Wow" Vicky said because she her brain couldn't process that information fast enough. If Nick McCarthy loved Sammy then that was... what was it? Vicky couldn't tell if it was good news or bad news but it was certainly new."And the cheque, it wasn't a mistake. It's compensation for what Jason did""Oh" could we please go back to the part about Nick being in love with you?Not that she would ever bring it up again until Sammy stopped feeling like the world was upside down, but she really, really wanted to know everything."I'm not going to take their money. I don't want anything from them, I don't need it" Sammy said stubbornly.She reached for the cheque where it sat on the table, she didn't think twice about it before tearing it in half. This was the last thing binding her to the McCarthys and now that was over.Vicky was totally going to agree with her friend but maybe saying she didn't need their money was a bit of an overstatement. The girl didn't have any job or any money and she would have probably been kicked out of this apartment if Vicky didn't step up to handle her bills.Which reminded Vicky why she had been so excited coming here today, she didn't know if now was the right moment to bring it up but Sammy wasn't crying anymore and a change of topic might do her some good,"Momma said you could come work at the diner until you find something better""Really?" she asked and sniffled,"Yeah. She also said we could come for dinner tonight but don't worry about it, we can reschedule" Vicky told her and she nodded. Sammy didn't honestly think she had it in her to go anywhere tonight even if it was dinner with Vicky's lovely family."I miss your mom" Sammy told her with a sigh. The woman was an angel, she hadn't hesitated to take Sammy in after her mom had passed. And she was nice and kind to Sammy even till now."I miss her too. I haven't had time to visit home in weeks""Because you've been taking care of me" Sammy said sadly. She felt guilty that she had robbed Vicky of her life by robbing herself of her life. And at the end of the day it hadn't even been worth it. Nick hadn't even been worth it."Yes, because I've been taking care of you. But that's okay cause you take care of me all the time. Have you had something to eat?""Yes I made a sandwich and everything" Sammy said and then looking over to the kitchen counter to show her before she remembered she had tossed it in the trash"You did?" Vicky asked in excitement, a sandwich wasn't a big deal but the fact that her friend whom she had practically been force feeding the past couple of months made something to eat without having to be told, filled her with pride."Yes" Sammy said and smiled which warmed Vicky's heart, no matter what had happened today with Nick she was sure that her friend would be alright."I'm super proud of you" she said and then gave Sammy a peck on the forehead. "I knew you would be"

SLEEP WAS NOW elusive and Nick couldn't blame it on his aching shoulders anymore. It was all her, it was all Samantha. How could he sleep when he was in the same city with her but still couldn't see her? When he was now a single-minded man with only the thought of her in his head.She had now made it her life's mission to haunt his dreams, when he managed to find the strength to sleep which was rarely, she was always there with her smiles... and sometimes frowns. There was no avoiding it and even if there were Nick wasn't sure he wanted to. Not when the only time he was actually at peace was in the midst of the turmoil of her invading his dreams, and even though most times he would awaken with an aching and longing heart Nick knew this was better than nothing at all.The despair was threatening to tear him apart, it was a feeling he didn't know how to handle, well that was the case with everything about Samantha, he never knew how to handle it. It was too bad he had promised Luca he wouldn't drink because he so much wanted to take the edge off. She didn't want him, more than that she hated him, how was he supposed to handle that? How was he supposed to handle the gut wrenching feeling every time he thought about her words? Which was basically every time.Nick was glad when his phone rang, it was a welcoming distraction and it also meant PJ had news for him. News about Samantha obviously.

It was a busy morning, Sammy thought as she counted the money in her hand, the tips were better than yesterday but that also meant she had to smile more today. Mrs. Taylor, Vicky's mom smiled at her and waved, Sammy smiled back. Was she seriously going to do that every time their eyes met? Sammy wondered as she headed back to the register. Sammy knew she was just keeping an eye on her because Vicky asked her to, they were both probably waiting for her to have a breakdown. She knew this because Vicky had come during her lunch yesterday just to help her clean tables and serve coffee, the girl hated the place so it was a miracle she did. She wished Vicky would stop worrying, but she knew it would take more than her coming to work to convince her friend she was alright.Mrs. Taylor waved her over to the kitchen where she was instructing the kitchen staff, Sammy stood and waited for her to finish.When people said spitting image, Vicky and her mom always came to Sammy's mind because the mother and daughter were a perfect example. The mother and daughter had practically the same face, just that one was now covered in wrinkles and had aged gracefully. They even made the same hand gestures when they spoke, Sammy observed while she watched the older woman pass information to her staff. Vicky was a lot taller than her mother, that she got from her father but everything else she got from woman."Is everything going okay?" Mrs. Taylor asked when she was done giving out instructions. Wrapping a hand around Sammy's shoulder she began to lead her out.See, worry. The woman had literally just seen her serving customers and getting paid but she still needed verbal confirmation that she was okay. Fuck you Vicky."Yes, everything's great" Sammy replied with a smile even though she wanted to roll her eyes."That's great" Mrs. Taylor said"so I was thinking, I know Vicky's coming here for lunch but you could maybe take a break now if you wanted, cause I see you're working really hard"Sammy did roll her eyes now, but she did it subtly so Mrs. Taylor won't see. It was the tone she was taking, like she was speaking to a child that disgusted Sammy more. 'Cos, I see you're working really hard?' what did that even mean? The other waitresses were working a lot harder but no one was speaking to them about taking early breaks."I'm fine Mrs. T" she said"Okay, okay" Mrs Taylor said with a nod and a smile,"I'm going to step out now but I've spoken with Fred, you can take a break at any time you wish and as many times as you want""Thanks Mrs. T, but there's no need for that" absolutely no need. She had come here to work and not to get pampered."I'm sure there's not but Vicky would kill me if I over work you""Okay, thank you" she replied just so the older woman would stop, she didn't intend to take advantage of their generosity. She was going to have a talk with Vicky about this later, but for now she was going to get back to work because just then a group of teenage girls came in noisily.

"There's a customer for you" the other prettier waitress came to tell Sammy as she stood waiting for the order she had just put in. Sammy couldn't quite remember her name so she settled to never call her by her name ever. it felt horrible because the girl had been really nice to her."I'll be right there" Sammy told her and then watched as the girl walked back.Sammy sighed tiredly, it had been a long morning, her feet were killing her, her back was hurting and though she had been tempted once or twice to take up Mrs. Taylor's offer she held steadfast. Her actual break was in less than half an hour and then she'd rest without feeling guilty about it before coming back for the lunch rush.She marched in with a tray in hand, she was glad there were only a few customers left at the diner. She looked over to her section and sighed tiredly again before plastering a smile she hated on her face. The couple stopped talking while she placed their order and asked them to call her if they needed anything else. And then there was the other gentleman sitting at the corner, waiting. She thought about giving him a minute to go over the menu before going to take his order, she hated when costumers made her wait because they were undecided. The worst was when they asked for her opinion, order whatever you want and leave sir/ma, I don't have the energy to pretend I care what you eat or if you like it or not.She decided not to wait, if he wanted a suggestion, she as usual would recommend the day's special even though she didn't know what it was today.He was looking out the window when she came to him, she was too tired to notice anything except how he was impatiently tapping on the table. "Good afternoon sir, welcome to Jessy's. I'm here to take…" she began to say and then he turned to face her and she startled. She frowned,"Nick?" she called quietly, she swallowed. He was the last person she had expected to see here today."What… what are you… what are you doing here?" she stammered.The last time she had seen him was a week ago and she'd explicitly told him that she never wanted to see him again, she had thought he'd have been long gone back to Texas or maybe Europe, so for her to see him here in Vicky's mother's diner was a bit unnerving."Can we talk?" he asked."I'm working" Sammy said trying hard not to fiddle with the notepad in her hand.

How dare he come here? To her place of work. Hasn't he and his family humiliated her enough?Without anyone telling her Sammy knew she looked like shit, it wasn't about the customary blue striped white short dress she had to wear for the job. Maybe it was a little bit about that too but that was just one of the reasons. She felt and looked exhausted because even though she was lying to Vicky about getting a solid five hours, Sammy was barely sleeping at nights, mostly because the sofa wasn't as comfortable as she'd hoped. She was sure there were bags under her eyes at the moment not that she had bothered to check. She hadn't had the time or the energy to visit a proper salon so her hair was a bit overgrown and it looked unkempt. She did brush it before coming into work today but that had been hours ago. Sammy took a moment to look at him, he wore a dark blue turtle neck sweater with a pair of jeans. He was looking good as always and she decided she hated him more for it."I know" he said.He knew"Okay then, can I take your order?" she asked trying to sound as professional as she could giving the circ umstances."I didn't come here to eat" he told her.Of course he didn't, people like him didn't eat in places like this."Then I can't help you" she replied and then turned to leave. She needed to be away from him as fast as possible."Samantha" he called. It was the desperation in his voice that made her stop and nothing else.She slowly turned around to face him. It wasn't just his voice that sounded desperate, it was the look in his eyes too. He looked... scared."Please" he said in a whisper-like tone.Sammy took a deep contemplative breath, she knew that whatever he wanted to say to her would leave her feeling worse than she was already feeling, it was Nick after all."Fine. Give me a minute" she said and left him sitting there.

Sammy went to meet Fred she hated that Nick was making her take up Mrs. Taylor's offer to go on a break she didn't need. Fred was very much obliging, which only made Sammy feel worse.She needed to prepare herself physically and mentally for the conversation ahead, knowing Nick it wasn't going to be an easy one.She ran to the dressing room and borrowed a hairbrush from one of the lockers, she didn't change into her regular clothes but she lost the apron. She hated that she was tempted to put on lipstick, she wasn't going to do that especially for an unappreciative jerk like Nick. She did brush her hair, hating how lengthy it was now. It wasn't really that lengthy but it wasn't as short as she'd have liked either. She liked wearing her hair short, it suited her well, at least better than it was now.

When she came out, he was staring out the window, the sight of him suddenly made her feel nervous which was stupid. This was Nick, the man that had made feel more horrible than losing a child did, the man she hated most in the world right now, there was nothing to feel nervous about. Except he was the same man that had told her he loved her merely days ago, the fact that she knew that wasn't true didn't change the nerves that attacked every time she thought of it.She walked slowly to his table, like a cow heading for the slaughter. He didn't look at her until she sat on the seat opposite of him,"Hi" he said and then cleared his throat. Sammy said nothing, she just waited for whatever had brought him here."How are you doing?" a basic question that nobody really ever cares for an answer to."Considering that your brother killed my child and blamed it on me, I'm great. Anything else?" she didn't mean for it to come out as harshly as it did but she was glad it did. Nick only knew her as the pregnant, weak and pathetic girl that had showed up to his home. Now she was no longer pregnant and she didn't want to feel weak anymore.Anger was a good substitute. It didn't let her remember the things she liked about him or the things she had felt for him. Nick cringed, that obviously wasn't the answer he had been expecting."I'm sorry" he said"You've said that before" she told him. He nodded, in a way that showed he was thinking about what to say"Nick what are you doing here? What do you want?" she asked impatiently"I miss you" he looked her right in the eyes and said.Those words however little they were Sammy found out, had the ability to immobilize her. This wasn't what he was supposed to say, he should have said something that would piss her off and make her more upset than she already was but instead he found a way to sound so sincere when he said that."I miss you so much it's driving me insane" she remembered using those exact words with him, feeling that exact way. "Nick please stop" she begged him hating that the more he spoke, the more he unarmed her with his words"Why?" he asked as if he didn't know"Because you don't mean it""Why do you say that?" "Because I believed the lies your brother told and that cost me everything, because your brother sat me down and told me things he didn't mean while planning to take my child from me" she aggressively wiped the tears that had refused to listen and stay in her eyes. It was too early in the conversation to start crying."I have nothing left for you to take Nick, so please just stop" she told him."I'm not lying to you. I never have and never will. I love you Samantha""That's not true" the tears just wouldn't stop coming, for reasons that were unexplainable to her she had become that pathetic girl again. She hated having him watching her while she cried so she tried her best to suppress the tears."It is"Sammy scratched her head in frustration, why was he doing this? She was out of his life, the baby was gone, what else did he want?

"You said you loved me back in Texas, yes?" she asked and he nodded slowly."I know for a fact that that's a lie. Nick if you'd loved me then, you wouldn't have said those things to me. You wouldn't have left me alone in that awful place at a time when I needed you the most, you would have trusted my word because ever since we met I have never given you a reason to doubt it""I'm sorry" he whispered"Can you please, stop saying that!" she half yelled and then regretted it immediately once she saw she had attracted some of the other customer's attention.She took a deep breath, a futile attempt to calm herself,"You love me and you knew what your brother did to me for months and you kept it from me. I lay crying and blaming myself for months and you never showed up. You don't love me Niklaus, love doesn't work that way""I should have come, the minute I found out what Jason had done I should have rushed down here to tell you but I didn't think you'd want to see me""I don't. I just want you to leave me in peace, I want to pick my life up and you constantly being here isn't helping" she told him"I can't do that. It is physically impossible for me leave you""You did it once, I'm sure you can figure out a way to do again"how he managed to look so hurt when he was the one that had hurt her was beyond Sammy."How can I fix this? How do I fix it? Just tell me what to do and I promise I'll do it"Sammy shook her head, wasn't he even hearing her? Hadn't he been listening?"I just want you to leave me alone""I can't do that Samantha" he told her for the second time, with a sad smile on his face and a shrug. "Nick I don't…" she was interrupted when her phone rang. She could already guess who was calling when she reached for it in her dress pocket, Vicky. She was probably already on her way over here, or worse she was already here. Sammy didn't want Vicky coming to find Nick in her mother's diner. Knowing her friend she was going to have some things to say to him and Sammy just didn't want that."Hi" Sammy greeted with the warmest voice she could muster at the moment. She didn't want Vicky knowing she had been crying merely moments ago."My mom just had a heart attack. We are at the hospital" Vicky said hysterically from the other end of the line."What?!" Sammy asked startled. She had just been with Mrs. Taylor a few hours ago and she had been okay, she had even been cheerful and didn't look like someone who was going to have a heart attack."What's wrong?" Nick asked from where he sat"Can you come?" Vicky asked"Of course I'm already on my way" she told her and then took down the name of the hospital Vicky and Mrs Taylor were."What happened?" Nick asked when she got off the phone.Sammy sighed,"Vicky's mum's in the hospital, I have to go" she told him already getting out of the chair."Do we know why?" he asked her getting out of his chair too."Vicky says she had a heart attack. Nick I really have to go, Vicky needs me right now""I'll go with you" he offered"You don't have to do that" she told him."I have a driver outside, he could take us" a tempting offer Sammy really wanted to refuse, but she was almost desperate enough to agree"That's not necessary, I can find my own way" she said instead even though she wanted to say yes."I know you can but please lemme help you"She took a deep contemplative breath before nodding her affirmation, there was no use pretending like she really couldn't use a ride right now. Plus, she didn't want to imagine Vicky alone in the waiting room of the hospital while she headed to the subway.

# CHAPTER 22

As usual the hospital was a depressing place that Sammy didn't want to be in, it didn't help that the first sight that assaulted her was a man carrying his infant boy crying that his child was dying. It was really sad to watch.The hospital was were horrible things happened and Sammy didn't think she'd be back in one so soon.They found Vicky, she was speaking to a nurse when they saw her, aggressively. Her hand gestures were scaring Sammy from feet away so she wondered what the cowering nurse was feeling."Ther e she is" she pointed and told Nick.She didn't understand why he had insisted on coming in with her, she would have simply been content thanking him for the ride and coming in alone to be with her friend. Now she was going to have to explain his presence here while Vicky was still worrying over her mom."Vicky!" she called and then waved when Vicky turned to look at her. She watched as the nurse used the distraction to sneak away."Could you wait here a minute?" she asked Nick, he nodded and then she began to walk to Vicky.She embraced her friend, to offer comfort but she was met with a distracted hug in return. Vicky gently pushed her away,"Is that him?" Vicky asked, she nodded. She could already see the daggers coming from Vicky's gaze."What is he doing here?" she asked, she still wouldn't take her eyes off him.Sammy scratched her head,"He was at the diner when you called. How's your mom?" she tried to change the subject"They wouldn't tell me anything, the dumb nurse over here doesn't know anything" Vicky said and for the first time noticing that the poor girl she had been emotionally terrorizing was gone.She shook her head,"why was he at the diner?" she asked"Could you please stop staring at him, he'll know we're talking about him" Sammy told her"I don't care if he knows, why was he at the diner?" she asked again"I don't know, he wanted to talk I guess""You guess? Fine, I'll talk to him then" she said and then started to walk,"Vicky" Sammy called bodily blocking her,"What? You said he wanted to talk, right?""I'm begging you"Vicky frowned and then huffed loudly, she folded her arms and then looked at her friend,"I just want to ask him nicely to leave you alone" she said.Sammy shook her head, the girl had no clue what asking nicely meant"He was kind enough to bring me here in his car, please don't embarrass him or me" she whispered"Fine" Vicky replied with a pout."I'm gonna go find out about my mom" she said before walking away.Sammy returned to where Nick was standing, waiting,"That's the best friend?" he asked and she nodded,"She seemed angry""She's just worried about her mom" she told him.He nodded,"I guess so but I mean she kept staring at me, I thought she was about to come beat me up"Sammy chuckled awkwardly and then shook her head,"She just went to find out about her mom""Okay" he told her with a nod.They fell into an uncomfortable silence waiting,"Thanks for the ride but you don't have to stay" Sammy told him after a few minutes of awkwardly saying nothing to each other."I want to stay, I want to be here for you"Please stop saying things like that.He was weakening her resolve to hate him and he obviously knew that, Sammy thought."Okay then, let's find somewhere to sit"

THERE WAS SOMETHING about a hospital bed that just made people look frail and week, Sammy observed when they were finally allowed to enter to see Mrs. Taylor. She was asleep when Sammy and Vicky came in but she woke up almost immediately, she smiled once she saw them."My girls" she called and they both went to either sides of the bed to embrace her."Mum, a heart attack? Seriously?" Vicky leapt immediately."I keep saying you should take it easy, let Fred earn his salary as the manager and you take a step back, but you never listen. What is wrong with you?"Sammy looked at her friend in disbelief, the woman still wasn't out of the woods yet and she was already getting a lecture."Vicky" Sammy called her friend and then shook her head when she looked.Vicky took a deep breath,"I was so worried about you, mom" she told her mom and then hugged her again."I know, my love. I'm sorry" Mrs. Taylor told her daughter. She knew her daughter had just spoken from a place of fear and nothing more and she hated that she had given her cause to worry ."What happened?" Vicky askedSammy watched Mrs. Taylor take a deep breath and then struggle with whatever it was she wanted to say."Your father happened. He mortgaged the diner to fuel his gambling habit and now we are almost seven hundred thousand dollars in debt""What?!" Vicky and Sammy asked simultaneously."I didn't know until this morning, he's been taking out money for years. Now the bank is threatening to take the diner" Mrs. Taylor told them bitterly."I'm going to kill him" Vicky said immediately. "Killing him won't pay the bank" her mom told her with a sigh, taking her hand."I'm so sorry Mrs. T" Sammy said."The diner has been in my family for almost fifty years and now I might lose it because I got married to an idiot""How long do we have mom?" Vicky asked"Not long enough, two weeks"Not long at all."How are we expected to come up with seven hundred thousand dollars in two weeks?" Vicky heaved"I don't know"This was just crazy, how could someone gamble seven hundred thousand dollars away? And Mr Taylor? Sammy wasn't as close to him as she was with his wife but he didn't seem like someone that would do this sort of thing and even if he had before Vicky never mentioned.

The ride back to Sammy's apartment was a lot less awkward than the one to the hospital had been but still awkward none the less.The doctor had said Mrs. Taylor had to stay to be observed overnight and Vicky had decided she was going to stay with her mom while Sammy went home to get some rest. Not that she needed any rest. She definitely wasn't going to get any rest with Mrs. T in the hospital like that.She was surprised when she came out to the waiting room to find that Nick had still been waiting. She had almost forgotten about him.It had been a nice surprise to find him sitting in the same exact spot she had left him hours later. And he smiled when he saw her, not a kind of 'I'm relieved to see you' smile but like an 'I'm genuinely happy to see you' one, it felt weirdly nice and comforting.

"Thank you for today, thanks for driving me and thanks for waiting" she told him when the car parked in front of her apartment building."Is your friend's mom going to be okay?" he asked"I don't know. The doctors think she might be able to go home tomorrow but she's about to lose the diner and I don't know what that will do to her" it was weird, she was talking about Vicky's mom not because she wanted him to have all the information but because it was Nick, she could try to deny it all she wanted but she liked talking to him. How could she not, he was being all nice an attentive and she was a bit reluctant to leave the car because she knew that once she got out of the car things would really be over, she would probably never see him again and she tried to remind herself that that was what she had wanted."I'm sorry to hear that" he told her. Sammy nodded,"Me too" she said and they fell back into the silence."I'm gonna head upstairs now" she told him after a while, it felt slightly awful that she wanted him to ask her to stay a little longer. If this was the last time they were going to see each other, wasn't it reasonable that they spent a little while longer together?"Your friend doesn't like me very much" he told her instead,"Who Vicky? Why do you say that?""I don't know, maybe because of the whole passive aggressive thing she had going on"Sammy faked a chuckle, it didn't even sound right,"What? Vicky? No, she wasn't being passive aggressive, she was just really worried about her mom" Lie."Okay, if you say so" he told her in a way that felt like he didn't exactly believe her.They sat in silence for a while before Sammy began to realise she was getting too comfortable around him and that wasn't what she wanted or needed,"I'm going to head upstairs now" she told him and hated that the look of disappointment on his face made her feel sorry."Okay," he said and then nodded,"I'm still in the city so we could maybe...""I'll be too busy helping Vicky out with her mom, plus we still have to figure out a way to save the diner so I don't think that's possible" it was best not to see him again. For his sake as well as hers.He nodded gently."Goodbye Nick" she told him with a sad smile on her face.

LUCA HAD SAID to show her and not tell, which in all honesty scared the crap out of Nick. He wasn't the hearts and flowers kinda guy and every time he thought about it, he felt sick to his stomach but he felt sicker at the thought of losing Samantha forever.She seemed different, like something had changed, maybe it was about losing the baby but being with her still felt the same. It still felt good.He rolled over in the gigantic bed that felt empty, the darkness of the room was soothing but not soothing enough to help him fall asleep. Of course, he had set himself up when he had decided to stay in the same room he had stayed with Samantha, she was everywhere and nowhere all at the same time. He would have hit the bottle but he had already promised Luca he wouldn't do that plus drinking wouldn't help him come up with a plan to win Samantha back. Nick cringed, win Samantha back, it sounded corny in a way that just wasn't him.But he was going to have to get corny if he wanted things to work out. He felt her thaw today, not completely though but enough for the hatred she had in her eyes whenever she looked at him to fade, enough for her to let him spend the day with her, so all that was left to do now was to convince her he wasn't lying when he said he loved her. He had been so worried about her not feeling it back that he didn't even consider the possibility of her not believing his feelings for her. Another thing that Jason had ruined for him. He tried not to think about his brother, thinking about him came with feelings of rage and anger and he didn't need those right now.So instead he sat up on the bed and reached for his phone, he needed to find out what was going on with the diner situation before deciding what to do next. But there was no scenario where he was leaving New York with things unsettled with Samantha.

THE LONG NIGHT gave way to a tiresome morning, Sammy knew she should have slept but the thoughts never stopped coming. She knew she should have been thinking about Mrs. T, of course she was worried about her but she couldn't think about anything else but of Nick. It was embarrassing, someone who had humiliated her in more ways than one and then all he had to do was show up and she was already back to the incessant thoughts of him. There was no winning with Nick not until she figured out a way to get rid of these feelings she had about him. It had felt better when she hated him- maybe that was a lie- but at least the thoughts she had of him then had often been murderous and hateful and those she could handle. Murderous and hateful thoughts didn't leave her missing him and pining after him, it didn't leave her wanting to consider if he meant what he had said even though she knew she couldn't trust that he did. She had trusted what Jason had said and that had cost her dearly so trusting another McCarthy would just be plain stupid.

Sammy put a quick call to Vicky when she finally found the energy to get out of bed. Vicky had sounded strange, a little distant and Sammy had thought she had maybe felt a little bit of that passive aggression Nick had spoken about last night but she wanted dismiss it, of course Vicky was allowed to sound strange with what she was going through. When she had gone through hers, she had totally blocked her friend out but that didn't stop her from worrying a little.Even on her way back from the farmer's market a couple of hours after the conversation Sammy still worried.The farmer's market, she didn't think she was going to go back anytime soon. That wasn't a place for her since she couldn't tell the difference between a zucchini and a cucumber, but she had really wanted to do something nice for Vicky and her mom but she realised halfway back to her apartment that cooking for them wasn't actually a nice gesture, it was a catastrophic one. Because even though the nice man from the market had helped her pick out everything she needed to make some chicken noodle soup, Sammy was sure she would end up poisoning her best friend and her mom which would be very bad.When she got back to her apartment building, she was still struggling to get the door open with the bags in hand when she got tapped on the shoulder. Startled she let go of the bags before turning around, it was Nick.He was standing unapologetically behind her with a smile on his face."Nick" she called with a little reliefIt was still too early in the morning for this."Hi" he said already picking up the bags she had let go off, good thing the contents didn't spill."What are you doing here?" she asked him reaching to take her bags from him, he held on and she wasn't about to drag it out with him."I was in the neighbourhood and I came to say hi" he said with a smile."Seriously?" Sammy tried to frown but it was really hard to do so when he was smiling at her like that."I was worried about your friend's mom, how is she?""The same. Thanks for stopping by, you can go now" she told him and made another attempt to grab the bags from him, he dodged by swinging the bags away gently."Nick" she called hating that she was not more upset by his presence."Samantha" he called in a flirty tone.Sammy sighed, she put her hands akimbo and then frowned while shaking her head at him."What are you really doing here?" she asked him, seriously."I told you, I was worried about your friend's mom. And I missed you" he told her.Sammy rolled her eyes, she stretched out her hand,"Give me" she requested"These? They're quite heavy. I'll take them upstairs for you" he offered, she shook her head"You're not going up to my apartment" she told him"Why not?"because being in an enclosed space with you right now is not a good idea."Because I have a lot of things to do today" she told him"Like what? I'll help""Nick""Samantha" she hated how she loved the way her name rolled of his tongue most times."Fine, I was going to cook something to take to the hospital""You were going to cook" he swallowed a chuckle, he puckered his lips in a way that showed he was trying hard not to laugh."I hate you" she told him and then he did laugh. Sammy pouted but only because she was trying not to laugh too"I hate you" she said again and then chuckled. It was pretty laughable, the notion of her cooking for an invalid or even a healthy person for a matter of fact."Let's see what we have here" he said taking a look inside the bag,"What are you planning to make?" he asked her"Chicken noodle soup""And how many times have you made that before?""A lot of times" she lied"Okay" he said and chuckled"I hate you" she said again with a smile on her face"Come on, I'll help you" he told her"I don't need your help" another lie, she desperately needed any help."I know, since you're such an expert on the dish right?" he was mocking her. She was almost tempted to tell him she hated him again but the phrase now felt like a semantic satiation."Fine, you can come up but only to observe. I don't need your help" she told him and then started to go in, he followed.

She had only met this Nick one time, the playful one that laughed at everything. It was during their weekend together and somehow, he was back today.She sat and watched him as he chopped up some onions, his fingers moved with such skill, she couldn't help but admire them. She had almost forgotten how pleasing it was to watch him cook, the way he held on to the knife when he chopped, the focus on his face when he calculated the ingredients in his head, it was just all... stimulating."Where's the garlic?" he asked as he dumped the properly chopped onions into a bowl."It's in the bag" she told him. He shook his head,"I took everything out," he looked at her"you forgot to buy some garlic, didn't you?" he asked and she shook her head. She didn't forget anything, more like, she didn't know it was even a requirement for the dish she wanted to make."I didn't forget," the nice man that helped me must have forgotten"they must have forgotten to bag it at the market""Sure they did" he replied with a smile."Do you have any here?" he asked already opening the cabinets, it was highly unlikely that he'd find any but she let him look anyway.As expected he came up empty,"We'll have to make do without it" he told her and then went ahead to begin cutting the other vegetables.Sammy sat and watched, helping herself to a slice of carrot even when it earned her a playful swat on the hand by him. She poured them both a glass of milk each and he thanked her even though he didn't touch his.She watched the whole process, from him sautéing his chopped ingredients to the preparation of the noodles and everything else that followed and by the end of it all she found that she was almost drooling and had learned nothing.The taste was divine as she knew it would be and for a second she thought about being selfish enough to forget Vicky and her mum, but she didn't. Instead she let Nick pack it up for her and agreed when he offered to escort her to the hospital.

Vicky was in an angry conversation on the phone when Sammy came into the hospital room, Mrs Taylor was asleep, she looked quite rested and most of the machines she had been connected to yesterday was gone now. Sammy sat and waited patiently for Vicky to get off the phone and when she did, she was met with a hostile;"What are you doing here?" an unexpected question and a confusing one too. It surprised her that Vicky would even ask that, Mrs T was in the hospital, of course she'd come."I came to check up on Mrs T. I brought some food for the both of you"

Sammy replied and she stretched out the bag she held." You bought some food?" Vicky asked,"No, I brought food" she corrected with a smile"You brought. From where exactly? The diner?" that was a stupid question since the diner didn't open on Sundays."From my apartment""From your apartment" she repeated sceptically. She still didn't take the bag Sammy was holding out."Why do you say it like that?" Sammy asked her,"Well because there's usually nothing edible in your apartment""I went to the farmer's market""You cooked?" Vicky asked, she didn't bother to hide her surprise"I had a little help"Vicky nodded her head in realisation,"The McCarthy brother helped you" why did she have to say it like that? Like it was the worst thing to happen on earth. Like it was something to be ashamed of.Sammy said nothing, there was really nothing to say on the matter."So he took you home last night, and then what? You crawled into bed with him again?" it was disgusting the way she said it that got to Sammy more than the actual words did. She had this frown on her face and this look in her eyes."That is not what happened" Sammy told her dropping the hand that had been stretched out waiting for her friend to take the food she had been so excited about a few moments ago, but now made her feel like she had committed a crime."So what happened then? He told you he loves you again so you let him fuck you again?""Screw you Vicky!""No, it's you who's going to get screwed over again. Knowing you, you'd just let him knock you up again and then when everything goes to hell, I'll be left to pick up the pieces"It stung like a slap, 'knowing her?' What did that even mean? She couldn't believe that Vicky had just said that right now. Was that really what her friend thought of her?"You forget so easily what happened the last time you mingled with those people," Vicky continued when Sammy said nothing, she was still too surprised at what her friend had said to come up with a response."the only reason you are standing here is because I killed myself to get you out of the hole you crawled into. And the first thing you do is to what? Let him in again? He cooks for you and you forget everything he did to you? Samantha that guy has been nothing but cruel to you since the first day you met him. Belittling you and making you feel bad about yourself and you think that you can walk in here and hand me the food that he made you and I'd take it and be happy for you? You are unbelievably stupider than I thought"Just then Mrs. Taylor opened her eyes and called to her daughter, she saw Sammy and then gave her a deep smile. This was the kind of reception Sammy had thought she was going to receive when she was on her way over."You're back" she said sitting upright on the bed.Sammy smiled weakly,"Yes, I brought some food but I'll be going now" she told the older woman"Oh that smells lovely" the woman said already stretching out her hand to receive it. Sammy looked over at Vicky before handing Mrs. Taylor the bag, part of her felt that Vicky would reach out and grab it away and then toss it in the trash but she did neither of those things, instead she just stood and watched her mother collect the bag."I have to get going" Sammy said and then she hurried out without waiting for a response from either of them or even saying goodbye.

Sammy felt like she was going to throw up, she knew she was definitely going to cry and she totally forgot that Nick was still in the waiting room, waiting for her.When she burst out of the room and their eyes locked, she cursed under her breath. He was on his feet and walking towards her immediately,"Is everything okay?" he asked when he got to herShe nodded,"I just want to go home" she told him"Did something happen? Is your friend's mom okay?" he asked"Yes she is, I just think it's time to go""Hey, what's wrong?" he asked taking her hand. Sammy sighed and then gently slipped her hand out of his, she didn't want Vicky to come out here and see them holding hands. It would only fuel her crazy theories some more.But were they really crazy theories? She had welcomed Nick into her home today and she had let herself forget all the reason why she had hated him. She had laughed around and played with him and then somewhere along the line she had let herself remember the things she had felt about him."Vicky is in a mood, I just want to go home" she told him tiredly."Can I take you?" he asked her"You don't have to do that, I wanna walk and clear my head" she really wanted to be alone right now"Let me walk with you, please"She nodded, even though she wasn't sure about it.

THEY WALKED SIDE by side in silence for the longest time and all the while Sammy reflected on what Vicky had said to her. She hadn't been wrong either and even though Sammy didn't want to, she knew she needed to put a stop to this."You can't show up to my apartment again," she began reluctantly"or to my work"He nodded slowly,"Why? Because of your friend?" he asked"Because of me" she told him"Samantha,

I'm truly sorry for everything that happened," he stopped walking and gently drew her to the corner of the road."I just want to make it better""I know, Nick. And if I'm being honest with myself, I think I might have forgiven you" she told him and it was the truth."You have?" he asked"Yes. But that is the problem, I went through hell the past couple of months. A week ago, I couldn't even get out of my apartment, I thought I was going to die, I hated you. But all it took to make all the anger I felt toward you go away was you just showing up and saying you're sorry""And I mean it" he told her"I think that you do, but I also think that it's best for us to leave it at that. I forgive you Nick, but I think we shouldn't see each other again"He took her hand in his,"Samantha I don't want that""I know, and I don't even know that I want that either but it is how things should be""Why?" he askedHe was asking an obvious question, an annoyingly obvious one."Because Nick we met when I was pregnant by your brother and then I had an affair with you, that is not just something we can look past" she told him."I can, we can""And then we become what? Friends? Lovers?" she asked"Samantha I want to be with you" now he was just being ridiculous."It's not about what you want, Nick" she told him and pulled her hands from his. It was getting difficult to think with him touching her."I know that""Do you? Because I thought I was going to die after the miscarriage, I was in so much pain that sometimes I actually wanted to die" she said with so much pain in her voice. It was hard to tell him but she wanted him to know."and do you know the worst part? It's that it wasn't even about losing the baby... it was about losing you" she gave a humourless chuckle and then took a deep breath."For months I couldn't leave my apartment, I couldn't eat, I couldn't sleep, I couldn't function. Nick I still can't sleep in my bed, I can't use my kitchen without thinking of you in it and you were just in my apartment for just a night.You say you want me now, but what happens when you don't anymore? What happens to me then?" she asked him"Samantha that won't happen""You don't know that""I do" he said it with a certainty that was kinda scary"But I don't. I can't trust you, I refuse to" she whispered already tearing up, she sniffled to hold the tears in check."Samantha please..." he said and then tried to reach for her"Nick I can't, I can't" she took a step away from him, she knew that if he as much as laid a finger on her, her body would betray her."this would never work out and I don't think I would survive it then. I don't think my heart could take it then""Samantha we could try" she was already shaking her head before he completed the statement."I don't have to try to know what the outcome would be, Nick. This hurts me too but it has to be done" she told him."I don't know if I can live without you, I don't think I can survive that" he sounded so sad which only broke Sammy's heart some more."You survived well enough since the miscarriage" she reminded him"Samantha I wasn't surviving," he shook his head,"I was merely existing in a constant state of an unending pain. Day and night, I thought of you and of nothing else. I drank to keep the thoughts at bay but even that didn't work, nothing worked because all I want is you""Nick please... stop" she wished he would stop, she hated the way his words were breaking her resolve inch by inch. She hated the way the honesty in the way he spoke just wanted to make her forget all the bad stuff and let him in."I can't. Samantha, I love you and I'm not going to stop saying it until you believe me" he told her"I don't know what you want from me but I...""I want you and only you""You had me, and then with one phone call I ended up with a broken heart. Nick, you had me, and then with one false accusation I ended up with a shattered heart. I'm sorry but I can't go back there" she shook her head tearfully."Why won't you just try?" he asked"Because I don't trust you" she whispered

"Then let me earn your trust" he pleaded,"You can't, Nick. Our story? It's not a love story, it's a cautionary tale. One I plan to learn from. Look at everything that happened because we got together""Because we fell for each other" he corrected like that somehow made it better"What we did was wrong and maybe me losing my child was karma" it had crossed her mind more than once before she found out what actually happened."It wasn't karma, it was Jason. He did a horrible thing just because he could and you can't let that ruin what we have""We don't have anything, we never did. Nick you didn't even like me, you could barely stand me when we met""That's not true," he told her with a shake of her head."I was taken by you and I was ashamed by it. I started dreaming of you the second night after you came to the manor and I tried to push you away but I don't want that anymore. I don't want to be without you"He was taken by her? This was news to her. Not even in their time together in New York did he mention this, and he had dreams about her too."you were carrying my brother's child and I was having all these feelings that I didn't know how to process or what to do about it""Nick...""Samantha wait, please wait" he begged"back in Texas, after the miscarriage the things I said, they were unforgivable and I wish I could take it back. But I said those things mostly because I was angry at myself, I thought that you had done that because of the things I said to you the previous night. But that doesn't mean that I didn't love you, because I did. I do love you Samantha""Maybe you do, but Nick I can't be with you, at least not yet. The miscarriage messed with me in ways I'm yet to recover from and if we tried anything now, it would just be setting ourselves up for failure and more pain""Samantha...""Nick please. I'm not saying never, I'm just saying not now. And if you love me like you say you do, you will let me go" she was the one who was now breaking her own heart,"if we are really meant to find each other again then we will"He opened his mouth and Sammy thought he was going to argue further, then he closed it back again. He closed his eyes and Sammy could see the pain all over his face. Was she making a mistake?This was real, he was really here wanting to be with her, wanting to make things right and she was giving it up for no other reason than because she was scared. But she barely survived the other time and it would destroy her if she let herself get sucked back into all of these and then he ended up realising that she wasn't what he wanted.She reached over and then gave him a kiss on the cheek, she let it linger because he wrapped his hands tightly around her waist."Goodbye Nick" she said sadly and this time she let a single tear drop before leaving him there and walking away.She didn't turn around because she knew that one glance could undo her resolve.

# CHAPTER 23

When Sammy got back to her apartment, for the first time in months she lay on her bed. She spread her arms and legs apart like a spider and enjoyed the feel on the bed underneath her. Her body enjoyed having enough room to manoeuvre for the first time in months and then she coiled into a ball and then she let herself cry. No weep.She wept because of the things Vicky had said to her, she wept because of the thought of never seeing Nick again and she wept because of that pain in her chest. The one that had started since that night at the hospital, the one that had refused to go away until yesterday when Nick had held her hand in the waiting room, it was back now and it somehow intensified. Would she never stop hurting? Because right at this moment it didn't feel like she ever would. It felt like she was going to be sad forever, like she was going to be in pain forever.It felt like she had always been crying, like her life was one puddle of tears and Sammy was tired. She was tired of everything, she just wanted to go back to a time where she was content with her life, where everything that happened in her life didn't just make her sad and miserable and teary. A time where she wasn't plagued with memories that hurt.She slept off with the tears still in her eyes and the pain in her chest, but that didn't last long because she awakened to someone pounding on her door.Nick. She thought almost sprinting out of bed.She rushed to the door and opened up immediately forgetting to ask who it was, but hoping it was him. It wasn't him. Instead it was a sober looking Vicky at the other end of the door.Sammy sighed on the inside, she didn't say anything instead she turned around and went back into her apartment but she left the door ajar for Vicky to entire if she wanted to. She knew she didn't have to knock, there was always a key under the mat for her to use whenever she wanted.Sammy walked to the kitchen, she poured herself a glass of water while mentally preparing herself for a fight. She had said nothing to Vicky when she said those things at the hospital only because she had been caught off-guard so she readied herself for whatever her friend was going to say now."You can come in, he's not here. Yet" she purposely added yet at the end after a second thought.Vicky came in slowly and then gently closed the door behind her."I brought this back" she told her holding out the bag Sammy had brought to the hospital.Sammy's heart sank, so they didn't eat it."Okay" Sammy said trying to pretend she was fine by her friend rejecting something she had worked hard to make."Momma said it was delicious" Vicky told her walking towards the kitchen"She ate it?" Sammy asked noticing for the first time that the bag didn't look as full as it had before."Of course she ate it, we both did. She was really impressed""I didn't cook it""I didn't tell her that" Vicky said and they both stood in awkward silence for a minute"I didn't mean it, what I said at the hospital," Vicky began breaking the silence"I'm sorry"Sammy sighed in relief, letting herself relax for the first time since Vicky had walked in. She was so glad her friend didn't come to fight."Then why did you say it? You hurt me" she told Vicky"I know and I'm truly very sorry. It's just..." she inhaled sharply and then scratched on her ear,"the bank called, they got an offer on the diner""What? I thought we had a week?" Sammy asked"Me too, but apparently someone made a very generous offer to the bank and now they are considering selling" Vicky explained."That's awful" Sammy said coming around to hug her friend."I still haven't told momma, I don't know if she can take it""It's going to be fine" Sammy told her friend, even though she didn't know that it was."did you hear from your dad?" she asked and Vicky sighed. She let go of her and rolled her eyes."He came to the hospital after you left last night but I kicked him out. I don't have time to listen to his useless excuses, momma is talking about a divorce""Oh God"Vicky went ahead to go and settle down on the sofa and Sammy followed,"Sam," she called"I was mad at you, at the hospital. That is why I said all that stuff""Because of Nick?""No. I just... I was just thinking about the cheque that you tore up"The cheque! Sammy didn't even remember that. That money would have gone a long way in saving the diner."I'm so sorry""Please don't apologise, I feel so terrible already. You have nothing to be sorry about""If I'd...""Don't even complete that statement. We didn't know that we would need that money and even if we did, I'd never ask you to do something you didn't want to. I was just in a mood at the hospital and you were an easy target, I'm sorry"Sammy nodded, she couldn't help but to feel bad about the whole situation. She had had the means to help and she had because of pride and anger ruined it. Vicky was saying now that was okay, but it wouldn't be okay if her mom lost the diner"Would you hold me?" Vicky asked and again she nodded and made room while Vicky placed her head on her bosom and let her cradle her."Nick and I are done. I told him not to come looking for me anymore" Sammy told her friend while still cradling her."You didn't have to that, I didn't mean those things I said" Vicky said raising her face."I know but I needed to hear them. I would have let myself get sucked back in, heck I let myself got sucked back in.Today, when it was just us, I started to feel things again and that's not right. I don't know if I can be able to live without him but I do know that I want to try. It hurts so much but that is how it's supposed to be, I'm supposed to hurt now so I can move on" she didn't believe a single word of the things she was saying. She didn't think there was any way she could move on from Nick, but she had to try to.Vicky nodded,"Can I tell you something selfish?" she asked and Sammy smiled with a nod."I'm glad that you're not seeing him anymore, I just felt like he was going to take you away from me""No one's ever going to take me from you" Sammy told her friend and it was the truth because no matter what happened and where she was, Vicky would always be her number one person.

It was late Wednesday afternoon when Nick got the call, he jumped out his seat at the same time it felt like his chest was beating out of his chest.She was calling him.That was something he wasn't expecting to happen anytime soon. She had said not yet and that was what had kept him going for two weeks, the fact that she had asked him to wait for her, so he had been waiting – not so patiently but still waiting nonetheless. But she wasn't the reason he was still in New York, at least not directly anyway. He had closed the deal yesterday but he thought he would have had a little more time before he saw her again, but that didn't mean he still wasn't excited that she wanted to see him.The plan had been to head to Europe Friday, but if things worked out with Samantha then he might have to change his plans. Richard would just have to understand and even if he didn't, Nick honestly couldn't care less, he could call by himself instead of asking his secretary that spoke like she had a piece of glass stuck in her throat.Samantha asked if he could stop by the diner Thursday afternoon, she did sound a bit down but that was going to change after their meeting, he knew that because he had a special surprise for her, one he had called in a lot of favours to get. But it would be worth it in the end once she forgives him and agrees to be with him.

SAMMY WAS WAITING, she hated that she nervous, but she was angry too so it was kinda cancelling out the nerves. She took another quick glance at her wristwatch and then back at the office where Mrs. Taylor was packing up her things and her heart broke a little more. She hated confrontations, it was something she often tried to avoid if she could but it was cruel what he had done and the worst part was that she could not say she was surprised. He had fooled her and hurt her again, just like she knew he was going to. What she didn't expect was that he was going to drag her entire family into it.Was this some sort of ploy to force her back to him? To bend her to him? But what had she expected? A man who was not used to taking no for an answer, a man who treated everything like it was a sort of business transaction, of course this was his response to rejection.Mrs. Taylor came out from the office, the sadness on her face was so overwhelming that Sammy had to gnash her teeth so she wouldn't cry again. She hated that everyone was in pain, Vicky had been running herself rugged trying to save this place and all of that had been for nothing because in the end, it had all been pointless. They still lost."Have you had anything to eat?" Mrs. Taylor asked.Sammy sighed, food was not a priority at the moment. Maybe later, her stomach was in too much of an upheaval to let keep anything down.She shook her head,"Maybe later" she told her"After you've spoken with him?" Mrs. T asked"How is the packing going?" Sammy asked changing the subject. The impending confrontation wasn't something she wanted to talk about before it happened, she was already too nervous as it was."I was going to go get more boxes but I wanted to know if you needed me to stay"Sammy shook her head,"You should go" it was better this way, being alone when he came would be better.Mrs. T nodded and then began to leave,"Are you sure you are okay?" she turned around and asked. That single question almost drove Sammy to tears. How was she the one been asked if she was okay when it should be vice versa? She was the reason everything was happening. She was the reason they were losing everything."I'm so sorry Mrs.

T. Everything is my fault, I'm sorry for causing you all this trouble" she gnashed her teeth harder even though her eyes were so watery now, because the alternative was breaking down into a puddle of tears and she wasn't sure she could handle that just yet.Mrs. T shook her head vigorously, she then sat down on the seat opposite the one Sammy sat."It breaks my heart that you think this is your fault""But this is happening because...""Shhh" Mrs. T silenced her. She took Sammy's hands in hers"this is happening because I married a selfish man that chose gambling over his family. Eugene has been doing this for years and I was too blind and busy to notice, so baby this is not on you okay?" Sammy nodded even though she still couldn't let herself believe what Mrs. T was saying to her."I love you, and that will never change" Mrs. T told her and then Sammy chuckled, even though a few drops of tears slipped out, it still felt good to hear Mrs. T say that. She reached over and then hugged her,"I love you too"

Not long after Mrs. T left, the door gave a little jiggle and in walked a very dapper looking Nick. Sammy was too angry to notice but he wore this huge smile on his face and if she was in a better mood, she would have remembered how much she loved his smile."Hi" he greeted, the smile never leaving his face"are you alone?" he asked like some creepy serial killer."Do you want to sit?" Sammy asked, she was still contemplating on how to begin.Nick nodded, for the first time noticing how glum she looked. The smile on his face instantly disappeared and was replaced by worry."Is everything okay?" he asked now sitting."No it's not. I just realised the extent you'd go to get what you what"Now he looked shocked, like he was surprised that she actually realised the kind of person he was."What are you saying?" he asked"I'm saying, the more I know you, the easier it is for me to hate you."Nick was so confused, he didn't know where all this was coming from. He had come here today for a reconciliation and instead he was getting hurtful words hurled at him."When you came to New York, I thought to myself, there was nothing else you could take from me. You and your family had taken it all, you took my baby, you took my dignity, you broke my heart and my soul. But I may have just underestimated how evil you are"It was the icy indifferent tone she was speaking in that was like little razors to Nick's heart."I don't know why you are saying all this but...""You bought the diner" she waited and watched the reaction on his face and then she confirmed what she already knew was the truth."You know" he said with a frown"How could you do that?""Samantha you don't understand""Oh I understand that I trusted you with what my family and I were going through and in turn you went and sabotaged our chances of saving our diner""Samantha...""I'm curious though, what did you think would happen? That this would force me back to you or what?""That's not what I was trying to do""So all along you just wanted to acquire a new establishment for Luxury." She inhaled sharply and then pursed her lips."when you said you loved me, I knew you were lying, but I was stupid enough to hope that maybe a part of you did. But if a tiny part of you felt anything for me then you wouldn't have done what you just did"Nick looked at her sadly,"So you really believe I'd want to hurt you like that?" he asked. He was clearly in pain, which was the part Sammy didn't understand. He had this magnificent ability to always look like the wounded one when he was the one inflicting the hurt."I believe that you have hurt me more times than anyone else ever has and I'm done allowing it. Nick I don't know what you set out to accomplish with buying this place but after today, I hope I never see you again in my life""Samantha you don't mean that" Nick told her"I do, because every time we see each other you find a new way to break my heart""Samantha, if you would just let me explain...""I don't want you to explain, I just want you out of my life... for good. And I hope you'd meet someone who would cause you as much hurt as you have caused me"Nick pursed his lips and he watched her; this was the first time Sammy was seeing him this close to tears but her resolve now was stronger than any emotion he could display. She was done now.He nodded slowly and then got up with the same pace, Sammy threw her face away, watching him walk away would be too hard. She didn't want to remember his lowly figure walk away when she thought of him, because she knew she would think of him. Instead she wanted to remember the cruel Nick that had went ahead to buy Vicky's mother's diner even when he knew how important it was to them.Nick reached into his jacket pocket and wrapped his hand around the envelope that was there, he dropped it on the table with a gentle thud and even then, she still didn't look at him. So, he walked away with the pain in his chest and the agony in his heart because he knew he might never see her again in his lifetime and the worst part about it was that this time, he knew had done everything he could to win her back.

VICKY CAME IN a couple of hours later, relieving Mrs. T. It had been one hell of an argument getting the older woman to leave. She said she wanted to spend as much time in Jessy's before everything was packed up, but truth be told, both she and Vicky knew Niklaus McCarthy was going to have to physically drag her out of this place when the time came.It wasn't until Mrs. T left that Vicky brought out the bottle of whiskey in her purse and then invited Sammy to come drown their sorrows together.Drinking never solved anything, at least never for Sammy but she joined her friend after a little persuasion. She didn't like drinking but the thought of getting a moment where she didn't have to deal with all the thoughts racing through her head and all her problems just made her take the bottle that was being handed to her. She took a mighty gulp with frown on her face before handing the bottle back to Vicky,"I thought we were going to continue packing?" she asked hating the afterburn at the back of her throat up to her tongue."How did the meeting go?" Vicky asked once had taken her own gulp. She handed the bottle back to Sammy.Sammy took the bottle and then poured more of the hot liquid down her throat. Maybe the booze was a good idea after all since she this wasn't a conversation she thought she could handle sober."It was a big waste of time" she told her friend and then took another big gulp and instead of handing the bottle back to Vicky she held on to it as she went to sit on the floor in a corner of Mrs. T's office. Vicky went ahead to join her on the floor, they sat in a way that they were facing each other and their knees were touching."What did he say?" Vicky asked."Nothing. He didn't even apologise" she took another gulp and then let Vicky take the bottle."I hated this place. Growing up I always wished that something would happen to it, but now that we've lost it, it makes me so sad" Vicky said before taking her own share of the misery liquid that was being passed to and fro. "He just sat down there and said 'you know', like it was no big deal. It just made me so angry" Sammy continued as she took back the bottle, she took another heavy gulp."I don't think my mom will survive this" Vicky said taking back the bottle"And once again I don't have a job" Sammy said and it was her turn again with the bottle."I wish I didn't have a job, I hate my job""My life changed that night I met Jason in that awful bar and it's like the more I try to get back to normal, the worse things get. And now I've ruined you and your mum's life""You didn't do anything wrong, that psycho Eugene ruined our lives and if it wasn't Nick, it would have been someone else buying the diner. Now stop hogging the bottle, I have a lot of sorrows to drown" she said with a smile before taking back the bottle."So you don't think he did anything wrong?" Sammy asked"Of course he did, he's a backstabber. But at least when they turn this place into another one of Luxury's hotel, we can come pee in the lobby as revenge" Vicky said and then giggled. Sammy immediately knew that her friend was now experiencing the effects of the booze but she laughed too because it was a funny idea and something her friend might probably see to the end.

Two hours later, they were both struggling to stand up straight as they decided to call it a day and head home. They didn't get any work done which was going to disappoint Mrs.

T when she came in tomorrow, or make her happy, it was always hard to tell with her."What's this?" Vicky asked as they began to head out. She was the one who had had most of the content of the bottle but she was still the one that looked the most normal.Sammy looked at what she was referring to, to find the envelope Nick had left earlier."Hush money, I think" she said and then scratched her head. She was definitely going to get a haircut tomorrow or she would start thinking about investing in some head bands."What do you mean hush money?" Vicky asked picking it up"Nick dropped it earlier. I think it's another cheque""You think?""I didn't open it but knowing him..." she trailed off, she forgot what she was going to say so she giggled. Vicky giggled too and then handed her the envelope."Put it in your... pursett... pocket... no purse. If it's big, big money, then we'll buy a...""A bar!" Sammy completed and they both laughed. Vicky nodded in agreement with her friend. It was concluded then, they were going to buy a bar once they sobered up. Problem was, once they sobered up this conversation wouldn't sound as brilliant as it did right now.

# CHAPTER 24

Sammy felt like her head was going to fall off, she had let herself over indulge after she had promised herself that the last time was the last time. At least she didn't wake up in a stranger's bed this time, she didn't wake up in her bed this time either but she was no stranger to Vicky's apartment.V icky was still asleep when she woke up so she snuck out of bed. Water. She needed water because her mouth felt like it had gone to a desert for an extended vacation. And she also needed a thickly brewed cup of coffee or a jug, it felt like she could finish a jug of coffee right now.She first got the coffee maker going before pouring herself a tall glass of water and downed it in one gulp, she poured another before remembering there was a possibility of a packet of aspirin being in her purse. She slowly dragged herself to the corner where she and Vicky had both carelessly dumped their purses and shoes and then picked up her purse. She dipped her hand into it and the first thing she felt was Nick's envelope from yesterday, before she could stop herself, she pulled it out. Headache and aspirin forgotten she dropped the bag back on the floor and then let her curiosity guide her when she carefully tore open the envelope. She vividly remembered how surprised she had been the last time she had gotten one of these from his father. At that time, she hadn't known what to expect so it had totally caught her off-guard when she saw his hefty cheque. But now she knew exactly what was in the envelope – maybe not exactly but she could guess. The envelope this time looked thicker and slightly bigger than the last time, so did that mean the money was bigger this time? She wondered as she finally unfolded the papers."Oh my God" she whispered to herself as she read through the contents of the papers she held."Oh my God!" she repeated, this time louder than the first time."Vicky!" she screamed but only because she wasn't believing what she was seeing and she needed someone else to tell her if she was hallucinating or imagining things.Did hangovers make people hallucinate? "Vicky!" she called again before friend staggered out looking like crap"What? What?" she asked looking around for what might be making her friend scream this early in the mor ning."Come take a look at this" Sammy requested her eyes never leaving the papers"What? You called me out of bed this early because of this?" Vicky asked frustrated"You need to see this""Can't it wait? I'm tired and hungover and I need more sleep before I have to go into work" Vicky whined"It can't" Sammy said going and thrusting the papers into her friend's hands.Vicky took them with a sigh of frustration and then Sammy watched as her eyes went from tired and bored to wide and shocked,"Oh my God" she whispered in just the same tone Sammy had merely seconds before and if Sammy hadn't still been in shock she would have found it a tad  amusing.Vicky looked up at Sammy,"Oh my God!" her eyes widening in excitement."what are you going to do?" she asked"I gotta find him" Sammy replied realising. She was already putting on her shoes before she thought about it. She picked up her earlier discarded purse and then took the papers back from Vicky and shoved it back into the bag,"I gotta go" she repeated and then hurried out.

SAMMY KNEW EXACTLY where Nick was going to be, at least she hoped she did. She knew he only stayed in one hotel when he came to New York and that was the hotel they had both stayed in, so she hoped to catch him there before he got out of bed.She took a taxi, there was no way she could sit through a subway ride, knowing what she knew now. She practically raced in when the taxi stopped her in front of the hotel complex. And when the receptionist told her that he checked out about twenty minutes ago, Sammy thought she was going to die. Checked out to where? She wanted to ask. Did that mean he had gone back to Texas? Or worse, Europe. Her heart sank at the realisation.With shaky hands she pulled out her phone and then dialled his number, it rang with no response for the first couple of times and then at the third ring the operator told her that the number was unavailable.Of course he didn't want to speak to her, not after the things she had said to him yesterday. She had been so rude and cruel, with the intentions of hurting him and by the look on his face when he'd left, she had succeeded. And now she couldn't take it back.She stood in the hotel lobby and tried to think of what to do. If Nick had already left for Europe then that meant she had lost him forever, she didn't want to lose him forever, she realised in panic. Her heart, she was sure wouldn't be able to handle it.Charlie!She dialled Charlie's number immediately and was almost driven to tears with relief when she picked up at the first ring."Hey beautiful" Charlie greeted with that her beautifully nice voice"Hi Charlie" Sammy replied with so much relief"It's so nice to hear from you. How are you doing?" Charlie asked and Sammy could hear Luca faintly from the other end of the line asking his wife,"Who is that?""It's Sammy" she replied and then back to Sammy,"Are you okay?" she asked"No. I need to  find Nick, I can't find him cause he's checked out of the hotel and I don't know where he is or where I can find him. He's not picking my calls and now the operator is saying his phone is not available. I don't know what to do, please help me""Samantha breathe" Charlie reminded her. She inhaled deeply and then exhaled the same way."Can you help me?" she asked"Of course. I don't think his flight's left already but I'm gonna call Peter from the airline. Can you make it to the airport?""Yes" Sammy replied desperately, she would make it to the ends of the earth if it meant Nick would be there waiting when she got there."Good. I'm going to text you his number, he's a friend of the family and he'll be waiting when you get there cause I'm going to call him, okay?"Sammy nodded and then realised she needed to use her words because Charlie couldn't see her,"Yes. Thank you, thank you."  "Sammy relax, you're gonna find him and then you two..." Charlie stopped talking and then she inhaled sharply"Charlie? Are you okay?" Sammy and Luca asked simultaneously "I think I'm in labour" she told them and Sammy could hear the excitement coming from her voice. Only Charlie would be excited about going into labour."Babe I told you, you need to stop this. It's not funny anymore" Sammy heard Luca reprimand her from the other end of the line"I'm not kidding" just then Sammy started to hear the water gush"My water just broke" Charlie said into the phone, her excitement more evident."Your water just broke?" Sammy asked"Her water just broke. Oh god!" Luca confirmed, he sounded so nervous and scared."Sam, head to the airport, I'm going into labour but Luca's still going to call Peter" Charlie instructed in a high-pitched voice."Me?" Luca asked nervously"Yes" Charlie replied"But I'm in labour" he told her"No, I'm in labour baby." She corrected"Okay that's true. You're in labour, I'll call Peter" he said as if realising that he wasn't actually the one going into labour."Sammy I gotta go, go get your man. I'll call you when I pop out this thing inside of me. Goodluck!" she hung up before Sammy could get a chance to say anything.Sammy smiled, Charlie was in labour. Sammy was glad she had witnessed it even if it was just a few seconds of it. Now, she had to go find her man.

Peter, a man in about his late fifties met Sammy immediately she got to the airport. He was super nice but it still didn't do much to ease Sammy's nerves. All the way down to the airport Sammy had thought of one thing and one thing only. Rejection. What if Nick didn't want her anymore? She had rejected him more than once when he'd told her how he felt. She'd treated him so badly, insulted him and kicked him out. It was an awful thing she'd done to him, so who was to say he won't return the energy? Who was to say he'd even want to see her?Sammy bit on her lips as Peter walked her to the tarmac,"Is he really there?" she asked him nervously"Yes. But they're scheduled to take off in fifteen minutes so we have to hurry" he told her.Sammy nodded,"Do you think he'd want to see me?" she asked him even though she was sure he wouldn't have the answer to that question.He looked sadly at her,"I think it's best Mr. McCarthy answers that question" he told her and then she nodded.Sammy sighted the Luxury plane from a distance, she knew it because she had been aboard it more than once. And then she saw him. He was talking on the phone, standing on the steps of the plane when she saw him. She couldn't help it when she yelled,"Nick!" he didn't hear her, she was obviously still far away so it was basically instinctive when she left her guide and broke into a run."Nick!" she called again and this time he did turn around. He frowned and then Sammy waved. She didn't stop running, even as he briskly walked down the steps towards her."Hi" she greeted when she got to him still out of breath.He was looking at her in confusion,"Samantha?" he called unsure"Hi" she said again struggling to catch her breath"What are you doing here?" he asked "I came to find you. The hotel receptionist said you'd checked out""You went to the hotel?""Yes. I missed you by twenty minutes" she said and then smiled. She was so happy that she hadn't missed him here again."What are you doing here?" he asked again, this time curtly."I came to apologise" she told him not letting his tone scare her off. She knew him better now, he was all bark and no bite."That's not necessary" he told her still being all courteous.

Nick put his hands in his pockets so he wouldn't touch her. He still wasn't sure if he was dreaming but Samantha was right there at the hanger for him.When he'd seen her running to him, he had for sure thought he was now hallucinating. That was the only thing he hadn't done when it came to Samantha. He'd dreamt about her often, and those times when he had been drinking, in his most drunken state he would let himself imagine that she was there with him. But she was standing there with him right now and she wasn't a hallucination. He didn't want to be presumptuous or even hopeful because he wasn't sure if he could handle one more rejection from her.God he wanted to touch her! He wanted to do more than touch her. Fuck!He stared at her, she looked unrested, like she had been awake all night. And Nick noticed she was still in the clothes she had been wearing yesterday."It's not necessary" she repeated and Nick watched the corner of her lips coil. She smiled."You bought me the diner""Yes" he swallowed, he wished she would just stop smiling suggestively at him because he didn't know how much more restraint he still had left in him."You bought me a fucking diner" she repeated"Yes""Why would you do that?" she asked him.Nick looked at her, did this girl really not know the things he was capable of doing for her?"You were sad at the thought of losing it and I couldn't stand by and let  you lose something that mattered to you" it was the truth. He had decided he would buy the diner  the night after he had taken her home from the hospital.

She smiled sadly at him,"You really do love me" she said it, like she was just believing him now.He didn't say anything, he just watched her and even though all he wanted to do was kiss her, he tried to act indifferent to her and her words, which was probably the hardest thing he had done in his life.

"And I was so horrible to you, I said all those terrible things to you""It's fine" it wasn't fine, she had hurt him deeply and had broken his heart."It's not. I'm so sorry, I should have let you explain. I didn't mean the things I said, I was angry and hurt and I thought..." she trailed off, she took a deep breath. She was obviously struggling with whatever it was she wanted to say and Nick knew instantly that she was trying to figure out a way to let him down easy."Samantha, it's fine. I have to go now, my plane is supposed to take off in less than ten minutes. Goodbye" he turned around because he knew that if he stayed any second longer, he would fall on his knees and beg her to take him back and he knew that won't work because she had already made up her mind that she didn't want to be with him. "Nick wait!" she called out desperately and then hurried around to his front."...I thought," she continued"that that meant you didn't love me. And that broke my heart – no, it shattered my heart""Why?" he asked and for the first time letting himself be hopeful.She looked him dead in the eyes and with all seriousness she told him,"Because I love you"It took a moment for her words to register but Nick still asked,"What?" he just wanted to be sure those words had come from her.Her lips coiled in a smile and then she rose to her tippy toes and then dragged his head down to mouth and then whispered into his ears,"I love you"Nick smiled and then grabbed her by the waist and lifted her off the ground in a tight embrace, she in turn wrapped her legs around him and her hands around his neck. His spun her round in the air and then enjoyed the tickle on his neck when she giggled before taking her lips in his.He kissed her, hard, long, soft, sweetly before gently dropping her back to the ground.

"You love me" he said again with a smile. She nodded with the most beautiful smile on her face."Good. Because I love you too" he kissed her again.He looked her dead in the eyes and became serious,"Samantha, I will never hurt you again. I promise that I will never doubt you ever again, and I will never leave you. You are the best thing that has ever happened to me and I promise that I will never take that for granted.""Do you mean that?" she asked him"I do. Samantha when you told me that you hated me, it had felt like someone was physically reaching into my heart and ripping it out, and when you said you never wanted to see me again, I didn't think I was going to survive it. Samantha, I love you and that's never going to change""Nick, I love you too and I am tired of pretending that I don't" she told him and then reached out and hugged him.

"Wait, how did you get here?" he asked her as if just realising,"I called Charlie, Peter brought me" she said looking back at where she had left him. He was still standing there, he waved awkwardly."Oh! I forgot, Charlie's in labour!" she told him"She says that all the time""No, I heard her water break""You did?""Yes, your brother's freaking out. He said he was in labour" she said with a chuckle.Typical Luca, of course he said that."Then we have to go""Go where?" she asked all confused."Texas, to the hospital. I was supposed to head to Milan but it would have to wait, Charlie's having a baby, we need to be there""We?""Yes, except you don't want to?""I do, it's just, I still haven't showered, I'm pretty sure I'm still a bit hungover and I'm still in the same clothes I was wearing yesterday" she explained"That's no problem, you could shower once we take off and when we land we could find you something else to wear"Sammy thought about it for a moment and then nodded,"Okay, let's go to Texas. But I have to call Vicky"

Sammy and Nick were ushered into the hospital room by a very cheerful nurse, Luca and Charlie were sharing the hospital bed, Luca was sitting with one leg dangling off the bed, he was holding the baby and staring at it like it was some alien creature while Charlie was laying half snuggling her husband. She raised her face when she heard them come in and then gave one of her very pleasing smiles,"You found him" she said in a hushed tone"I found him" Sammy replied in a tone matching hers and then she waved slightly. She smiled at the cozy little family in front of her. She repressed the bout of jealousy that was beginning to rise in her, she reminded herself that today wasn't about her or the baby she had lost, today was about being happy for her friend."I didn't know you guys were coming""Are you kidding me? My best friend's having a baby, I wouldn't miss it for anything the world" Nick told her going to give her a hug. He kissed her hair"why didn't you call me?" he asked"I thought you'd be busy, I didn't think you two were going to get out of bed until Calla starts talking"Nick rolled his eyes at her playfully,

"Calla?" Sammy asked "Come meet our baby" Charlie said sitting up properly and taking the baby from Luca while motioning for her to come closer.Sammy's heart swelled at the sight of the tiny creature wrapped in a tiny blanket."It's a girl" Luca told them, his pride emitting from his voice."Her name's Calla, after the flower. It means beautiful" "She is beautiful" Sammy whispered and she couldn't help the emotional tears that started to swell in her eyes."Calla meet your godparents" Charlie said"Godparents?" Nick and Sammy asked at the same time"Yes. Nick was always supposed to be her godfather and we were thinking, maybe my sister Sandra but after you called this morning, we decided it was going to be you two. It made more sense, you two make sense." Charlie explained loving the look of joy on both their faces and they didn't miss her underlying message even though she wasn't trying to be subtle about it."But Nick you can't be my child's godfather if you are going to take off a million miles away and never come back""I told you I'll be more present this time, I'll come home more. I promise" he told her and then smiled,"I'm a godfather" he whispered excitedly."Are you sure?" Sammy asked"Of course, we're sure. Welcome to the family Samantha" it was Luca that replied and he went to her and engulfed her in a hug.When Luca's hands wrapped around her briefly, Sammy thought she might burst out crying. But not the sad tears she had now gotten so used to, happy tears. She was just so happy, happier than she had been in a long time."Thank you, this means so much to me" she told both parents with a sniffle."Do you wanna carry her?" Charlie asked,"Of course I wanna carry her" she replied going ahead to carefully and gently take Calla from her mother.

The instant Sammy held the baby she knew she was in love, she was in love with the tiny human that lay in her arms without a care in world. She instantly felt her heart heal and get whole again when Calla looked at her and then smiled. Smiled at her. It was unexplainable, the feeling she was getting from just holding the baby but she felt peace and serenity and she was loving that feeling. Those were feelings that had evaded her for so long but right there in that room with Calla in her arms, she knew she was going to be okay."Are you okay?" Nick asked coming to stand next to her"Yeah, why?""You're crying" he told her and just then she began to notice the wetness coming from her eyes."I am," she said with such realisation as she touched the liquid on her face with her free hand.She looked at him and smiled,"I'm happy," she told him and then to Charlie and Luca she said,"thank you for including me in your joy".

NICK SAT WITH Luca in the lobby and waited as he got off the phone with Richard, they had left both women cooing over the baby to go call the rest of the family. Mara Augustine, Charlie's mum promised she was taking the next flight out and Alex wouldn't stop screaming so hard that Luca had to hang up mid conversation. And Chase was in France, probably with a woman, he said he was happy for them even though he wouldn't be able to make it for several days."Richard said he's heading over the day after tomorrow, he's in Tokyo" Luca informed his brother when he got off the phone."Good for him" Nick said nonchalantly, he was still a little pissed at his father, or at least he was trying to be. This was the longest he had ever gone without having any communication with the man."He asked about you" "He's just worried about his stupid winery""He's worried about you" Luca told him. Nick rolled his eyes, he didn't believe his brother, but only because he knew their father well enough. Richard McCarthy was a man who made everything about business, so Nick knew that if his father had really inquired about him it would be because of something work related."I wish you'd just talk to him and then you'll see how much he cares about you""I'm not talking to him unless it's Luxury related""You can't be serious""I am. As a matter of fact, I don't wanna talk about him either, so can we change the topic?" Nick told his brother; he was getting cranky and he didn't like it."What would you rather talk about? Samantha?" Luca asked and Nick couldn't help the smile that crept onto his face. He hated that he immediately started to feel giddy and for a moment he thought he might just burst into giggle and that scared the crap outta him. Disgusting! What was he turning into?!"She came to the airport" he told his brother trying and failing to control himself."Yeah, I know. She called Charlie all frantic this morning""She loves me" he said and his smile grew wider."I suspected," Luca told him "so what are you going to do now?" he asked."I'm going to marry her" he said because he realised in that moment that this was how he wanted to feel for the rest of his life. Giddy and happy.